DEEP IN THE DRAGON STRONGHOLD

The commandos spread into the intersecting corridors. All reports were the same. Frozen lizard corpses were everywhere. The ice dome was a dragon mausoleum.

"*Doc!* Over here!" Windy stood on the other side of the corridor, fiercely wiping frost off a storage case. "We got people!"

Everyone gathered around the platoon leader and helped him to brush off the adjacent cases. It was difficult to see clearly through the maze of tiny cracks. The bodies were naked and upright, and for the most part hairless.

Sam winced at the entombed humans. "Maybe this is what became of the Cro-Mag—"

Scott screamed. He clamped his hand to his mouth and uttered low, guttural sounds like the cough of a wounded animal choking on its own blood. Enough of one female was exposed to show a cadaverous face and a head of long blond hair.

Doc rushed to his side. "My boy, what is it?"

Scott wanted to scream again, but his throat was paralyzed . . . In a halting voice he finally blurted, "She's my sister. . . ."

NO FUTURE FOR
◇ DRAGONS ◇
GARY GENTILE

ACE BOOKS, NEW YORK

This book is an Ace original edition,
and has never been previously published.

NO FUTURE FOR DRAGONS

An Ace Book / published by arrangement with
the author

PRINTING HISTORY
Ace edition / September 1990

ISBN: 0-441-58336-9

Ace Books are published by The Berkley Publishing Group,
200 Madison Avenue, New York, New York 10016.
The name "ACE" and the "A" logo
are trademarks belonging to Charter Communications, Inc.

PRINTED IN THE UNITED STATES OF AMERICA

10 9 8 7 6 5 4 3 2 1

NO FUTURE FOR
◇ DRAGONS ◇

CHAPTER 1

Scott signed off his work crew by manipulating his fingers in dragon finger speak. Natives gathered the tools and trash, and carried everything away. "That's it, Doc. The core change is done."

Tapping the checklist with an errant finger, Doc looked up and cocked one bushy eyebrow. "I thought it was going to be a much more complicated procedure."

Scott tucked a screwdriver in his belt pouch. "I have to give the dragons credit where credit is due: they were technological geniuses, especially in design and construction. They built products to last, and assembled them so they were easy to service."

Doc nodded. "Their machines were wonderful; it was their machinations that led to the destruction of their civilization. I have often thought that if they had not embarked upon a course of world domination, the Cretaceous never would have ended, and they might have continued uninterrupted as the dominant species on this planet. In a way, they were responsible for their own demise."

"The dragons didn't shape the world the way it is today, Doc. You did."

"I played my part." Doc shrugged and rubbed his white beard. "We all had our roles. We still do." His forehead wrinkled in consternation. "But my mind is full of wonder and trepidation. Are we indeed actors on the stage of life, exercising free will; or are we merely puppets locked in an unalterable script written by cosmic prerogative?"

Scott took Doc by the shoulder and urged him out of the reactor room. "Let's base our plans on physics, not metaphysics. Besides, if you truly believed in predestination you'd simply lie back and let the world run its course, instead of working so hard to alter its direction. And nobody has made more earthshaking changes in the world than you."

Doc allowed himself to be led along the corridor. "You instill me with confidence, my boy."

1

"We all need our strokes. But this is the first time I've ever seen *you* lacking self-assurance."

Doc shuddered, as if a blast of icy wind had struck him across the back. "Perhaps that is because in the past my method of attack was somewhat spontaneous. I did not have time to envision the potential consequences of my actions. Now that we have all the time in the world, this premeditated campaign has me justifiably concerned. I have no idea where—or when—this path will lead us."

"One never does. But that won't stop us any more than it stopped the caveman from playing with fire. He burnt his fingers a few times, I'm sure. But if he had been the kind of man to run and hide from what he didn't know, or understand, we'd still be living in caves. Instead, he took his chances and learned to harness his fire. We aren't just walking blindly into the future, we're being pushed by our heritage."

Doc thought that over as they turned at an intersection and followed the curved corridor along the outside bulkhead. "That is very clever of you to paraphrase my own words."

Scott laughed out loud. "It's impossible to psychoanalyze a psychologist. You're always one foot ahead of me."

"For one in your condition that is a curious use of words."

Scott exaggerated the clumping of his prosthesis on the plastic flooring. Long pants hid the bulky brace strapped to his right leg. The only part of the artificial limb that was visible was the plastic extremity that extended below the cuff, and the padded heel plate. "Some things you have to learn to live with."

Doc ignored the twinge of pain in his bad leg. "And you have done quite well, my boy." When they reached the ramp and ascended to the next level, Doc leaned forward and pushed harder on his cane. "With my tapping and your padding, we make quite a duet."

Scott laughed as he threw an arm around the smaller man's shoulders and hugged him tight. "Yes, but we're playing an overture, not a swan song."

"I will remember that as we charge headlong into perpetuity— or oblivion."

"Doc, let's not start this operation on the wrong foot."

Now it was Doc's turn to laugh. "It seems to me you made that very same statement once before. Your sense of humor in situations of imminent peril or dire straits is indeed an inspiration."

"Part of my charm." They passed another landing, then got off the ramp when it next leveled out. "Hey, Death Wind. How goes it?"

The Nomad pulled his head out of an electrical cabinet. His long black hair was pinned back in a ponytail. He wore a tool pouch over his loincloth, and held a screwdriver and pliers in his hands. "I am tightening all connections to the power grid."

Scott nodded. "Did you draw a schematic for the auxiliary focusing nodes?"

"On vellum. Jane is inputting data into computer."

"Great. But I want a hard copy kept in a safe place—just in case."

Death Wind stared back expressionlessly. "Level Two lock-box."

"That's fine." Scott slapped Death Wind on the back. "Keep up the good work."

Scott and Doc continued along the corridor. They had to wind through the bustling horde of natives who were storing supplies in the rooms and compartments. Although they chattered constantly in their newly discovered language, whenever their hands were empty they continued to use sign as an adjunct to speech. It was not only a matter of habit; it allowed them to be understood above the racket.

"Doc, I can't believe how much progress these people have made." Scott yelled in the doctor's ear in order to make himself heard. "It seems like only yesterday they were a rabble of cow-eyed slaves. Now they're men and women with a will, infused with the desire to work and learn and run their own lives. The change is amazing."

Doc waited until they reached the central ramp and left the hubbub behind before commenting. "Freedom has a strange effect on people. Even the most slothful flourish with zeal when liberated from the bonds of captivity."

"I understand the process. But I never thought they would react so—explosively. These people have burst out of oppression like lava from a volcano."

Doc shrugged. "Look at yourself. Did you ever imagine that once released from the confinement of Maccam City you would have become who you are?"

Scott led the way up the circular ramp. "Well, I used to dream about escaping into the world above—"

"Howdy, pardners. You all ready fer the launchin'?" Windy

was clad in beige attire of his own manufacture. The shirt's long sleeves were rolled up past the elbow, the pants were bloused at the ankles, the moccasins were made of heavy-duty dinohide with reinforced soles.

"I do say, Windy, you look positively resplendent in uniform." Doc eyed the ammunition belt around Windy's waist. Clipped to the synthetic material were water pouches, one-shot stun guns, and ditty bags for provisions. "That is an ensemble any soldier would be proud to wear."

"Thanks, Doc. We got ever'thin' but the medals. Decided we ain't gonna have none. We'd haf to do a whole passel o' damage to catch up with you fokes, so we'll jus' stay 'nonymous."

"The true mercenary spirit."

"How's the name calling?" Scott asked, smiling.

"Me an' the boys thought up a coupla monikers. Split ourselves inta company units with separate captains, 'stead o' jus' one big army. Figgered that kinda structure'd give us more leeway. Mine's the Texas Rangers. The other chaps're callin' themselves the First Fusiliers, under Broderick."

"I'm sure they look dashing."

"Their outfit's darker 'n ours so's we kin tell us apart. Got lots o' natives to join up, too. More 'n makes up fer the outsiders that 'lected to stay behind with their wimmenfoke. Even got a squad full o' ladies callin' themselves the Femme Fatales. That was Sandra's idee. Hope I don't hafta tangle with 'em; they're real scrappers."

Doc and Scott exchanged guffaws. Doc said, "Who is in overall command?"

"The vote was fer Death Wind, but he din't want no parts of it. Kinda independent like, that feller; fancies bein' a scout. So Sam gots the job. We call 'im the Gentleman Gen'ral. Kinda fittin', doncha think?"

"I'm not sure he would agree," Doc said. "Although he *has* got a good sense of humor. In any case, I suggest you keep that honorific for private consumption."

"It don't make no never mind. He's a good egg."

"But he can't take a yolk." Scott went on quickly as Doc rolled his eyes, "Windy, this bird's almost ready to fly. Who's taking care of the crew list? We don't want to leave anyone behind."

"Me an' Broderick's responsible fer our own outfits, but Sam's got the main printout on the bridge." Windy jerked a thumb upward. "He's double-checkin' it now. Some job, too, 'cause most o' the natives never had names before, so they don't know who they are when they're called. Anyhow, I gotta do a last-minute weapons check. Catch ya later."

As Windy descended the ramp, Doc and Scott continued on up to the command bubble: the superstructure dome that perched atop the saucer-shaped flyer. The bridge was a large hemispherical room whose lower bulkheads were crammed with control panels full of switches and annunciator lights, and whose upper works consisted of alternating windowpanes and computer screens that went completely around the perimeter. In the middle sat an octagonal console with eight terminals facing outward.

Rusty glanced up from the command seat. "I'll be right with you. The diagnostics test is still running." He looked haggard; fine lines grew under his eyes, and his curly red hair was long and bushy and hung down across his forehead and around his ears.

Scott nodded, and walked across the bridge to where Jane sat at an auxiliary terminal. He leaned down and kissed the top of her head. "How's it going, sweetie?"

Jane smiled, tilted her head, and offered her lips. Scott kissed her again. Her fingers flew across the keyboard without missing a key. "It is much easier since you declawed the equipment."

It had been a comparatively easy task to redesign the input pads with pin extensions that conformed to the tips of human fingers; now programming and data entry could be handled without taloned gloves. Scott huddled up to Jane, rubbing her shoulders. "Anything to make life easier for you."

Doc cleared his throat. "I think I'll leave you two lovebirds alone." He winked as he sidled around the central console. On the opposite side, Helen tapped control keys at an identical station.

Sam leaned over her with his eyes glued to the monitor screen. "Okay, honey, that's enough. Give me a printout."

"You know, you could learn to do this yourself."

Sam shook his head. "I *can* do it myself, but it takes twice as long. My motto is 'always hire an expert.'" Sam looked up at Doc's approach. "What do you think, Henry?"

"I think Rusty prefers that I keep my bromides to myself." Doc nodded in the direction of the youth, who was deeply enmeshed in his work and made no sign to indicate he heard Doc's words. "He says they put him to sleep."

"Does that mean you're going to quit prescribing them, or make them more complicated?" The printer clacked as sheets of white vellum spun out of the burning tube. "Never mind." Sam grabbed the top sheet and slid a black-faced reader under it. The holes seared through the vellum stood out as legible typeface. "I'll bet the dragons never thought their computers would be spitting out orders in English."

Helen said, "I'll bet they never knew someone as brilliant as Rusty could crack their matrix code and reprogram it."

Rusty made no movement at the mention of his name. He was completely preoccupied.

Sheets of vellum continued to drop into the collection bin. Sam skimmed each one. "Well, folks, I'd say the People's Expeditionary Force is ready to get under way."

"Sam, how is our star genius?" Doc tilted his head toward Rusty. "I am quite concerned over his health and psychological well-being. Since we began this project he has concentrated enough energy on it to kindle a small nuclear furnace."

"And he still has power to spare."

Helen leaned against the chair's makeshift backrest. "He seems to have retreated into himself. He doesn't talk about anything but the mission. We have to force food into him. When he becomes so exhausted he can't work, he sleeps at his console. He hasn't left the bridge for days. He keeps digging for data in that crystal, as if it contains all the secrets of the universe. I have the feeling he's harboring some deep dark secret—as if he's discovered something he's not yet ready to reveal. Whatever he knows—or thinks he knows—he's keeping to himself. And it's eating him up inside. Frankly, Dad, I'm worried about him."

Sam raised his eyebrows. "I've been keeping an eye on him, but I guess a mother's observations are instinctively more astute than a country doctor's."

Helen swept her hand past the surrounding viewscreens. "This computer has become his whole life. He sits there for hours on end, running programs, accessing data, making computations. I understand that the work needs to be done, but without dragons breathing fire down our necks, we've got all the time in the world to do it."

"Henry, it's almost incestuous the way he fondles that keyboard. But I can't say that it's necessarily bad for him. He's naturally introverted anyway. Scott's the only one who can get through to him; they grew up together. And Rusty took it pretty bad when the dragons gassed his family and friends. It turned his whole life around. Emerging from the womb of Maccam City into the reality of a dragon-infested planet was quite a shock for him, and a blow to his security. Maybe he's just working out those pent-up emotions by delving into the sanctum of his mind. These mental exercises are probably as important to him as physical therapy is to Scott. Both need to stay in shape: one mentally, the other physically. Rusty *might* be headed for a nervous breakdown; or he might be on the road to catharsis."

Doc pursed his lips and squeezed his beard. "That's a well thought out medical opinion for one who professes to be only a country doctor."

A broad grin split Sam's bewhiskered face. "I *have* been keeping an eye on him. The diagnosis is subject to change, if there's a change in the subject."

"I'll change the subject," said Helen. "How about some chow? The granary is overflowing, the galley is stocked with fresh fruits and vegetables, the last of the livestock has been butchered and salted, and the freezer is full of prepared meals. And when I passed by there earlier the galley slaves were baking bread."

"I'm easy," said Sam.

"You always were," Helen chided. "Father?"

"There is rarely a time when this stomach is not grumbling. But with all these good victuals so handy, I'm going to have to watch my waist line. Starting tomorrow." Leaving Sam and Helen laughing behind him, Doc tapped his cane across the deck. "Scott. Jane. Would you care to join us for a mild repast?"

Scott looked up from the monitor. "I'm as hungry as a dinosaur."

"You always are." Jane pushed back her chair and stood up, surrounding Scott's midriff with her arms. "He is an eating machine."

"Good." Doc pattered across the orange plastic deck to where Rusty sat in front of a bank of terminals and viewscreens. The redhead was completely absorbed in the dragon line language flashing intermittently on the display monitors. Doc was barely able to focus on the coded symbols before they disappeared and were replaced by others, but he knew that Rusty was scanning every line with complete understanding. Doc slipped his hand between Rusty's face and the computer screen; he waved to gain attention. "My boy, do you think you can break away long enough for a bite, and perhaps a short rest? You look awfully run-down."

The blank stare that was returned seemed to be a million miles away—or a million years off. Rusty's face was gaunt and haunted, and his tan had long since faded. He squeezed his eyes tightly, opened them, then blinked several times. "Wha—what?"

"As friend, physician, and father-figure, I heartily recommend some time off."

"Time?" The lone word lingered in the air like the dying croak of a frog. Rusty blinked some more. His eyes were red with the lack of sleep. "Time?"

"We cannot take off on this venture with our bodies debilitated by fatigue, any more than we can fly this saucer in a state of disrepair. We must be fit to meet every demand. I think, perhaps, you are overtired."

There was silence on the bridge.

Rusty squinted as he surveyed those around him. "Tired? Of course I'm tired. And you know what I'm tired of? I'm tired of legendary lizards and prehistoric monsters ruling my life. I'm tired of dragons popping up in every millennium. I'm tired of living in fear of what tomorrow may bring. I'm been on the run too long, and I'm not running anymore. The dragons have reigned supreme one time too many. We chased them out of the present, we destroyed their past, now we're going to make *damned* sure there's no future for dragons. One time they came after me; now they're hiding. This time I'm going after *them*—anywhere, anywhen. And this time there will be no survivors."

CHAPTER 2

"I christen thee *Ark*."

Helen officiated the ceremony. After delivering the incantations and pronouncing the name chosen for the modified dragon flyer, she smashed a plastic container of local manufacture against the telescoping entrance pedestal. The jar broke, splattering water over Helen, the landing pad, and the loading ramp.

A great cheer arose from the throng crowded in the shade of the saucer. The overhanging undercarriage bristled with lifting cones and double-acting focusing nodes, now quiescent for the commissioning. The casemates were hinged open, and the guns protruded from their blisters like giant insect stingers. The warship was fully charged, the weapons systems functional, and the power train operational. It was ready for launching.

"I can't wait to try this baby out." Scott grasped Rusty's forearm in the Nomad greeting style. "Now we can really make some time."

For the first time in weeks, Rusty had the strength to stand up straight. He thrust back his shoulders and worked out the cramps. The forced feeding and round-the-clock snooze had done him a world of good. He was able to face the future with renewed energy and outlook. "I'd be willing to forgo the pomp and circumstance and get on with the performance trials."

"Don't worry about that. The *Ark* will pass the tests with flying colors. She'll do her job anywhere, anytime."

Rusty nodded absently. "I believe in execution, not theoretical prediction."

"She's a machine, Rusty. More sophisticated than most, but still a machine. And like any other machine, she'll do exactly what she was built to do. You don't call it a prediction when you press the trigger of a laser gun and it burns a hole through a bulkhead, or when you drop a ball and it bounces on the ground. It's called design and natural law. The *Ark* is simply the greatest machine and the grandest design ever conceived, operating on sound principles of natural law."

9

Scott's enthusiasm was gradually breaking through Rusty's self-doubts. "I'm sure you're right, Scott. I'm just afraid of being disappointed."

The slap that Scott landed on Rusty's back nearly bowled him over. "Come on, you old skeptic. Is this the same Rusty who programmed missiles to knock down dragon flyers and never thought twice about success?"

Rusty forced a grin. "The same one, but older and wiser."

"Then fight off senility and get with the program. We've got to stay one foot ahead of the dragons." Scott tapped his peg leg on the landing pad. "Tyrannosaurs, too."

"How can you joke about something like that?"

"I can't let it get me down. Life is what you make of it, not what it makes of you."

"Have you been taking proverbial lessons from Doc?"

Scott bowed in laughter. "I guess a lot of him has rubbed off on me."

"Me, too." Rusty reconnoitered the crowd. People were celebrating the event like Roman soldiers marching off to war. "Uh, listen, Scott, I'd like to avoid the festivities and take care of a few last-minute details. Will you make excuses for me?"

"No way. You're staying right here. With the amount of time we've got ahead of us, the detailed minutes don't count." Scott glanced around at the merrymaking. "Sandra." The jollity was so loud that his voice was lost in the hubbub. "Hey, Sandra!"

She was only a few feet away, clinging to Death Wind like bark to a tree. She saw Scott, waved with her free hand, broke her husband away from the mob, and piloted him to the corner of the entrance ramp where Scott and Rusty huddled out of the stream of well-wishers. "I've never been to a party before, but this is an awful lot like they looked on video. Hey, sourpuss, did you have a nice nap?"

The corner of Rusty's mouth turned up in the semblance of a smile. "Thanks to a potion that someone slipped into my salad."

Sandra held up her hands, palms outward. "I'm innocent. I've been exerting all my feminine wiles on my husband. He thinks just because I'm—" She rubbed her hands over her distended abdomen. "Well, never mind. It's just an old Nomad custom that I'm not accustomed to."

Death Wind looked on expressionlessly.

"That watermelon seed you swallowed looks like it's about

ripe." Scott pointed a finger at her belly. "Have you thought of a name yet?"

"No, but we're working on it." Sandra's hair was growing back in. When she swept the loose strands over her ear the frizzled ends brushed her shoulders. She leaned close conspiratorially. "Death Wind Junior is *not* among the choices."

"No offense meant, but I'm glad. That's too much of a mouthful for a godfather to say." Scott held his hands out like a supplicating priest. "So how do you like our pincushion. Think it'll get off the ground?"

In addition to the lifting beams of original installation, the *Ark* was equipped with all the focusing nodes from the dismantled time transport structure, as well as the battery packs to operate them. The extra cones were mounted atop as well as beneath the saucer, and along the curved perimeter. Only the gun turrets, command bubble, and landing platform were uncluttered by force-field units.

Sandra jabbed Scott with her elbow. "I think the *Ark*'s gonna show us a great time. Whoops, sorry, I'm slipping into dialect. Going to show us a great time. The hardest part about teaching language to the natives has been cleaning up my own lingo. If I don't speak properly or enunciate correctly, they pick up my bad habits."

"Have you chosen your replacements?"

"A local gal we named Susan is taking over for Jane in basic; it's important to have someone who understands finger speak and tone talk in order to converse with the natives. An outsider named Bethany is taking my place in advanced." Sandra shook her head. "I never thought I'd be an English major."

Scott winked. "You're only a captain, but there's still hope."

She faked a scowl. "You may think you're funny, but you don't have a kernel of wit."

Scott groaned as he buried his head in his hands.

Rusty roared out loud. "She got you that time." He could not stop laughing.

Even Death Wind smiled.

The noise attracted Doc, Jane, Sam, and Helen. Jane slipped her arms around Scott's chest. Sam and Helen lounged in each other's embrace. Doc pinched his eyebrows at the continuing laughter.

"Is this a private conversation, or can anyone join in?"

Rusty completely lost control. He laughed so hard his cheeks hurt. Scott fell back against Jane as if in a fit of weakness. Sandra joined in with a chuckle.

Doc was still nonplussed. "I fail to comprehend the nature of such merriment, but the condition is certainly infectious."

Natives and outsiders clustered about and joined in the revelry. The commissioning ceremony was more than the simple naming of a renovated aerial warship, or the official transfer of control to human hands. It was a preflight gala, a celebration for those about to embark on a mission of mercy—and a campaign of all-time war.

"Can you give me a general idea what it's all about?"

Rusty bent over double; his sides ached as he bellowed and cried at the same time. Grinning broadly, Sandra shook her head. Death Wind was no longer the stoic Nomad: he was taken over by a deep-throated snickering. Sam and Helen joined in the rejoicing, but did not know why. Jane had her hands full with Scott.

When Rusty got control of himself, he managed to squeak out, "It's a matter of corporal punishment."

By this time everyone was roaring uncontrollably. The townspeople who now owned the erstwhile dragon city caught the fever and cheered their compatriots who were about to leave for battle. Those who elected to remain behind had responsibilities, too. They had the backbreaking job of adapting the city for human habitation; of starting a new civilization from available resources; of teaching a new generation about freedom, fraternity, and individuality; of learning the rudiments of dignity.

They named the city Charon—after the mythical boatman who ferried the dead across the River Styx to eternal life in the underworld. The modern-day Charon was the departure point for mankind, the portal through the Stygian flux of time into the great unknown of dragon purgatory. Little wonder that the eve of decampment should be attended by such jollity—otherwise, dread and depression might prevail.

The revelry went on until long after sunset, under the artificial light provided by minimum power to the lifting cones. The stroboscopic effect kept the cabal in high spirits: singing, dancing, and enjoying the last night before battle.

Later, after it was all over, Rusty returned to the command bubble and shut down the outside power circuits. The flyer's plastic insulation stifled the clamor of Rangers and Fusiliers bedding down in the barracks, of couples slipping into their rooms. The bridge was a refuge of silence and solitude.

"No one but us bachelors to mind the midnight watch."

Rusty spun around at the deep-throated voice. "Doc, I didn't hear you come in."

"My bones may creak, but I still retain a modicum of stealth." Doc tucked his cane under his arm and eased himself into the copilot's seat. His lion's mane of white hair and his bushy bleached beard were damp from a recent shower. The luxury of indoor plumbing was one of which everyone partook. "It is my resolve that reverberates."

"Don't tell me *you're* having second thoughts."

Doc humphed. "The wise man never stops having thoughts, for then he is undone. In this case, however, it is my imagination that runs riot. When one contemplates the paradox of time travel, one realizes that in an infinite universe in which one may roam at will, there is time for as many thoughts as one wants. All this confabulation about alternative continua and parallel universes does not conform to my primitive, nonmathematical concept of space-time. The complexities are paramount. I remain agnostic to the notion that the cause-effect of our actions is interdependent upon our origin as well as our destiny. Going backward and forward in time has altered my perception of reality."

"Time isn't a treadmill with a beginning and an end. It's a simultaneity. Mathematically, space and time are two coordinates perpendicular to each other. There are many spaces, and many times. Events can occur at one space at many different times, or at one time at many different spaces. By definition an event is something that occurs at a specific space at a specific time. It's a mutual exclusivity."

Doc raised thick eyebrows. "And your explanation, my boy, lacks pellucidity."

Rusty smiled. "Sorry, Doc. I wasn't trying to be pedantic. It's just that you're used to traveling in space, but not in time. I'm sure our existence is equally incomprehensible to a being who travels in time, but not in space."

"Do you postulate such an entity?"

"I admit only the possibility because time travel has the same mathematical validity as space travel. The dragons' time transport structure is a prime example. It has the capability of moving objects anywhen in the time stream, but it's static in space. That's why we filled in the area with twenty feet of poured plastic: it invalidates the use of the TTS for as long as that space is occupied. The time dragons can't suddenly appear in our midst. The force of a material object recoiling off already occupied space would destroy the sending unit with incredible devastation.

"Let me give you an example of apparent nonsimultaneity. Once we were prisoners in this flyer, now we command it." Rusty held out his hands. "Is that a paradox?"

Doc shook his head.

"That's because the events occurred at different times. Easy enough to understand. But suppose I said we are sitting here and we are lying on the deck in the brig."

"You're merely confusing the issue with semantics—"

"No, I'm not, because the statement is true. I just left out the time axis referent. But that's not cause for invalidation. I could just as easily have left out the space axis referent by saying you are six years old and you are sixty years old."

Doc cleared his throat ominously. "Neither of which is true."

"Both of which are true—sometime, somewhere, but not anywhere at the same time, or anywhen at the same place. We can't be two places at once any more than we can be twice in the same time. That's a universal given."

"In other words, you can't bump into yourself."

Rusty grinned. "Doc, you have a knack for reducing the most complicated concepts to simplistic analogical terms."

"A minor talent."

"But let me go one step further."

"Do we have to?"

"I'll keep it simple. Besides, it was you who said that time is an endless river with no past or future, only flow."

Doc brightened measurably. "How nice of you to remember."

"I always pay attention to wisdom."

"Thank you, although that may have been one of my less lucid apothegms. I believe I was just being philosophical."

"Nevertheless, it was an astute physicalistic statement. Between you and me, Doc, you know a lot more than you let on, and understand more than you allow."

Doc pursed his lips, but made no comment.

"Anyway, in spatiotemporal terminology, the flow of time is more accurately defined as upstream and downstream. We think of it as backward and forward for the same reason we think of north as up and south as down—that's the way we draw our maps. We relate to time according to our psychological orientation to it. Since our movement through time from birth to death gives our bodies existence on the time axis, we imagine time to be moving.

And it *is* moving relative to the cosmos, the same as the Earth moves through space: rotating on its axis, revolving around the sun, spinning with the solar system through the Galaxy, swept along with the Galaxy through the universe. But we're not aware of all that motion. All we can perceive is that the ground beneath our feet is steady.

"If you were to view events in time from an external frame of reference equivalent to that of a station master able to see what was going on inside every car of a train, they would all appear to be occurring simultaneously. You'd see me sitting here in front of you, you'd see me running from a tyrannosaur in the Cretaceous, you'd see me attacking the Outpost, you'd see me living in Maccam City, you'd see my birth—and you'd see my death. Every event in the time stream is visible from the proper perspective, which means that every event is universally simultaneous. It's the same as standing on a mountaintop and observing four different people, one in each quadrant. Those people can't see one another; in fact, they have no awareness of the others' existence because they are out of sight from each grounded observer's point of view.

"So here we are flowing downstream in time, sighting each event as we pass it by. Now the dragons have invented a machine that can journey through time the same as an airplane flies through space. It's not quick enough to reach simultaneity, and paradox, but it permits us to go faster than our life flow allows, and permits us to go further in either direction. You can't walk to China: your life line isn't long enough, and the physical barriers are insurmountable. But a jet can fly you there in a few hours. The dragon time transporter works the same way, but along the time axis instead of the space axis."

Doc said, "Then you are assuring me that, even with the refinements you have incorporated, the fabric of space-time is not so fragile that mere mortals can disrupt its continuity."

"Exactly."

Doc inhaled deeply. "I guess that is what I needed to hear."

"Good. Now we both feel better."

CHAPTER 3

The throttle control was an electronic rheostat operated from the pilot's console by a series of buttons, or tap switches, each of which applied eight times the thrust of the next lowest button in line. Rusty made sure the perimetric gyroscope had reached full stabilization before switching on the electric drive. He tapped the lowest button once. A light appeared on the flight annunciator panel, denoting a single increment of vertical thrust.

He tapped it again; another light came on. A dazzling array of gauges and digital readouts fluctuated slightly with the added energy potential. A third tap caused the bridge to shudder, like a sail struck by a gust of wind. Rusty glanced at the anxious faces around him. He realized that he was holding his breath.

"It must be all the extra weight—"

The fourth tap brought a bump. Rusty studied the screens whose linked cameras brought external images into the command bubble. The power nodes glowed dimly. Thermocouples registered outside temperature readings, while telemetry equipment sufficed where hardwire was impractical.

"I think this is it." Rusty tapped again and felt the floor push up against his feet. The inclinometer did not waver. The momentary pressure eased off; there was no more sense of motion. Rusty broke into a broad grin. He could not keep the elation out of his voice. "The *Ark* is airborne."

A loud cheer rose up around him, but he had to ignore it in order to keep his mind on the unfamiliar controls. As he continued to tap the vernier buttons the thrust grid lit up by degrees.

"Way to go, Rusty!" Scott, in the copilot's seat, kept his eyes on the readouts. "Look at the down monitor. You can see the ground getting farther away."

"Steady as she goes." Rusty kept all the power on the vertical axis. Until the *Ark* had more altitude, he did not want to drift off the landing pad and fry the surrounding buildings. Onlookers had been warned to maintain a safe distance during takeoff. Reprogrammed transponders gave the elevation in Arabic numerals. "Relative altitude is just passing a hundred feet."

"The sky's the limit," Scott shouted.

"Is it?" said Sam. "How high will this thing go?"

"She's not a rocket, so she can't fly in a vacuum. The power nodes need to push against a substance. The thinner the air, the slower her rate of ascent." Scott pointed to a sectional viewing screen. "The altimeter is calibrated to about twenty-five thousand feet, but there's no reason to think that's her true ceiling. After that, she probably becomes increasingly unresponsive to vertical lift."

"Passing two hundred." Rusty gulped as he tapped the next highest button. The power input jumped by a factor of eight. His stomach dropped into his pelvis, giving him a queasy sensation that he had never felt before.

"Hey, what're you trying to do, cause a premature birth?" Sandra gripped her belly with both hands, fingers intertwined, as if she were making a cradle for her unborn offspring. "You'd better slow down unless you want a baby born on your bridge."

"Sorry."

Jane stood behind Scott, rubbing his shoulders. "I have climbed walls, but never air. It is strange."

Rusty flipped on the external microphone. The vibrant thrumming of the lifting beams filled the command bubble, lilting in cadence with the purple pillars of light that coruscated along the needlelike energy focusers.

"That's a sound I never thought I'd be happy to hear," Helen said.

Doc exaggerated a shiver. "It still fills me with apprehension. The depths of emotion are not readily overridden by reason, nor can a lifelong association of that sound with death be shrugged off so simply."

"I've got a few chills myself." Rusty tapped the level two thrust button again. Another burst of power surged through the *Ark*, launching the flyer upward at ever-increasing speed. Less than half the lights on the flight annunciator panel were aglow—there was power to spare. "Altitude one thousand feet, elevation nine hundred." The hundred-foot difference was the height of Charon above sea level. "Scott, you want to start displacing thrust from the vertical axis to the horizontal?"

"With pleasure." Scott manipulated the axial displacement controls that tilted the energy needles off their baseplates in any selected direction, thus providing lateral thrust. The copilot's console contained a flight panel similar to that of the pilot's console, except that the lights glowed in accordance with power applied to the horizontal axis. The vernier buttons controlled angular thrust. "Honey, this may get a little rough. You'd better tell everyone to hang on."

Jane was the communications officer. "Okay." She squeezed Scott again before taking her place at the intercom station. Dragons did not possess the laryngeal apparatus needed to issue vocal commands; all audio transmission was given in the form of musical tones played on a stringed instrument, or, in the case of shipboard intercommunications, on a digital synthesizer. Jane typed the appropriate coding signals. Loudspeakers in the rooms and corridors below decks chimed the message.

Scott flexed his fingers. "Going for level one displacement." He selected his direction from the gyrocompass and locked it in. "Headed east."

As Scott tapped the lowest vernier button, Rusty added another increment of power from the fusion drive. The result should have been a smooth transformation from pure vertical rise to vertical rise with lateral movement. The actual consequence was a sudden drop in altitude because the energy cones were deflecting their power at a slight angle, propelling the *Ark* laterally, and not enough power had been added to correct for the loss of upward motion.

"Add power! Add power!"

Rusty responded to Scott's shouted entreaties by tapping rather casually on his control panel until the altimeter leveled out. "Looks like we've got a three or four to one ratio for vector translation. At least, at this altitude. Air density probably makes a difference."

Scott wiped sweat off his brow. "Didn't mean to panic. I just don't like feathers in my stomach."

"I think this is going to take some getting used to." Rusty decreased power by flipping the reverse switch and tapping the power buttons. Lights faded off the flight panel. "Reading the manual isn't the same as flying."

"You said it." Scott studied the gauges spread before him. "We're headed east at about one mile per hour."

The *Ark* maintained an even keel, without pitch or yaw; the gyromechanisms were functioning perfectly. The ex-dragon flyer glided smoothly across the landscape. Starting at city limits and heading away from the plastic structures, it soon cruised over thick green jungle along the bank of a broad river.

"Let's practice our maneuvers at two thousand feet." Rusty flipped back to positive feed, tapped, and brought the *Ark* to the determined height. "That'll give us a safety margin in case I'm slow on the draw."

"I don't want to hear talk like that," Sandra said.

Scott smiled at her. "Don't worry. There's an emergency kill switch that immediately transfers all power to vertical lift." He touched the lever lightly.

The sarcasm in her voice was feigned. "I feel much better."

Beside her, with arms folded across his chest, Death Wind watched the proceedings wordlessly.

Rusty explained. "Of course, we'll still coast on the same bearing until friction brings us to a halt. Forward motion is canceled by retroversion: tilting the cones in the opposite direction and exerting a compensating thrust. This crosshair base recorder"—he indicated a graphic monitor—"bounces a laser beam off the ground so you can judge your drift."

"What happens if you're over the water?" asked Helen.

"It doesn't matter. The beam reflects off bedrock whether it's at the top of a mountain or at the bottom of the ocean. But the most complicated maneuver is turning. When thrust is applied at a different orientation, the machine describes a curve that's the result of both directional components. Well, as long as there aren't any peaks to bump into, let's put the *Ark* through the paces."

Death Wind glanced over his shoulder. The leading edge of the *Ark* was barely visible through the jungle canopy: a gold rim in a sea of green foliage. He readjusted the bow and the quiver of arrows slung across his broad, naked back, and continued the slow jogging pace he could keep up for hours.

He felt free in the woods, the kind of freedom he had known as a youth, before he had become a brave and his life had changed so abruptly, so drastically, and so irrevocably.

After such a long spell living the life of a city dweller, shrugging off the reins of civilization was like tossing aside iron shackles. As a captive in Charon, a guerrilla in dragon land, or a liberated citizen, he was confined to the indoors: a situation he bore with patience and Nomadic stoicism. Science and technology did not hold for him the fascination of the woods, the lore and the lure of the open spaces.

The air caressed his bare skin with silken pleasure, the woodland odors assailed his nostrils like perfume. He loved running free. He prized his physical prowess. The heaving of his chest, the dripping of sweat, the ache of muscles too long restricted, all brought back memories of simpler, happier times. The touch of lush ground cover under his moccasined feet was pure ecstasy. The faculties of reason were important to him, but his body was life itself. In the jungle Death Wind was at home.

His peripheral vision captured the minutest details around him: birds flitting in the treetops, insects buzzing among the branches, tiny lizards slithering underfoot. He ran on and on. He leaped over logs, slogged through the wet marsh, sprinted madly across the glades where he could put his mettle to the test. He was so sorry when, after an hour of independence, he heard sounds in front that were not natural to the forest.

Death Wind crouched by a thick bole, his bow unslung. Whoever, or whatever, was approaching did so with slow deliberation. Others were farther back. They were spread out at intervals as even as the trees and terrain allowed. They were quiet; hardly a twig cracked. But the Nomad's sensitive nose detected them with unerring precision. Confidently, Death Wind waited until the point man came into view.

The Nomad made his presence known. "Greetings!"

Like a felled oak the man dropped to the ground. He crawled behind a clump of tall grass. Only the battery pack protruded above the green stems. From all around came the clatter of weapons and falling bodies.

Death Wind made no foolish movements. Scared men were too quick on the draw, too likely to shoot at the merest provocation or hint of danger. He remained snug against the tree trunk until an unnatural silence reigned supreme. He sensed half a dozen laser barrels pointed his way; they were close enough to cleave the tree from its roots.

The Nomad waited for a bird to stop trilling. "Men stick together. It is code."

Death Wind heard rustling in the underbrush. Then he saw a head pop up above a bush.

"It's a Nomad." The startled expression matched the surprise in the man's voice. "It's a goddamned Nomad."

Death Wind stood tall and stepped into the open. He held up his right hand, palm outward. "Greetings, Ned. Many moons have crossed the sky since we last spoke. And much has happened."

CHAPTER 4

"You sure gave us a hell of a fright. I mean, buzzing over the city like that reminded me of before, when you folks were taken away." Ned threw his arms around Sam and hugged him tight. Tears flowed unabashedly. "And you— We thought the dragons got you years ago."

"They tried to interrogate me, but all they got was an icy stare." Sam winked at his wife. "Helen gave them the cold shoulder, too."

Ned pushed away from Sam so he could hug Helen again. "You don't look a day older than when I saw you last."

"Aging is arrested during hibernation, while the healing process is promoted," Helen sniffled. Tears of joy rolled down her cheeks. "Dad says the preparatory chemical injections shift the body's hormone balance."

"A diagnosis partially substantiated by computer scan of dragon medical records," Doc explained. "I followed their prescribed therapeutic procedure to thaw out the few corpsicles left behind after the dragon exodus, and they all revived in better condition than when they were frozen."

Ned used his short sleeves to wipe his face dry. "I'm still stunned. This reunion—and what I know from the quick briefing Death Wind gave me on the way here—well, it's just incredible." He swept his hands around the bridge. "This flyer." He shook his head. "And a time machine." He rolled his eyes in awe. "And you went back to the Cretaceous. It's just—unbelievable." He faced Doc. "Only your outfit could have pulled it off."

Doc shrugged. "My own part was relatively small."

"Although he did have a few earthshaking moments," Scott added.

"The most frightening part of the whole venture," Sandra tendered, "was Scott's humor—or attempt at it."

Scott tapped his stump on the deck. "I lost a few bones in the past, but not my funny bone." He gripped his upper arm. "Despite my loss, I've kept my humorous disposition."

Sandra rolled her eyes. "Uncle Ned, are you sure you missed all this?"

Ned laughed uproariously. "Every bit of it. I love you people. And the town will go wild when they hear about your return—and your revenge. Abolishing the fear from the past will offer hope for the future."

"Do you think your squad's had enough time to reach the Outpost and warn them?" Rusty fidgeted in the pilot's seat. "So we can get going?"

"Oh, sure. Death Wind met us about halfway, and we walked back pretty slowly. I kept prying him with questions."

"Jane. All aboard." Rusty spun around and faced the console. He checked the power grids while Jane toned the departure warning. When the all-clear signal came back from the entrance ramp, Rusty tapped the vernier buttons. With a week's flying under his belt, the *Ark* lifted off so smoothly that not a single stomach fluttered. This time, too, he did not forget to actuate the hydraulic ram that withdrew the telescoping landing tube into the body of the saucer. "Next stop, the Outpost."

Ned seemed unaware that for the first time in his life he had left the ground. Mentally, perhaps, his head was already in the clouds. "Sandra, what's happened to my little girl?"

"I grew up."

"And out," added Scott. "If she gets any bigger she won't fit through the doorways."

"You're just jealous because I'm having our baby before Jane's having yours."

"No, I just like teasing you. It's one of life's little pleasures."

Sandra ruffled Scott's hair. "I think I liked it better when we fought all the time. Sometimes I miss seeing you cringe."

"And no two people fought longer than we did—all the way from the Cretaceous onward. Ned, did anyone else ever get away with calling her Toad?"

"Watch your tongue, you!"

Scott smiled. "Never mind. I got the reaction I wanted."

Sandra hit him playfully on the arm. "Careful, blondie, or I'll crack your humorous humerus."

"If you do, I'll slap your gluteus maximus."

"Don't you wish." Turning to Ned, she said, "You can tell we love each other. We quarreled constantly before we got married— to our prospective mates. Honestly, Jane, I don't know what you see in this hunk of flesh."

Jane opened her mouth, but did not join the repartee.

"Sandra, please. You two can spar later. Let Ned tell us what's been going on since we left."

"Not much, Jane. Fortunately, Scott and Rusty trained enough people in reactor maintenance that we've been able to keep the electricity going. I mean, we're holding our own, all right, but we haven't made much progress in converting the Outpost, as you call it, into a human habitation. Oh, we've got some of the houses renovated, but since the Nomads left, and then you were taken away, that left us shorthanded and not very motivated. We didn't know when the dragons might come back again and recapture the whole town, so we've been living on the edge ever since. Got quarters near the city limits, and moved the whole armory into the jungle for safekeeping.

"We've been concentrating our efforts on cultivating the crops and repopulating the swamp with dinosaurs. I know that's what the dragons wanted to do, to change this world into a latter-day Cretaceous, but we don't have much choice. We need meat, and without any other stock, dinosaurs will have to be the fare for the future."

"I could eat one right now," said Scott, from the copilot's seat.

"You always could consume a triceratops right down to the shield and horns. I see you haven't changed any." Ned ran his hands through his hair and wiped them off on his shorts. "So what's this Death Wind was telling me about computer crystals and seeding farms? That fellow still don't talk much."

Doc snickered. "Once a Nomad, always a Nomad. Despite his recent education, he still harbors his native ways. But then, I guess we all do."

"Thanks for answering my question, Doc."

The aging doctor shook his head and came out of his reverie. "Sorry, I have a tendency to wax philosophical these days."

"No comment," said Rusty. The *Ark* skimmed along the top of the jungle just high enough so the energy needles did not singe the upper branches. Once the course, speed, and elevation were established, and locked into the automatic pilot, there was little to do but sit back and watch the gauges and monitors. Coordinated ground-scanning radar maintained at all times the *Ark*'s height above the ground, while lateral proximity sensors warned of oncoming cliff faces that might obstruct passage.

"As you were saying," prompted Ned.

Doc stroked his cottony beard. "I never understood how love

could conquer the world, but in this case it has certainly given us the weapon to do so."

Ned stared openmouthed. "Huhn?"

"We have Scott and Jane to thank for that. Scott for demonstrating his love so thoughtfully, Jane for requiting it in such fiercely feminine fashion. It was the diamond that prompted so traditional an engagement: a diamond that was a crystal memory lattice and the key to the future."

"Oh, sure. That makes perfect sense."

"Forgive me if I ramble, but so much mental disorientation has occurred in recent months that those events seem like ancient history. We are now engaged in a totally different but every bit as serious battle with dragons. They lie in wait for us in the future—our future. And world domination is again the stake for which we are playing."

"It's getting clearer already."

Doc continued on his own track, gazing most of the time into space. No one offered to prompt him. "Death Wind's thumbnail sketch undoubtedly covered the destruction of the time transfer structure in the Cretaceous, and the disabling and dismantling of the TTS in Charon. But the latter action merely ensures that dragons cannot suddenly reappear at that specific space-time coordinate. The information contained in the crystal brought back from the past along with Jane's slender neck confirmed Rusty's deduction that, while the geographic location occupied by the TTS in Charon was the same throughout the ages, other way stations existed along the time stream. The Charon TTS was not a terminus, but a stopover point operated for the specific purpose of making the land fertile for later dragon occupation. A seeding farm is what we call it; the Outpost was built later for the same purpose. More plantations were planned, but never reached the construction phase."

"Whoa. Hold on a sec." Ned held his hands out in front of him. "I'm more bewildered than ever. Can we go a little slower."

"For us, time is no longer of the essence. I do understand that, not having spent countless hours discussing the probability of events, the issue must seem somewhat perplexing to you. Let me add detail. You see, Ned, soon after the dragon's serendipitous discovery of time travel, came the startling revelation that their race as well as their rule was doomed to extinction. They did not know how, nor how soon, only that despite their best efforts it must occur. They firmly believed in the absolute inevitability of events; that is, they perceived the flow of time as an immutable conveyor belt that began when the universe was created, and that will end when entropy causes the universe to run down.

"Rusty, here, possesses no such preconceived notions. He has been instrumental in convincing the rest of us that nothing in the universe is absolute except the zero mark in the scale of atomic motion: that point at which all nuclear activity ceases, and when for all practical purposes the structure of the atom collapses into a form of degenerate energy."

"Uh, Doc, you're getting a bit beyond me."

"An unnecessary digression. To clarify, atomic motion is what we perceive as temperature. Its relevance to the present is metaphysical and somewhat out of context with our initial and for now primary purpose. I was musing in terms of the Grand Design of the Universe. To resume, on their very first downstream time jump the dragons descried that warm-blooded dinosaurs and cold-blooded lizards had relinquished their predominant place in the scheme of life to an order of animal that had previously been considered little more than a nuisance: the mammal. Dinosaurs died out altogether, while lizards survived in a subservient role. The erstwhile tiny protomammals would shortly grow to great proportions and evolve competitive intelligence. Am I boring you?"

"Not at all. I'm sure it all means something."

Doc frowned. "I will try to be more specific. The dragons, despite their dogmatic acceptance of the unalterable flow of time, were quite understandably loathe to yield either their lives or their power. They conceived a master plan that was commensurate with their credence: to populate the Earth at some future time when the climate was suitable to their way of life. Only one thing stood in their way."

"Let me guess. Us."

"A minor impediment, which they abolished without quibble or qualm. Dragon shortcomings lay not in the technologies of mass murder or obviating the time barrier, but in the humanitarian sciences. No, the chief hindrance was an unstoppable geological process leading to global glaciation: what we refer to as the Ice Age."

Ned sighed and glanced at the others on the bridge. "The Pleistocene Epoch?"

"The same. And what may eventually come to be referred to as the Pleistocene Epic. You see, when the dragons laid siege to our time period, the Quaternary, they did so with the knowledge that the last of the Pleistocene glacial advances was over. That was why they selected this particular interregnum in which to make their invasion. It made little sense to start some millions of years into the Tertiary Period knowing full well that most of the Earth would someday lay buried under billions of tons of ice.

"Biological survival was not the problem. Many species have lived through the four glacial advances that occurred during the Pleistocene; many also died. Most managed to cope by adapting to conditions, a process known as evolution. But the dragons did not want to evolve, or be forced to undergo the hardships of living through global freeze-ups lasting hundreds of thousands of years. They wanted to maintain the status quo of their civilization, and eventually transport it in its entirety to a ready-made Garden of Eden. They did encounter a few problems, however, in carrying out their stratagem.

"They had all of time to dabble in, but their time transport apparatus was limited by two constraints: power and imprecision. This station, what we have termed the Holocene Station, represents the furthest time downstream that their equipment in the Cretaceous could reach."

"You mean, they couldn't focus enough energy to punch through more than sixty million years?"

Doc was taken aback. "Why, yes."

Ned smiled at the sea of faces. "Go on. It's beginning to come to me."

"It is?" Doc cleared his throat. "Of course it is. In any case, their problem was not the lack of raw power, but, as you surmised, the technology required to concentrate enough energy through the focusing nodes to further penetrate the barrier of space-time: in correlative terms, to get further into the future than our own present. At the time of their demise, it appears that the dragons were on the verge of making the technological breakthrough that would have allowed them to extend their temporal range with ease.

"But the reptilian intellect operates differently from the intellect of mammals. Just as the ectothermic body is more primitive than the heat-producing body of the mammal, so is the structure of the lizard brain more primitive. Dragon gray matter has vast potential, but it works more slowly. What this means in evolutionary terms is that dragon progress, both biological and cultural, takes place over a period of time we would consider abnormally long."

"I'm way ahead of you," Ned said proudly. "Dragon verge is not the same as human verge, am I right? Industry that took the dragons hundreds of thousands of years to develop could be invented overnight by man."

"Perhaps an oversimplification, but approximately true."

"Which means that given dragon science and technology as a starting point, mankind can push ahead dynamically and accomplish what dragons could never even dream of. The good old hyperactive human bean is better than the dragon noodle."

"Vegetative aspersions aside, yes."

"Which means that we're going places while the dragons are still making up their minds to blink."

"I wish you would not make it all sound so elementary."

"Doc, you didn't have to go through all that rigmarole to arrive at a simple conclusion. All you had to say was we got what it takes, and they don't."

Doc raised bushy eyebrows at his companions. "I'm afraid I have gotten completely off the subject of our goals, both short-term and long-range. Ned, you must understand that we do not have complete knowledge of the dragons' latest activity or state of advance, because the crystal salvaged from the Cretaceous was a backup crystal stored in a data retrieval facility. However, the fact most clearly delineated and not subject to change was their plan of campaign. And while we have destroyed both dragons past and present, there are others that exist in a time frame that can still do us harm.

"What we need to do immediately—if you will allow a word which within the parameters of time travel has no relativistic meaning—is to spike the Outpost's TTS in order to prevent dragons from entering this particular spacial reference, and to recruit an army to track down all surviving dragons—wherever and whenever they may be—and stamp every last one of them out of existence." Doc wiped sweat off his brow. "That may sound pathetically brutal, but given the history of dragon intrigue and tenacity it is the only choice we have. Dragon and human cannot coexist. There is space-time for only one of us."

CHAPTER 5

"Father."

"Son."

"Men stick together. It is code."

"It is code."

Death Wind and Bold One clasped each other's shoulders in the traditional Nomad familial embrace.

"You come in flyer," Bold One stated flatly, not just as an observation, but as a summation of all it implied.

Death Wind did not need to concur. "Much has happened."

Bold One waited patiently for an explanation. The hot sun beat down on the open prairie, baking the sandy soil. The grass was withered and dry except along the banks of the nearby creek. There was no wind to rustle the brittle stems, or to sift through dark, shoulder-length hair. Except for the creases of age, father and son were as alike as two kernels on a cob.

The land felt good under Death Wind's moccasins. A deep-seated longing crawled out of the soil and held him there like the roots of a quaking aspen. Here, with his father, with the rest of the tribe looking on, he was home. That other world, in the dragon flying machine, surrounded by space-age technology, no longer seemed real. That was where he lived, this was where he belonged. Death Wind was suddenly homesick for the freedom and lifestyle of his youth.

"We fight. Many dragons die. Take flyer. Fight more. Need help."

Bold One stared long and hard. He held the finely crafted spear in front of him, butt on the ground, and stood as tall and immobile as a cigar-store Indian. His naked chest was broad and bronzed, his belly flat with abdominal muscles finely delineated. His stance was that of a warrior about to pounce: legs spread wide, knees slightly bent, upper body tilted forward at the waist.

Dark, fathomless eyes peered out from under a wrinkled brow. "Come. We talk."

Bold One spun on his heel and took off at a jog. Death Wind

31

Gary Gentile

followed his father at the same pace. The tribe was spread out among the bushes, out of sight to all but one experienced in the ways of the Nomad. Death Wind strained his eyes to pick out the protruding arrow here, the tip of a spear there. The men and women themselves blended in with the terrain; the children lay huddled under the leaves of shrubbery, or behind the trunks of stunted trees. They were the wraiths of the plains.

The older Nomad stopped in the middle of a shallow depression. He jammed his spear into the loamy soil, cupped his hands, and emitted a loud call that was the perfect imitation of a hoot owl. Slowly people came out of hiding. They emerged from the ground, they crawled out from under blankets of leaves, they descended from the low pinon pines. First the braves: men and unattached women; then the young and elderly; then mothers with children and babes-in-arms.

Death Wind kissed his mother and exchanged greetings of love.

"Son, you have come home."

"Not to stay, Mother. Take away. In flyer. Fight dragons."

Slender Petal nodded once, almost imperceptibly. "More?"

"We find. We must destroy."

Slender Petal nodded again.

The tribe gathered in the hollow. Bold One, as their chief, raised his arms skyward for attention. There was no noise or clatter, no fussing or fidgeting—only the occasional whimper of diaper-clad infants and the choral cooing of their mothers. The air was still.

Bold One's voice was deep and sonorous. "Death Wind speaks." He dropped his arms and stepped aside.

Death Wind took his father's place. He gazed at the faces of the people—his people—making eye contact with each and every one before opening his mouth. He had never spoken to the tribe as a member of the council of war. Yet, he felt no anxiety or lack of resolution. Many times during his youth he had squatted while others offered counsel. They were always treated with respect, and their ideas were taken with great regard.

"I have come far in dragon flying machine. Since we last met we have killed many dragons, we have captured other city, we have destroyed their homeland. But others exist to menace us. Not now, but in future. We build great army to fight them, to rid them forever from our world, to make this land free for our children for all time. To do this we need help. I have pledged my tribe to conquer dragons because men stick together. It is code."

Every person of speaking age repeated the litany. The intonation sounded like one voice with a hundred different pitches.

Bold One raised his arms once again. "Members speak."

There was but a moment's hesitation before the first brave, a woman, stood up and jabbed her spear at the white, puffy clouds. "Fight!"

A wizened, old man bent with age climbed unsteadily to his feet. "Fight!"

One by one, then en masse, the tribal members jumped up. Men and women, young and old, warriors all, shouted their subscription to wage war against dragons. It took but five minutes to gather weapons and personal belongings, to load the travois, to start the march toward the shimmering golden saucer that perched serenely on the horizon like the rising sun. Once before, against their will, these people had been herded into such a flyer; now, by their own prerogative, they rushed forward eagerly to meet their fate, and to play their part in deciding the fate of the world.

The surface of the Earth was a dizzying patchwork quilt of muted colors some six miles below. The images received on the downward viewscreen were interspersed with puffy cumulus clouds. The lateral viewscreens showed a faded blue stratosphere and fleecy strands of cirrus; the sky above was a deep purple canopy punctuated by the bright, untwinkling pinpoints of stars.

"It's a complex formula that took me months to develop, despite the fact that I knew both the problem and the solution: that is, where/when in space-time the dragons departed, and where/when they arrived. What I had to determine was how to get from one synchronistic point to the other. In actuality, I worked from both ends toward the middle, or, in scientific terminology, from one synchronism to another."

"Rusty, I don't think of myself as an ignorant man, but talk like that humbles me." Ned scratched his balding head. He wore an expression of perplexity that was fast becoming his normal mien. "If it hadn't been for Scott boning me up on your gobbledygook I'd be a regular flibbertigibbet."

Rusty squinted hard. "Huhn?"

Now it was Ned's turn to laugh. "I've been picking up some of Windy's argot. It has a right nice twang to it."

Scott raised his eyebrows innocently. "He didn't ask for a course in spatiotemporal navigation, just for the short version of why we're practically going into orbit to make the jump."

Rusty rolled his eyes. "It's not easy to condense a textbook that hasn't even been written into one easy lesson."

Still smiling, Ned urged him on. "If I get stuck on the big words I'll let you know."

Rusty looked from one to the other, took a quick glance at the flight grid, gauges, and control screens, and inhaled deeply. "I'll try to make it as simple as possible, but I've had to make up words to describe some of the transtemporal phenomena."

Scott winked. "You don't need sixty million years to take him from the Cretaceous to the Holocene, but you don't have to do it in two high intensity minutes, either."

"Actually, the transfer through time is instantaneous in both the objective as well as the subjective sense because universal isochronism dictates the parameters—" Rusty stopped with his mouth open, realizing what he must sound like.

"Just take it slowly," Scott warned.

"Right." Rusty took a deep breath. He paused for half a minute before proceeding. "Okay, look at it this way, Ned. The mathematics of physics recognizes four dimensions which as descriptions of convenience we call length, breadth, height, and the passage of time. Understand, however, that these measurements are artificial representations designed to fit human perceptions: finite quantities that portray a picture of infinity. Are you with me so far?"

Ned screwed up his face. "Just barely. Are you saying that dimensions aren't real?"

"Almost." Rusty wagged an index finger. "What I mean is that dimensions lend corporeity—no, forget that." Rusty held up his fist and circled it with a bent finger. "Here's an electron spinning around an atom. All of this in here is empty space. But when we put millions, or billions, of atoms together, with their outer shells touching, we get this chair. It's tangible, something we can see and feel, but we know it's made up mostly of tiny bits of matter held in place by electromagnetic force."

Ned nodded slowly. "I got you so far."

"What we perceive as solid is composed of a bunch of hollow spheres whose shells are jammed together like a bag full of soap bubbles. And we don't even know if protons and electrons are solid—they too may be forces whose subatomic interaction is manifested as humanly perceived solidity."

"I'm not sure—"

"Forget it." Rusty dissolved his hydrogen atom and waved his hands in the air. "Just think of the universe as a force field, not as a physical substance. But let's use our dimensions to create an analogy." Rusty placed a dragon writing pad on his lap. With an etcher he drew a square on the plastic facing. "Here's a two-dimensional world that exists on a single plane. It has length and breadth."

"Not bad breadth, I hope," Scott intruded.

Rusty sighed, but otherwise ignored his friend. He slid his finger along the pad. "To a two-dimensional stick figure the interior of the square is hidden." His finger bumped into the etched lines on all sides. Then he raised his finger in the air above the pad, and slowly brought it down inside the square. "But a figure that exists in three planes can see and touch any point in the square."

Ned's face brightened measurably. "Hey, that's pretty neat."

"Now just take that one dimension further, and you begin to understand how points of view exist that we can never be aware of. But it doesn't mean that with the proper instruments we can't detect those points of view, or that with sophisticated enough technology we can't utilize forces we can't comprehend. We can't see electrons move through a conductor, but that doesn't stop us from using electricity. Our eyes perceive only a narrow band of light, but we have detected and used the entire scale of electromagnetic radiation. Short waves existed before the invention of the radio. Our ears translate pulsations—"

"Okay. Okay. I get the point. Molecules vibrate when a tree falls in the woods, even if no one is there to hear it."

"Very good. Now let's assume that time is another dimension. We don't pay any more attention to it than we do of the Earth speeding through the Galaxy. We just take it for granted. We're a kind of universal flotsam, or an interstellar plankton, swept along with the tide of space-time. And we're stuck there just like this square is stuck to the pad. As three-dimensional observers, it's easy for us to understand that the square could invent a machine that could lift it off the pad.

"And so the dragons discovered a way of stepping through time. They stumbled over the physical principle that allowed them to peel off the three-dimensional world in one spot, and drop back down in another."

Scott interrupted his friend. "You see, Rusty. You don't *have* to use all that technical jargon. We'll make a teacher out of you yet."

"Don't do me any favors." He redirected his attention to Ned.

"But as long as I'm on a roll . . . The dragons didn't want to drift aimlessly with the currents of time. They never operated in random fashion. They had a specific goal in mind—a direction, a purpose, and a destination. They knew about the two-hundred-fifty-million-year-ice-age cycle. If they were going to begin a new civilization, why not begin after the next glacial advance? That's when they ran up against technological problems. The state of development of their time transfer equipment was extremely crude."

"Stay away from feedback gap circuits and use the cog analogy," said Scott. "Ned isn't an electronics expert."

"I was going to." Rusty rankled at the intrusion. "Picture a wheel whose rim is a series of teeth. Two wheels: one is the wheel of time, the other a machine wheel." Rusty held both hands in front of his chest, fingers spread wide, and interlocked them. "When you put the two together you've got a time machine, because you can move freely from one to the other and back again. But the number of teeth on the time wheel is infinite, while the manufactured wheel has only as many teeth as the dragons were able to machine. The teeth are all the same size, but they can mesh only at certain intervals. Are you with me so far?"

Ned frowned, but nodded silently.

"Okay, the dragon cogs are about a million years apart, give or take a few hundred thou depending on space-time variables we needn't go into. That means they couldn't go anywhen they wanted, but were forced to jump to times that coincided with the circuitry of their time transfer equipment. They were on the threshold of refining the infinite-time transfer vernier, that would have given them ultimate precision, but they met their maker first. How's that, Scott? Did I use simple enough words?"

"I like it."

"Now I get the picture," Ned said, his voice lilting. He stabbed a finger at the redhead. "And that's what you discovered."

"Extrapolated is more accurate. The dragons already had the raw data; all I did was carry it one step further. Even then, I probably wouldn't have thought along those lines—"

"Or space-time continua," interposed Scott.

"—if it hadn't been for Scott coming up with the idea of removing Charon's TTS focusing nodes, mounting them outside the hull, and reversing the polarity. Converting this saucer into a flying time transport structure was a brilliant concept—"

"I thought so."

"—that revolutionized transportion. Now we can move through time *and* space—"

"Now, or then, or simultaneously."

"—with equal impunity. At least, as far as our power resources allow. The *Ark* is the perfect all-continuum vehicle—"

"I was partial to naming her the *Magic Carpet*."

"—because it can move in—"

"*She* can move."

"—all four dimensions. We can circumnavigate the globe here and now, or then and there. We can go wherever we want whenever, or whenever we want wherever. All the reaches of space and time belong to us."

"The world is our oyster, time is our pearl."

"And that's what brings us to this altitude, and my calculations."

"Our rate of ascent is slowing down dramatically." Scott leaned forward and fiddled with some dials. "We appear to be leveling off at about thirty-four thousand feet."

Rusty glanced at the flight grid and saw that all available power was being translated along the vertical axis. "The data in the crystal gave the coordinates of the dragon retreat. The spatial reference is the same because their time transport structures are fixed in space. When they left Charon in droves they didn't go all the way back to the Cretaceous. That would have required incredible energy for the number of transfers they made. Instead they went back only one click in their time wheel—to a TTS they had installed in the Pleistocene—a short jump, relatively speaking.

"The equation for calculating a course to those coordinates is complicated—it has to be integrated in four dimensions—so the comptime is incredibly long. The other factor is power output, which is a function of the distance traveled in time, the mass of the object, and friction. Just as dynamic drag slows down an object moving through the air, so a time transfer is affected by the density of air at its point of arrival. When a vehicle moving through space contacts a solid object, it crashes; when an object transferred through time tries to displace too much matter at the point of its arrival, it backfires explosively and destroys the transfer capsule—in the dragons' case, the TTS.

"That's the reason for the force field: the staging area is partially evacuated so that fewer molecules need to be pushed out of the way when the transferred object arrives. By climbing into the stratosphere we are doing two things: making sure we don't transport ourselves into the middle of a mountain, and reducing the friction at the other end of the transfer.

"But you don't have to worry." Rusty cocked an eye at Ned. "Remember what I said about instantaneity. If there is something in our way at the other end of the time tunnel, we'll never know it."

CHAPTER 6

The *Ark*'s bridge control octagon was crowded for the big moment. Rusty and Sam sat in the command seats, Jane took over the communications console, Doc monitored the reactor station, and Helen and Sandra held places at data input terminals.

Scott stood by the all-important time transfer post that he had rewired from an auxiliary steering station. "I wish we had time to check this baby out." Dragons designed all their systems with triple redundancy, but when Scott cannibalized Charon's TTS he found the equipment so massive that there was room in the *Ark* for only one working model.

"We're taking the time, right now," Sandra scowled. "And we have all the time in the world."

"You know what I mean."

Sandra jerked a thumb at Scott while she glowered at Jane. "You see how serious he gets when it's *his* shirt on the line."

Jane smiled demurely.

Like a skulking lion, Death Wind padded off the last curve of the circular ramp. "Preparations complete. The crew is ready."

Since the saucer was constructed as an armed troop transport, and since dragon psychology permitted only a strictly utilitarian use of space, the *Ark* contained no amenities that would have been built into a human warship. There were no wardrooms, game rooms, or scuttlebutts. Whoever did not have an assigned battle station was forced to remain in quarters, or to roam the corridors.

"Okay, Sam, put us into a glide so we don't drop like a rock when we shift power."

"Don't take more than ten percent of the load," cautioned Rusty.

Sam tapped the vernier buttons and gradually transferred energy from the vertical drive cones to the lateral thrusters.

"Let me know as soon as we're stable, Rusty." Scott kept his eyes glued to his station monitors. "I want to lose as little altitude as possible. The thinner the air, the better."

"Gyros are on full, deviation is zero."

"Halfway there," said Sam as the thrusters diverted five percent of the available power.

"Let's not rush it." Scott wiped sweaty palms across the front of his vest. "I want to make a last-minute check of the chronometry circuits."

"Stop biding your time," Sandra quipped. "I'm not getting any younger."

Jane switched on the external mikes. The thrumming of the lifting cones whined down while the thrusters emitted a low, deep-throated roar. The *Ark* flew too high to detect any visible motion across the green jungle below.

"We're at maximum glide," said Sam.

Doc looked up from his monitors. "The reactor is still making little atoms out of big ones."

"Remember not to look directly at the screens," said Rusty.

Scott took his last Holocene breath. "Infinity, here we come." He jammed his finger down hard on a button that needed only to be tapped.

Deep within the bowels of the *Ark* huge contactors shunted the main transmission lines so that all generated nuclear energy flowed into the time transport circuits. The interval of diversion lasted either an instant or an eternity. The bridge lights dimmed. The lifting cones and thrusters went dark. The revamped flyer dropped suddenly. The inverted focusing nodes burst into full brilliance with the speed and intensity of a high-power strobe light, and discharged as quickly with a loud clap that sounded like a truncated peal of thunder. Power reverted to its normal mode. The bridge lights brightened. Lift and lateral thrust were restored. The *Ark* cruised on.

Scott inhaled deeply. Despite sealed ventilation ducts and electrostatic filters, the air was tainted with the pungent odor of ozone. "Well, something happened." He scanned the gauges and digital readouts. "We lost a hell of a lot of stored power. The capacitors are reading zero potential, and every battery in the ship is stone dead. All that electricity must have gone somewhere—or somewhen."

"Or maybe *it* stayed there and we went," said Sandra.

"The fabric of space-time does not tear easily." Doc tapped a few buttons on his console. "The reactor is straining under the load demand."

Rusty issued orders in a raised voice. "Sam, cut the thruster power completely. Doc, switch off the charging circuits till we reach the ground. I'll cut back on the cones so we can drift down. Jane, tell the crew everything's under control. Helen, run a logic check. Sandra, get Sirius."

"I'm always serious."

Rusty grimaced. His fingers flew across his keyboard. He repeated a phrase that was still on his mind. "You know what I mean."

Sandra lolled back in her seat. "Hey, redhead, I don't need to fix our position relative to the Dog Star to know that we've moved." She stabbed a finger at the viewscreens in front of her. "A sun sighting will tell me that."

Each console had its own set of external camera monitors. Rusty looked up, frowning.

"Either we've been in slumberland for eight hours, or somebody moved the sun on us. It was morning when we left—where we left."

The words poured out of Scott's mouth like molasses in winter. "Hey, she's right."

"The logic circuits check out," Helen said perfunctorily. "But there's a memory gap that looks as if the computer couldn't find itself for a microsecond or two."

"Look at the downscreen," Sam screamed. "It's all white."

Rusty was standing now, crouched over his keyboard while he craned his neck at the monitors. "Clouds?" He tapped the power grid in reverse; the *Ark* lost altitude in a controlled rate of descent.

"No way, man. The sky's clear as glass." Sandra waved her hands at the cluster of viewscreens. "The only nimbus out there is around the *Ark*."

The purple halo was the result of raw energy from the lifting cones being swept away in the downward rush of the flyer. Ionized vapor curled up around the saucer's rim, glowing in conjunction with St. Elmo's fire.

"I believe the monotonous expanse of bleached achromatism is a broad blanket of snow." Doc smiled proudly. "As we drop lower we should see some relief—"

"Hey, I got something on radar."

Scott leaped to Sandra's station and engaged the image enhancers. "Nothing on visual."

"It's too far away for proximity warnings, but it's coming our way." Sandra was unruffled by Scott's intrusion. The blip hung in the lower left-hand corner of her screen. "What the hell is it?"

"Climbing fast." Scott skipped around the bridge like a nervous chipmunk. "Sam, what's our lateral speed?"

"We're still in a slow glide, momentum only. Say, fifty mph."

"Rusty—"

"I know. It's altering trajectory to match our course. Whatever it is, isn't natural."

"Jane, tone out a warning."

"It's closing vectors." Rusty's downscreen showed a growing blotch of red.

Sandra shouted. "Hey, the damn thing's gonna hit—"

"Brace for impact!"

The object suddenly filled the downscreen, then wiped it out. The *Ark* reeled with the concussion, bucking like a bronco with a burr under its saddle. The perimeter scanners showed chunks of metal and bits of plastic flying off into space like broken toys from a shattered pinata. The *Ark* absorbed the shock and the damage, then settled down with a slight wobble.

Scott was bounced momentarily off the deck. He hovered in the air for a second, then touched down on the toes of his one foot like a performing ballerina. "What the hell—"

"That was a missile!" Rusty yelled.

Sandra was laconic. "Strange way of saying your prayers."

"Not a missal! A missile!" Rusty realized how stupid he sounded. "A *guided* missile."

"Jane, get a damage report from below." Scott shoved Rusty back into his seat and stood behind him with his hands gripped on the backrest. "How's our flight pattern?"

Rusty pounded out instructions on his keyboard. "Everything's operational. We lost a few cones and some focusing nodes, and the gyro's a little out of kilter. Lucky the damn thing was a dud."

"We might not be so lucky with the next one." Sandra drew attention to the radarscope. "There's another blip rising to the occasion."

"If you'll pardon my intrusion at this time of emergency, I suggest that we consider evasive maneuvers. The dragons obviously have a launching pad stocked for immediate delivery."

If Rusty heard him, he paid no mind. "We're coming down too fast. I've got more cones short-circuiting." His fingers were a blur across the keypad. "I can balance the load by increasing power to the other cones, but we're destabilizing. The gyro—"

The *Ark* wobbled sickeningly, like a child's top running down.

"It's getting close," Sandra warned.

Jane played her keyboard like a piano. Melodic tones went out over the ship's loudspeakers. "I'll tell the gun crews to shoot."

"Great idea," Scott said feverishly. With Rusty at the conn, and the other navigational consoles already staffed, there was nothing for Scott to do. He made a continuous circuit around the octagonal control center. "If the warhead goes off even close—"

"Do you suppose it's atomic?" Sandra said.

"If it is, we haven't got a chance."

Sam screamed, "Rusty, give me some power. I'll take a random course."

"Take as much as you want. I just need enough to smooth out the oscillations. Let's go into a controlled dive, the faster the better."

As Sam applied full tilt to the thrusters, Rusty counteracted the circular gyration and nosed the *Ark* downward. The saucer picked up speed. The g-forces were noticeable as the *Ark* plunged into the thickening atmosphere.

With the downscreen out of action, the alien missile could not be traced visually from the bridge. It appeared only as an electronic blip on Sandra's radarscope. She locked on the ranging circuits, normally used to determine distance to the ground or surrounding obstructions, and forced the digital evaluations onto the tracking monitor. "It's gonna be a close one."

Laser cannons pivoted down in their sponsons. Gun crews opened fire while the speeding missile was still out of range. Unlike ballistic cannons, which required close calculation due to the lag between the time the projectile left the barrel and the time it reached the position of a moving target, laser fire was instantaneous: it was not necessary to lead the mark.

Sharp thrusts to port and starboard skewered the *Ark* haphazardly. Energy bolts fired at will seared lightninglike tracks in the air and left jagged condensation trails. But it was neither the skillful handling of the craft nor the accuracy of the fire that saved the *Ark* from calamity. The saucer's power dive was so fast that the missile could not alter its trajectory fast enough to catch up. The rocket-powered projectile flew harmlessly past the *Ark* in a tight curve that forced it to spiral back down to earth miles away.

"Whew. That was a close one." Rusty wiped sweat off his brow.

"Pure luck," Sandra said calmly. "But the next one seems to be coming in low enough to intercept our dive pattern."

"There's another one on our tail?" Scott dashed frantically

around the bridge and stared at the radarscope. Death Wind stepped back out of his way. "Damn."

"Rudder response is slow," said Sam. "I don't have much chance of avoiding it."

"Jane, tell the gunners it's up to them." Scott did another lap around the bridge. "If they don't blow that missile out of the sky, you'll be playing your harp in heaven."

The electronic tones went out over the intercom. In the lateral viewscreens Rusty watched the guns swivel on their trunnions as the latest threat became visible to the naked eye.

Jane monitored the return messages. "Cannons are not firing."

"What?" Scott screamed. "What's wrong?"

Doc supplied the answer. "I'm afraid the first artillery barrage drained our firepower. And since warping time depleted our energy reserve, I can recharge the cannon capacitors only at the expense of the propulsion units. We can either run, or fight, but not both."

"I'm for fighting," said Sandra, without hesitation. "Give 'em all the power they need."

Rusty shook his head. "The *Ark* isn't a hot-air balloon. It won't float."

"If we didn't outrun it before except by a stroke of luck, we won't do it now against a better aimed missile," said Helen.

"Make up your minds." Sam fiddled with the controls. "We got about two minutes before we'll be wearing uranium."

Scott spun Rusty around in his seat. "Just take the power you need to keep us from going into a tailspin and let the guns have the rest."

Rusty immediately saw the logic in it. "Agreed. Doc?"

"Shunting." Doc threw switches and twisted dials. "Jane, you may let the gun crews know that they have been resupplied."

The tones went out over the loudspeakers.

Sandra said, "This better work, 'cause I didn't bring my parachute."

"The hull is heating up," Helen said.

Rusty turned back to the controls. "Altitude is fifteen thousand. The friction's not slowing us down any, but it's adding calories to the heat shield." A thermal-resistant lamination protected the undercarriage from ablation and from heat generated by the lifting cones. "Sam, cut the thrusters. Doc, give me a tad more power so we don't hit the ground like a blazing meteorite."

Doc executed the transfer. "Use it sparingly."

As Rusty leveled out the *Ark*'s glide pattern, the craft began skipping on the dense atmosphere like a flat stone across the surface of a pond. "The saucer shape is amazingly aerodynamic. I'll bet from a high enough altitude we could glide halfway around the world. Even with all the extra weight—"

"Save it for the after-action report," Sandra chided.

The first laser cannon blast reverberated throughout the bridge, the sound carried by the external mikes. To Rusty, with the downscreens out of action, the dogfight was a mental exercise. He felt a strange tingling sensation creep up his spine. The *Ark* was flying faster than in any of the trials; any moment he expected the shear strain to split the hull apart at the seams, or the deck to bulge up beneath him from the explosion of a warhead. One part of his mind reveled on the genius of dragon construction—until he realized that the attacking missile must also be of dragon manufacture.

"Hey, catch the rearscreen."

The missile was just visible, captured by the video camera's wide-angle lens. Then it popped into the portscreen as well. The missile was nosing over to intercept the *Ark*'s predicted position. Rusty threw the saucer into a steeper dive, hoping to duck under the missile's path as he had done the last time. But this missile was staying right on the *Ark*'s tail, changing its heading to compensate for the *Ark*'s drastic loss of altitude.

"That thing's going ten times faster than we are," Scott breathed.

"Beam propelled," added Sandra. A long streak of blazing blue flame followed the shiny warhead like a pencil under an eraser.

The forward battery was frustratingly silent. Only the rear and the two lateral cannons could keep the missile in their sights; they pummeled away as quickly as their capacitors recharged. The gunners must have jammed the firing mechanisms in the on position while tracking the target.

The missile leveled out. As the *Ark* dived toward the ground far in excess of what Rusty thought must be its design speed, the missile closed the gap from the rear. "I'm out of tricks." With the ice-covered ground dangerously close, he raised the bow. The screaming sound coming through the intercom was the wind whipping past the microphones. "It's up to the gunners, now."

Bolts of energy lashed out, but not far enough to reach the missile. The gunners checked their fire to conserve power.

"Broderick is handling the men like an expert," said Sam.

"Once that missile gets in range, they're not gonna have much time to hit it." Sandra watched the digital readouts on the radarscope. She rubbed her bulging abdomen. The baby inside might not survive to see the new world. Death Wind stole up behind her and gripped her shoulders. She tilted her head to the side to kiss the back of his hand. "I feel so helpless."

Half the screen was filled with angry blue flames. The missile looked close enough to leap through the lens. Then all three bearing cannons opened fire at once. Laser beams crisscrossed in front of the silver cone and kept up a deadly barrier of energy. The missile flew blindly ahead, right into the web of beams. It was hit by two charges at once, and another a split second later. The double-barreled cannons let loose a second salvo that raked the missile's sides. The explosive charges penetrated the hull. The missile blew up in a titanic ball of expanding gas. The picture went blurry as the yellow incandescence overtook the after rim of the *Ark* and melted the lens.

The next explosion came from inside the bridge, when everyone leaped up and cheered. Even Death Wind let out a war whoop. Doc stood up without his cane, waving his arms over his head. Scott scooped Jane off her feet and swung her around in a circle. One advantage of dragon building dimensions was that, because of their tall, bulbous bodies and long tails, there was always plenty of room on the human scale.

Jane disentangled herself from her husband, gave him a peck on the cheek, and sat down at her console to tone out the all-clear signal.

Sandra clutched her belly and screwed her face into a grimace. "Uh-oh."

Smiles melted into frowns. The *Ark* plowed along on its own.

Sandra leaned toward the radarscope. Her hair fell forward and framed her face.

Scott said tremulously, "Another blip?"

"No, it's—" Her eyebrows formed twin steeples. Slowly she raised her head. "In front. Half the screen—"

Rusty looked up sharply at the forward viewscreen. He saw a huge expanse of white that was hardly distinguishable from the cloud-filled sky. Only a single jagged, windswept peak gave it away. "It's a mountain."

CHAPTER 7

Rusty plopped into the pilot's seat and slammed his fist down on the uppermost vernier button. Instantly, full available power was applied to the lifting cones. "Doc, give me whatever you can spare."

The cones that were still working burst into purple brilliance. The deep thrumming sound echoed in the bridge. Forward momentum was unaffected, but the *Ark* rose upward on dancing electric beams. With the gyrostabilizer out of kilter, and the energy levels to the cones no longer controlled separately, the saucer pitched and yawed.

Without sitting down, Doc worked the controls at his station and transferred all reactor output to the guidance systems. "It's yours."

The snow-covered mountain loomed closer. The summit was a black granite point unbelievably high. The *Ark* could never gain enough elevation to clear the frozen ridges on either side.

"I can't hold her steady and keep her climbing at the same time," Rusty shouted.

Scott picked up Rusty bodily and deposited him on the deck. "I'll take over." He cut the power to the perimetric gyroscope. The *Ark* no longer fought its mechanical directive to fly parallel to the ground. The wild circular plunging stopped immediately. The port side of the saucer dropped due to the inoperative lifting cones destroyed by the first missile. "Cut the lights, Doc. I want everything."

"Good idea. I should have thought of it myself."

The bridge blacked out. The darkness accentuated the glow of control panel lights, annunciator globes, and computer display screens. Below decks, isolated batteries switched in automatically to energize the emergency lighting system.

Scott took advantage of the drop. He added power to the forward and starboard lifting cones. The deck tilted sharply as the *Ark* careened port side down. Because the forward cones pointed at an oblique angle, the *Ark*'s bow was jetted to port. The saucer

47

turned in an arc like a fighter plane peeling out of formation. Momentum kept people and objects within the *Ark* oriented to the deck.

The picture through the viewscreens was out of whack. The port screen showed the dirty striations of an enormous glacier's medial moraine; the starboard screen showed nothing but overcast white and occasional patches of blue. Looking forward, the mountain was a crazily canted monstrosity of rock and ice. The angulation was making Scott dizzy.

"Helen, peel back the awning."

Rapid-fire typing on her keyboard actuated the dome port. The opaque filter opened like an iris, flooding the bridge with ambient light. The mountain loomed large and menacing above the saucer. Scott used the black and white checkered face as a visual reference until the *Ark* inclined so far that the horizontal axis lay perpendicular to the earth.

Rusty picked himself up off the deck and stood behind the pilot's seat. "I think it'll work."

"It better," Scott said grimly. "Or we'll be eating rock."

The *Ark* described a high-speed parabola that brought its radiant undercarriage dangerously close to the cliff face. Purple beams melted a broad swath through the snowdrifts and started an avalanche. The ridge curled toward the speeding saucer, matching curves. Scott transferred more power to the front cones, forcing the *Ark* into a tighter turn. An overhanging rock face momentarily blotted out the starboard screen. It looked for an instant like the saucer's bow would crash into a snowdrift. The cliff dropped off into a bergschrund—the crevasse separating the solid ice pack from the living, flowing glacier—and the *Ark*'s port rim sliced through it, taking off a few layers of white fluff.

Ahead was open sky.

Scott sank into the seat like a snowman in a furnace. "I don't have the energy to cheer."

Apparently, neither did anyone else.

Scott squinted several times and dug his fists into his eyes. "Doc, you can return power to the auxiliaries. Sam, hit the forward thrusters." Scott manipulated the energy levels to the cones, reactivated the gyrostabilizer, and brought the *Ark* onto an approximately even keel. "Let's see if we can find a place to land this baby."

Rusty pounded his friend on the back. "I'll bet that's one maneuver that's not in the crystal."

Sandra sat limply in her seat, hugging her belly. "Great work, Scott. I thought we were gonna get stoned for sure."

Scott looked at her askance. His face was a mask for at least five seconds before he grasped her meaning. Then he managed a weak smile. "Never take anything for granite."

While she groaned, Jane circled the bridge and threw her arms around Scott. She gave him a resounding kiss on the cheek.

"Please, Jane. Not in front of a crowd."

"Go ahead, Jane," laughed Helen. "He deserves it."

Scott pushed himself out of the pilot's seat. "Rusty, can you take the conn?"

"If you'll let me have it." There was no sarcasm in his voice. "I'm sorry I had to relieve you of command, but—"

"No apologies necessary." Rusty took his seat, nodded to Sam as he transferred power from the flight grid to the thrusters. "You saved me from engraving our tombstones with hull plate."

Death Wind said, "Scott has saved our bacon."

Scott slowly turned his head, an expression of amazement on his face. "Where did you ever hear an expression like that?"

Death Wind smiled proudly. "From Windy. He is full of vocalisms."

Scott jabbed a finger at the Nomad's chest. "Don't go falling for any of that dialect that he has the effrontery to call language. His kind of talk will throw English back into the Stone Age."

"I hate to burst your bubble," Sandra said. "But if we went when we were supposed to go, we're *in* the Stone Age."

Scott held up his hands. "I know. I know. The world out there is full of Neanderthals and Cro-Magnons. But just because we're in their space-time doesn't mean we have to start acting like them. Windy's a nice guy, and I like him a lot, but he just won't knuckle down and learn to speak properly."

"Only Neanderthals have arms long enough to knuckle down."

"If you will pardon me from interrupting your customary repartee, I would like to point out that the terrain below has changed from an icy, windswept polar panorama to a luscious, uxuriant green verdure." Doc gestured to the viewscreens. Then, pointing upward, he added, "And the sky has taken on a delicious shade of blue."

Sandra said, "How did we get from the Arctic to the tropics during the course of a conversation? We're not going that fast."

"My dear, I do not wish to comment on your loquacity. But while you were engrossed in digressive palaver, we flew out of the mountain regions and are now descending into a broad valley where Ice Age glaciers have not yet reached. If we can find a suitable clearing in which to land, I daresay we will find the countryside not only charming, but free of dragons. Perhaps we can settle down to effect repairs, and to plan our next course of action."

"Whew. And you accuse me of being long-winded." Sandra rolled her eyes. "But I like the part about being free of dragons." She patted her belly lovingly. "I don't want my children growing up under reptilian rule. So what're we waiting for?"

"For one thing we don't have a downscreen, so I can't see what's below us, and for another the landing pylon hydraulics aren't working." Rusty watched the speed indicator. "With all this extra weight, I don't know if the balance stanchions will hold us. Crushing the lifting nodes would have an adverse effect on future liftoffs."

"I get the picture, already. So what do we do about it?"

"Come on, Death Wind. Grab your tool pouch and we'll hop down to the cargo bay." Scott took an instrument kit out of a storage bin and slung it over his shoulder. In the aftermath of battle, in the release of stress, he was euphoric with the feeling of vivid animation: almost a resurgence of life. "Jane, tone some techs to meet us there and tell them to be snappy about it." Scott scraped his stump across the deck. "This is no time to drag our feet."

"Scott!" Sandra singsonged.

He winked at her as he left the bridge. Death Wind was right behind him. They followed the circular ramp down to the upper platform deck, then took a corridor to one of the perimeter ramps. The center of the flyer was the reactor room and machinery spaces, with limited access points. They met Windy on the lower level.

"You boys sure had us shakin' down here. I was in the for'ard turret with Broderick an' some o' the boys when you was playin chicken with that mountain. Why, I thought them rocks was gonna shear off the barrel. The port turret's plumb full o' snow."

"It was a close one," Scott acknowledged. "We've got enough gray hair on the bridge to weave a carpet. And I want to compliment you and the gun crew. For your first time in battle you did a hell of a job. And a moving target, no less."

"Weren't nuthin' to me. Was the boys in the back that did it." Windy shuffled along with a stiff-legged, stooped gait. His wiry beard only partially hid a craggy, rough-hewn face whose blanched features expressed more anxiety than his words allowed. A slight stutter, perhaps in dire memory, confirmed his agitation. "I smell a ra-rat. Where the hell d'you figger that blasted missile came from?"

"The dragon stronghold, no doubt. We've got the whole thing recorded on tape. We can triangulate the launch site when we review the log. But why they should be prepared for an aerial attack is beyond me. The local landowners can't be that much of a threat to them."

"Never underestimate dragons," Death Wind said. "They are smart."

"That's fer damn sure. Them guys in the capes always got somethin' up their sleeve."

"Windy, I've been meaning to ask you if you'd like to sit in on Sandra's advanced language course."

"Me an' her had a confab about that already. I don't think I got much to teach them native buggers from Charon. Leastways, not in the manner o' talkin'."

Scott wearily rubbed his temples. "That's not exactly what I had in mind. I was thinking more in terms of her, uh, let's say, helping you with your vocabulary, and diction, and whatnot."

"You tryin' to tell me I don't speak good?"

"In a manner of speaking, yes. There's no reason you can't improve your communication skills. Death Wind used to talk in clipped Nomad dialect, but under my tutelage he learned modern English. Now, Sandra's taken over the English department, and she'd like you to join in for a few lessons." They arrived at the mechanical room above the telescoping landing pylon. "Never mind. We'll discuss it later."

Several men and one woman were waiting inside. They had already removed some of the cover plates, exposing the electrical wiring and hydraulic lines. Scott had trained them well.

Scott climbed down into the maintenance pit. He crawled completely around the plastic cylinder, then poked his head up. Some of his golden, curly locks were smeared with grease. "No structural damage."

Death Wind touched a test probe to terminal screws and buss bars. "Disconnect okay. Leads hot."

"Probably a hydraulic break, then." Scott was in his element. He checked pressure tubes and vacuum gauges until he found the leak. "It's just a crimped pipe that split and lost some fluid.

Windy, tone Rusty I've located the trouble and will have it fixed in a jiffy."

"You got it, boss." Windy stayed by the intercom and toned back and forth with the bridge.

Scott left the actual work up to his technical staff, most of whom were Charon natives. They needed the practice. In short order the pylon was ready for deployment. Jane telegraphed the order to stand by for landing. Scott, Death Wind, and Windy stood by the pylon pump.

"Someday, when I have time, I'm going to replace the tone lines with telephones."

Death Wind took off his tool pouch and stuck it into a storage nook. "You always want to repair, or renovate."

"I love machines," Scott allowed. He understood machines. They were predictable and perfectly logical. When they broke, they could be fixed. A mechanical fault could be reduced to a formula that was as straightforward as a mathematical problem, except that there were no unknown quantities, no irrational numbers, and no unsolvable equations. He felt secure dealing with man-made, or dragon-made, devices. He pounded the bulkhead with his palm. "Especially this one. She's my baby."

"She is hurt."

Scott's face clouded. "Yes, the dragons didn't treat her very well. But I can heal her. That's what I do best. And, you know, Death Wind, you're becoming pretty good at maintenance and repair yourself."

Death Wind shrugged. "It is necessary." He watched calmly as the pylon descended smoothly. Despite the radiant heat of the lifting cones, a blast of cool air found its way up the ramp and blew dark hair off his shoulders. "I always do what is necessary. That is the way of life—of long life."

The fat cylinder extended twenty feet down. The cargo bay was filled with the thrumming of the lifting cones; the purple glow flooded the opening, shedding a garish light on the three faces staring down at the verdant green forest.

"But you don't like it, do you?" Scott said. "You don't really care about machines and mechanical marvels."

The Nomad shrugged again. "Life does not concern itself with likes."

"I go along witcha on that," Windy piped up. "Ya live one day fer the next, an' don't plan any further."

Scott shook his head. "As an animal, for sure. As a prisoner, perhaps. But as an active, free-thinking, imaginative human being, the future is something we dream about. It's not a full belly or a grassy pasture that keeps us going. We've become creatures of intellect. And *that* is what humanity is all about."

"If it's all the same witchu, I'll take the simple life."

Clutching a handgrip, Death Wind leaned out over the void. The *Ark* slowly settled into a clearing. Emerald fields of grass were burnt; long, knee-high blades shriveled and died, never to live again. But beyond the perimeter of deadly flame stretched a verdant, virgin forest that had never known the step of man. The simian, quasi-human creatures that lived in the Pleistocene were too wrapped up in their own individual survival to appreciate the woodland beauty.

Death Wind did not shrug, but his manner shrugged for him. "Different people have different dreams."

CHAPTER 8

Scott snipped the wires at the base of the shattered lifting cone, peeled them back, and applied a dollop of molten plastic to the ends; this prevented a short circuit in case the electricity should be turned on by accident. He shoved the still-warm capping tool into the holder on his waist, then coiled the copper conductors into the junction box. The terminal block was damaged, but reusable.

"How bad is it, my boy?"

Scott climbed down the ladder and propped his prosthesis against a lower rung. Too much standing or walking often sent twinges from his nonexistent foot. Phantom pain hurt just as much as the real kind. "Not as bad as it looks. One advantage my profession has over yours is the availability of spare parts. When thine cone offends thee, I pluck it out and replace it."

Doc fluffed his snowy white mane and aligned his face with the breeze. His long beard was blown under his chin. "Is that why they call you the mechanical medicine man?"

Scott laughed. "You've been eavesdropping on my technical crew. Great bunch of guys and gals."

"They look up to you, and not just when you're on a ladder."

The clamor of activity was getting louder. Work crews shuffled back and forth with materials, Bold One was forming a scouting and hunting party, Windy and Broderick were setting up a perimeter defense, and Jane was gathering women to forage in the woods for fresh fruits, vegetables, berries, and exotic plants of medicinal value.

Scott stepped aside as one of the technicians clambered up the ladder with a wrench. The totally demolished cones and nodes were being dismantled. The big dent in the undercarriage was the imprint of the missile's nose cone. Surrounding it the lifting cones and time transfer focusing nodes suffered varying degrees of damage.

"Let's go for a walk." He led Doc beyond the perimeter of the *Ark*. The sun shone down with a warmth that took the bite out of the air. Scott enjoyed the crispness, but was thankful for the long-sleeved shirt. The scent of pine was strong, wafting across the glade with the freshness of a newborn world. Scott swept out his arms to bespeak the surrounding forest. "You know, this all seems too good to be true."

Doc nodded knowingly. "It is easy to be struck by the pristine splendor of the land, by the flush and fragrance of flowers, by the chirping of birds in the trees. After the primeval world of the Cretaceous, the Pleistocene assumes the appearance of utopia. Keep in mind, however, that the presumption of innocence is based on our anthropomorphic concept of the world. Those birds—"

Gaily plumaged swallows flitted through the branches, chirping merrily. Warblers sang out in repetitive song, clung to tree limbs with delicately clawed feet, fed fledglings in their woven nests, or stood by their aeries high in the upper canopy. Squirrels and chipmunks added their high-pitched calls to the strident sounds of insects. The whole was an orchestration of nature supreme.

"Those birds," Doc continued, "do not sing for pleasure, either ours or theirs. The virtue of their song is a human conceit. The wild cacophony you interpret as exhilaration and content is the fight for survival: a signal for danger, the bid for a mate, the mark of territoriality. Underlying the melody is a strain of fear. There is brutality in these woods, there is unseen suffering, there is death and destruction. Everything has a purpose, and everything is not as it seems."

"Come on, Doc. Don't put on such a downer. I'm feeling guilty enough about enjoying the scenery. Don't make it worse."

Doc uttered one of his curt harumphs. "I did not mean to spoil your zest, only to break your enchantment. Certainly this world has not yet known the depravity of biblical man, or the civilized cruelty of the twentieth century. But remember that the brutality of survival often exceeds the cultured torment and mental anguish we inflict upon ourselves. Then, too, there is the malignity of dragons."

"Another cheering thought." Scott kicked away the clinging underbrush and climbed onto an angled slab of rock that was partially covered with red cusps of lichen. He perched his hindquarters on the cold stone. "Do you want me to share your melancholy?"

They were slightly higher than the command bubble of the *Ark*. Looking through the clear canopy Scott detected motion on the bridge, but was too far away to distinguish faces. The saucer rested on its wide landing pylon, balanced by the four outriggers. Wary gun crews remained at their stations in the blisters and kept a strict vigil. Beyond, the mountain they had almost become part of dominated the southern horizon. Most of the steep facing lay in shadow: a barren, icy, hostile, but somehow alluring mass of rock.

"Such caveats are merely the signposts of reality." Doc's speech was punctuated by short gasps for breath that did not slow him down in any way. He planted his cane on the granite surface, pivoted around it, and slid to a sitting position with practiced ease. "Let's look on the brighter side. This untarnished world is a cornucopia of delights, with continents to explore, new lands to settle, wildlife to tame, a civilization to build. We are here to witness the dawn of man, undoubtedly the most stimulating time in the history of this planet."

Scott rubbed his hands together quickly. The friction warmed his skin. "That *is* pretty exciting. I've been wondering what I'll say to the first caveman I run into. Probably 'ugh.' Maybe instead of trying to educate Windy, I'll try my tutorial skills on the local population."

"You've done it before with great success. Perhaps you should."

Scott thought for a moment before responding. "Well, I don't know. I don't want to do anything here and now that will upset the apple cart later. I think we should avoid any contact with Cro-Magnons. The Neanderthals don't matter, I suppose, because they're going to die out anyway. But I sure wouldn't want to create a paradox by doing something to stymie the evolution of Homo sapiens. We may wake up some morning and not be here because we accidentally killed one of our ancestors."

Doc tilted his head back and gazed at the faraway summit, some ten thousand feet high. "On the other hand, if we do not eliminate the dragons from this time zone, they may cause our preextinction for us."

"The age-old dilemma: is action more desirable than inaction?" Scott pursed his lips. "Sometimes I think we should just forget the whole thing and get on with our lives in the future—that is, the future as described from now. After all, when you think about it, we wouldn't be here if the dragons succeeded in taking over this time zone. I mean, we couldn't have evolved if they wiped out our Pleistocene progenitors. The very fact that we exist proves that the stock we descended from lived through the reign of dragons as well as the snow of the Ice Age." Then, after a moment of dubious introspection, he added, "Doesn't it?"

"I see that you and Rusty are not of the same mind."

Scott snickered. "Let's say that I don't have his confidence in the unalterable flow of time, or the immutability of events. I'm on your side there—or then. Maybe we can't tear the fabric of space-time apart, but suppose we put a nick in it that runs the entire length of the continuum? That's what scares me. I'm willing to admit only that the past *implies* the future, that perhaps it does not predetermine what we perceive as follow-up events. And I have to admit that because I've experienced its consequences. But this time selection business shatters my comfortable, preconceived notions about what's happened in the past, and how that'll affect what *may* happen in the future."

Doc drew his knees up to his chin. "The three of us have such different attitudes. I was brought up in the world of dragons, and in full knowledge of their existence. The nonimpermeability of time was forced upon me as observable fact. You, on the other hand, were raised in ignorance of such empirical data, and have been forced to accept abstractions foreign to your experience. But, Rusty—"

Doc wrapped his arms around his shins and tucked himself into a tight ball. Zephyrs carried the chill off the mountain slopes and into the fertile valley. Scott imitated Doc's position, then stuck his hands between his legs. Despite Doc's admonitions, the animal sounds did not seem in the least bit ominous.

"Now, that boy grew up in your environment, with no more appreciation of the outside world than that of a mole—uh, no aspersion intended."

"Sure, Doc." In order to keep the draft off his legs, Scott smoothed his pant legs and held the cuffs closed.

"Yet, he has leapfrogged both of us in grasping the conceptual significance of space and time not as disparate functions of the evolution of the universe, but as simultaneous points of view of equivalent phenomena."

"At least, he thinks he has." Scott rolled his buttocks. The cold from the coarse rock was seeping through the material of his trousers. "I don't care what he can prove mathematically, there's got to be a cause and effect relationship between everything that happens in the universe."

"Oh, I don't think Rusty has any argument with that. He allows for the inclusion of both cause and effect, but he believes that a specific effect may not be the consequence of what we may perceive as the cause. In other words, there may be causes of which we are unaware affecting future events. And, if you grant the idea of simultaneity—that is, that more than one event can occur at the same time in the same place—then that lends credence to his theories."

Scott shook his head. "I don't buy that parallel universe concept because it implies that you can cross over from one to the other like changing lanes on a highway. Traveling through time is difficult enough to comprehend, but jumping tracks in the space-time continuum is a bit more than I can handle."

"Because we do not like or understand an idea is not sufficient reason to discard it."

"That's not the problem, Doc. It just doesn't make sense. We've already got an infinity of space and an eternity of time, why complicate the cosmos with another endless variable? We may as well postulate universes of different scales: electrons as planets revolving around atomic suns, and our own universe as nothing more than a microscopic dot in some vaster, greater universe. There has to be a stop to it somewhere."

"Believe me, lad, I sympathize with your grief. But we cannot restrict the possibilities of the celestial sphere because of limitations inherent in the human mind. Don't you think nuclear scientists were more comfortable when they could describe the atom as an electron revolving around a proton, without having to account for scores of subatomic particles and the interaction of nuclear forces? It was mathematics that discounted the simple model of the atom, just as Rusty's mathematics quantify a universe more complicated than the human senses perceive. What bothers me is the indeterminacy of his formulas. They can be read two ways: either as a synchronism of events, relying on the mutual exclusion principle, or as an effect without probable cause. He will read it whichever way he thinks I want to hear it. But I am on to him."

Scott rested his forehead on his knees. He was getting a headache from the intense cerebration. "I don't know why the dragons chose such an inhospitable time zone anyway. They *hate* the cold. And cold-blooded animals can't survive in the cold. Hey! That's it." His head jerked up with the light of an idea. "Maybe they didn't intend to come here. Maybe it's all an accident."

"Where else could they go?" Doc countered. "Their TTS was anchored in space."

"No, I mean, maybe they didn't intend to come now—to this time zone."

"Dragons never do anything without good reason."

"Dragons can make mistakes, too. They've made a couple of big goofs already. Or, maybe they came to this TZ out of desperation. We had them on the run, they had to escape, and they chose sometime close; sometime when they wouldn't use up too much energy getting here—now. And maybe later on, without our intervention, they'll meet their end naturally, because they couldn't adapt to the cold."

"And perhaps they used the TTS to bring them to this time zone, with the idea of using a space machine to carry them to a more temperate climate," Doc countered. "Remember that their choices were limited by the crudity of their time transfer technology. But more important than why they chose this TZ, is why they felt the need for a remote storage facility."

Scott shook his head. For the moment the cold was forgotten. "If the crystal had only been a more recent backup . . ."

"That is why we must find out for ourselves. Dragons are not devious. Their thought processes are straightforward; it is just that their minds work in a manner that is alien to our way of thinking. And while I may be confused about space and time and other things, I am wise enough to know that we cannot afford to underestimate the grand design of their scheme. I am sure the dragons have a purpose that we have not as yet divined. And even if we do not succeed in killing a single dragon, we must at all costs discover what that purpose is. Only then can we be armed for the future."

CHAPTER 9

"You do not have to go."

Scott threw the combination battery/backpack over his shoulder. Food and supplies were carried in a satchel attached to the top of the laser gun's battery pack and capacitor module. "Yes, I do."

"But, you are needed here—" Jane pleaded.

"The tech crew can handle all the repairs. There are enough spare lifting cones and focusing nodes in the hold to build another ship. And Rusty can take care of any problems that crop up."

"But—"

Scott cut her off. "I have to go. I *need* to go. I need to get out there in the wilderness and prove to myself that I can still handle it. The *Ark* will be here when I get back."

Jane was silent for a long time. "Then, you know that I must go with you."

Scott took a deep breath. The air was clean and cold, redolent with the smells of nature. "I know, Honey." He bent down, ruffled her long, straight hair, and kissed the top of her head. "I'm sorry you feel compelled to watch over me."

"It is not—"

He smothered her face against his furry greatcoat. "I know what it is. And I want to have you along. I love you, and your company. I'm just sorry that my stubbornness is forcing you to go on this mission. I'm sorry for placing you in such danger—"

"I have lived my whole life with dragons." Jane pulled back and smiled at him pertly. "It may be that I can offer advice born of experience."

"Did you get that phrase from Doc? Because if he's been brainwash—"

"Did I hear my name in vain?" Doc strode into the staging area with his own greatcoat draped over his arm. All around men and women prepared for the assault on the dragon fortress, packing warm clothing and checking arms and supplies. "My dear, you cut a handsome figure in that outfit. A black beaver pelt, is it not?"

Jane smiled. "I stitched it myself. Scott's too."

"A smart-looking lad." Doc made a show of donning his own garb. "I rather fancy the glistening auburn coat of a curious and so far unnamed horned rodent, although I would not like to fight one of the creatures for its skin. They grow upward of three feet, you know, and have claws like daggers. Thanks to the Nomads' trapping skills and Helen's expertise as a seamstress, I have a tailor-made garment that is the rage of fashion." He looked askance at Scott. "My boy, you are going to suffocate in that attire until we get out of the lowlands—"

"Doc, I know you're trying to change the subject." Scott struggled out of his greatcoat and bundled it into a ball for packing. "I was only trying it on for size. Now, what kind of stories have you been telling my wife?"

Doc pooh-poohed Scott with a wave of his hands. "I was merely pointing out that a well-rounded army has the advantage over an enemy whose tactics are known and whose strategy is predictable. We are stronger for our diversity of arms and nuance of attack. Primitive as spears and bows and arrows are, the Nomads can use their weapons effectively, and perhaps in cases where our supposedly superior firepower is impractical."

"But what does that have—"

"If y'all pardon the intrusion, the Texas Rangers are pullin' out." Windy paused at the top of the ramp long enough to toss off a salute. "My outfit's havin' a conniption 'cause Broderick rallied his troops ahead o' ours. Got some time to make up."

"I will be tagging along with the supply train." Doc stepped aside as the heavily burdened soldiers tramped out of the *Ark* on their way to war. He turned to Scott, and faked a look of disdain. "It goes against my grain to let others lead the way. All my life I have been in the forefront of the fight against dragons. Now, I am relegated to the rear guard as 'honorary chief brave.' It seems that youth has privileges that rank has not."

"It also has the strength of two good legs." Helen stepped out of the mass of marching men. "And while I understand that both of you need to prove your manhood, you should be mature enough to know that you aren't judged by your physical prowess, but by your strength of character. Dad, at your age, haven't you yet gained that inner security. And, Scott, where is that sense of humor of yours?"

"My boy, I think we have been had. Lead me to the house of dragons, but deliver me from women."

Scott said, "I'm just eager to get going. I've felt guilty sitting around for the past week doing nothing but making plans while the rest of the gang's been out hunting and trapping and scouting the route."

The last of the Rangers filed down the ramp. Doc's raised voice rang out in the sudden silence. "Planning and forethought are paramount in any campaign, and are equally as important as the work of the foot soldier. With an enemy already entrenched, we must rely on siege tactics rather than hit-and-run guerrilla warfare. Speed is not essential; stealth and stamina are what will win this battle."

"Uh-oh. Now you've got him started." Helen led the way down the ramp. "We'd better get on the trail before we have to listen to the book of proverbs."

Scott hefted his bulky pack and slung it on his back. He jumped up and down a couple of times to settle the weight and adjust the straps. Then he stretched out his right leg and tapped the deck. "I guess I'd better put my best foot forward."

Helen looked back over her shoulder. "There's the Scott I used to know."

Jane shouldered her own smaller pack and disembarked with the others. Down on the ground she hitched herself to her travois. The plastic frame was jury-rigged from spare parts; wheels built into the trailing poles made it easier to haul through the woods and over the ice. The netting was piled high with tools, clothing, and camping gear. The army carried only a small amount of food, expecting for the most part to live off the land.

Doc doffed his greatcoat and lashed it to the frame of Jane's travois. "My dear, I want to thank you for volunteering your services."

"Youth has not only its privileges, but its responsibilities."

Doc's jaw dropped. He ogled Jane as if she were a figment of coalescing ectoplasm. When he finally found his voice, his words came out cracked and rasping. "I suppose a mentor should be honored by his student's emulation, but I find it a bit embarrassing."

Scott laughed raucously. "Serves you right."

"Dad, you may have created a soul in your own image."

"Hey, if you guys're finished lolling your tongues, we got a show to get on the road." Sandra stood fiercely, with her knuckles tucked on her hipbones. She wore a knee-length smock that disguised the evidence of her pregnancy. The sun striking her black hair made it glisten like the feathers of a starling; her voice was as harsh. "I don't like lagging behind my own platoon. Now let's move it!"

Scott looked at Doc and forced his lower lip to tremble. "She scares me more than the wild animals."

"I believe the commission has gone right to her head. Such is the influence of newly promoted authority."

"Coming, Lieutenant," Scott singsonged. He traipsed along behind Jane. Doc was by his side. Helen cinched down her harness straps and followed behind with another heavily laden travois.

"Mother, are you sure that's not too much of a load for you?"

Helen shook her head. "I tried it out yesterday. I can handle it. Where's your father?"

"Out in front, as usual. With Bold One. The Nomads are leading the parade, with the Fusiliers and the Rangers spread out behind 'em on parallel tracks—assuming the Rangers catch up. We're bringing up the rear. Early camp, today. Jane, if you get tired with that rig, let me know so's I can relieve you."

"Thank you, Sandra."

Scott squinted in the golden glow of the sun. From the edge of the forest he glanced back at the *Ark*. The top of the giant saucer was cleverly camouflaged with brush and branches piled so deep that the upper time transfer focusing nodes were visible only upon close inspection. "Where's Rusty? I thought he was out here seeing everyone off—"

As if on cue, the redhead stepped out from behind the trees. He carried a sheaf of papers in his hands. He peeled one off and handed it to Scott. "I was making sure everyone got a map, in case they became separated. This is the final update. When I reviewed the tapes from the flight recorder I noticed some discrepancies between the printout and what the Nomads drew from their scouting excursions. It has to do with sight angulation. I used a computer simulator to interpolate the actual elevation changes in the terrain—"

"I get the picture, already." Scott tucked the smooth vellum into an outer vest pocket and buttoned the flap. "I'm sure the topography will conform to within a fraction of a percent. Now, listen." Scott wagged a finger at his companion. "You take care of my baby. I want her in tiptop shape when I get back. And if you have any problems, call me."

"The tech crew will take care of it—"

"*Her*. She's a ship, and deserves the respect of her calling."

"It's a machine. It doesn't have a sex—"

"Then why, when you were under the stress of escaping those missiles, did you refer to her by the feminine pronoun?" Scott watched Rusty's discomfiture with pleasure and with a growing smile. "Ah-*ha*. You thought I wasn't paying attention."

"I never—"

"Then play back the audio flight recorder. It's all on crystal."

Rusty deliberated, casting his eyes down at his feet. "All right, I'll take care of—her. But you take care of yourself. All of you. And don't leave us out of the picture. Keep in touch. I want twice daily reports; more if you encounter anything unusual. Britt will be monitoring your channels at all times. Both of us will be sleeping on the bridge, so one of us will be on watch—"

"She's a nice gal, Rusty. Do you think you can keep your mind on your work with her around."

Rusty's face turned the color of his hair.

"Stop teasing him," Helen said.

"What do you think, Doc?"

Doc turned the corners of his mouth into the caricature of a smile. "I think we had better get moving before our computer whiz suffers from a downloading fault—and before we incur the wrath of an impatient platoon leader."

"You got that right," said Sandra.

Scott took his cue. He waved one last time to the ever-alert gun crew, sitting inside the blisters, and ducked into the cover of Pleistocene foliage. It felt good to be starting out on a journey—even if it was a crusade from which not everyone was slated to return.

Time would tell many things.

CHAPTER 10

The gently rolling savanna stretched out as far as the eye could see. Dense groves of evergreens alternated with open vistas that were dotted with lone birches and aspens and small stands of elms. Tall oaks dangled lofty branches high above waving fields of rust-colored grain. Rock outcrops were carpeted with lush moss in a kaleidoscope of muted oranges, reds, and greens. Long-stemmed purple flowers grew indiscriminately.

Dominating the foreground was a solitary mammal the size of a small elephant. It used it flattened tusks like twin shovels, rooting through the damp grass along the bank of a clear, shallow stream. It raised its head and grunted every minute or two, as if calling to the yellow sun that hung in the cloudless sky.

In the distance a herd of shaggy musk ox, whose drooping horns made them look like a gaggle of lugubrious women, grazed quietly. They paid no attention to giant birds soaring overhead on wings the size of plywood sheets. Even as one teratornis swooped down and plucked a two-foot-long, needle-nosed rodent from its mound of dirt before the squawking creature could scrabble into the safety of its hole, the musk oxen, oblivious to their surroundings, chewed their food with a dull, vacuous stare. They were too big, and too many, to care about the screech of a bird or the squeal of a rodent.

It was a world that was far from idyllic. Predator and prey waged a constant battle for survival against the forces of nature; predators fought off starvation, prey scrounged for nourishment while trying not to become the nourishment of others. The world offered no securities, nor made any guarantees: it bequeathed hunger to the inept, death to the unobservant. Life was fraught with sickness, disease, pain, and suffering.

Death Wind held no illusions. He recognized the perils of the wild. He also understood, in a great, blinding flash of insight, what the world must have been like before there were dragons—or men—to desecrate it.

Not more than a third of the Pleistocene landmass was ice. Most of the Earth was cold, windy, and raw, but so alive. It was also rampant with wildlife that had adapted to prevalent conditions. This time zone was the Age of Mammals and, except for the last stronghold under dragon control, was soon to become the Age of Man.

Death Wind knew this from his history studies. And looking out over the land, he could well understand how mankind could take root here. The Nomad in him saw a world of plenty in which to roam free. The savage inside saw, instead of herds of musk ox or fields of grain, an endless supply of meat and bread. The Cro-Magnons were lucky to have been born in such a time, with so much room for expansion. Little wonder that they were unwilling to share the land with ignorant, backward Neanderthals who lacked the sensitivity to feel the exhilaration of the wild.

With a tingling in his groin, Death Wind also knew that unless he and his companions rid the Earth of dragons, mankind could never come about.

It was a terrible responsibility that only a brave could bear. Even as he thought it, Death Wind knew that he would fight to the death for the near humans of this time zone. Men stuck together despite the barriers of space and time, for that was the code of Nomad tradition.

Thus it was with great sadness that he watched the small band of Neanderthals creeping through the tall grass, stalking the shovel-tusked elephant. Even if they succeeded in bringing down the beast and supplying the tribe with fresh food, they were ultimately doomed to extinction. The history books said it was so, and so it must be.

The amebelodon raised its mighty trunk into the air and trumpeted a baleful warning. The base tone echoed from the hills and lingered in the distance like a returning call. There was a flurry of motion in the reeds, and a cloud of dust that erupted from the ground as if a mine had exploded under the grass. A huge orange blur vaulted through the air toward the startled amebelodon.

The elephant reared on mighty hind legs that were like two hairy pillars. Massive forelegs punched the air crazily. The thunderous trumpet was met with a high-pitched caterwaul. The orange bundle of fur, five times the size of a man, raked the amebelodon's barrel chest with outstretched claws. At the same time the elephant fell forward so its padded forefeet struck its attacker's long back. Then the orange predator was crushed under the full weight of the elephant.

The shrill cry continued, and the next moment a giant cat slithered out from under the trumpeting amebelodon. With light-ninglike speed the cat bounded away, but not before its hindquarters were stabbed with long ivory tusks. The cat's body slewed sideways. It was knocked halfway to the ground, but it quickly regained its stance and ran straight away without once looking back.

For the amebelodon the fight was over. The cat's claws had barely penetrated the thick hide of its breast. The ancestral elephant thumped across the savanna to seek more solitary grazing grounds.

The giant cat's speed was so great that in seconds it covered several hundred yards. It skidded to a halt close under Death Wind's rocky perch, and in the midst of the stunned Neanderthals. The cat was so stunned that for a moment it just stood tall, tail flicking, dark eyes observing. Slowly it fell back into a crouch and uttered a hiss that sounded like a broken steam line. It bared its teeth, revealing a pair of long canine teeth that jutted downward like upside-down tusks.

Death Wind knew at once that this was not just an oversize cat, but a saber-toothed tiger.

The Neanderthals posed like cigar-store Indians, apparently frozen in fear. Fist-sized rocks held in limp hands were no defense against the fangs of the great cat, even if the subhumans had the nerve to fling them. The tableau lasted but a moment. Then two things occurred at once. The saber-toothed tiger leaped at the nearest Neanderthal, and Death Wind notched his longbow.

Muscular arms bent the still-green wood until the ends nearly touched. The plastic, dragon-made string was as taut as spun steel. The shaft was mated to the bow at the base of the knapped flint. Death Wind led the charge and released the arrow. Bird feathers—real bird feathers—guided the yard-long arrow through the air. The deadly missile caught the cat in midair and buried itself into the brawny shoulder blade.

Fangs aimed at a Neanderthal's throat missed their mark as the tiger's head twisted around and snapped at the sudden cause of agony. The cat's forward momentum did not change. One paw the size of a bushel basket rasped the subhuman's abdomen with telling effect. The claws eviscerated the hapless creature in an instant.

The remaining Neanderthals dropped their rocks and bolted. The enraged cat spun in circles, screeching and biting. By the time it succeeded in breaking the shaft in two, another landed in its midriff. A third soon followed.

Then came the Nomad war whoop as Death Wind leaped off the low precipice. Well-toned legs absorbed the shock as his moccasins struck the soft soil. He dashed forward like a pole vaulter, leading the charge with the tip of his spear. The saber-toothed tiger struggled to gain its legs. It had time to lean back and hiss only once before the thick steel point slipped beneath its head and entered its heaving breast.

The tiger whirled with uncommon strength, catching Death Wind unawares. The violent reaction knocked him off his feet and sent him tumbling. He hit the ground hard enough to knock the wind out of him. Instinctively he rolled away in order to clear those swiping, taloned paws. When he came up against a mound of dirt he climbed to his feet; he still had not been able to force an inhalation. He whipped out his knife and poised defiantly.

The cat charged him, seeming to ignore the spear that was buried in its heart. The butt of the thick wooden shaft caught Death Wind in the belly and bowled him over. He wrapped his fingers around the spear. Relentlessly, the tiger crawled forward, kicking great clods of earth out from under its four paws. Death Wind hung on for his life. His body was lifted and pounded into the ground; he plowed a furrow across the grassy plain as if he had been strapped to the end of a seesaw that was being pushed by a bulldozer. The saber-toothed tiger refused to die.

Death Wind felt his strength ebbing away. He was losing his grip on the shaft. Still the tiger came, reaching out with one paw, digging its claws into the earth, pulling itself forward at the same time it kicked with his hind legs. It did not hiss, it did not screech. It just kept coming.

As Death Wind's muscles weakened, his arms slowly unbent. The length of the spear was all that kept him and the tiger apart. Slowly they were drawn closer together. The tiger kept crawling, step by painful step, pushing the Nomad's weakening body ahead of it.

Lightning struck Death Wind's calf: a seering, numbing pain leaped the entire length of his leg. He jerked his knee, but his lower leg was pinioned and would not move. Death Wind had made two mistakes: first in attacking a fully grown saber-toothed tiger, then in being rash enough to face off the wounded animal.

This time he was lucky. The tiger died.

Two two-inch-long claws were embedded in the muscle of his calf: puncture wounds that would heal with time and proper treatment. If the cat had had the final strength to pull back its foreleg, it would easily have ripped off Death Wind's foot.

The Nomad lay like a corpse for many minutes before he regained the strength to move. Then he folded his body at the waist so he could reach his trapped leg. The tiger paw lay on him like an oversize mop armed with spikes. He studied the cat's exposed claws in order to determine the curvature. Then, he eased the sharpened talons out of his leg. It was less painful than he expected.

For five minutes he sat without moving. Although he was battered and bruised and felt a stabbing pain in his ankle, he was not seriously injured. Finally, he rolled over onto his hands and knees, and pushed himself up off the ground. He felt woozy at first and knelt back down on one knee. When the nausea passed he stood up again, slowly.

He stumbled back along the tracks gouged in the topsoil. It looked as if a backhoe had dug up the ground. Steel glinted in the sunlight. Death Wind groaned as he stooped to retrieve his knife. At the end of the trail lay the Neanderthal. She was ripped open from breastbone to groin; her intestines and most of her organs lay in a puddle of blood alongside her body. Yet she breathed.

Death Wind crouched by her side. She was big-boned and brawny, and covered with a thick mat of hair. Her arms and legs were long and muscular, her chest broad, her hips wide, her feet large, her toes splayed. Two ponderous mammary glands sported tiny pink nipples that protruded through the thatch.

Her head was much larger than the human head, and contained a brain that was larger than a human brain. But sheer bulk of gray matter was not the sole measure of intelligence. The structure of the brain was as important as its capacity. Neanderthals lacked the essential ingredient that was the quantum difference between racial genetic imprinting and individual learning ability.

Death Wind touched her jugular with extended fingertips. The pulse was faint. He left his hand where it lay as he surveyed the damage done to her body by a single swipe of the saber-toothed tiger. Her entrails had not been surgically removed by those monstrous claws, but had been torn to shreds as well; they could not be scooped up, replaced in the body cavity, and stitched in. Even Doc, the greatest healer Death Wind had ever known, did not have the medicine to save this one.

The Nomad recognized the organs strewn in the bloody froth. The intestines were shredded like confetti, the stomach had disgorged the contents of its last meal, the liver was split in two. And the uterus . . . The heart still pumped, the blood still flowed, and that wet, pulpy sac that was the womb still quivered with life. Even as he looked, with his fingers frozen on the throbbing jugular, tears in the uterus spread the mass apart. A tiny, dark foot kicked through the outer lining, followed by a hand. All at once the sac burst apart and spilled out a nearly grown fetus. The hairless doll kicked a few more times, and then lay still.

Neanderthal eyelids fluttered. Black eyes peered out from under protruding brow ridges. The female stared sightlessly at the blue sky. Slowly, painfully, the eyeballs moved in their deep sockets. With gimlet eyes she looked directly at Death Wind. Expressionless, she stared for a long time. After an eternity, her arm struggled up against the awful pull of gravity. Fingers weak from shock touched the Nomad's throat. He felt a sight pressure. The hand dropped as if it had been given a brick to hold, but subhuman eyes held their grip.

Death Wind saw in those silent orbs a prehistoric creature with no hope for the future. Already her unborn child was dead. Her own death was inevitable, and not far behind. Soon, her entire race would follow the path to extinction.

The Nomad understood her feeble gesture. As she watched him, begging for mercy, he pressed down harder on her jugular, spread his fingers until they encircled her hairy throat, tightened his grip. He stopped, but his eyes urged him on. He squeezed delicately, not choking, but embracing her larynx with a love and a strength he did not know he possessed.

Her primitive anthropoid brain desired release. And in that simple wish was more meaning, more comprehension, more humanity than could possibly exist in the mind of a mere mammal. As primal as she might be, she commanded the faculty to pray for death despite the animal instinct for survival.

At last her eyes closed. Her chest heaved in convulsions as her lungs screamed for air. With tears streaming down his face, Death Wind held her tight. In a few moments her body ceased all movement, her blood no longer flowed, her veins no longer pulsed. Her face, brutal and atavistic by modern standards, took on an aura of hushed tranquillity.

If her kind had the imagination to conjure the hope for life after death, and to invent the concept of God, then the soul of this unnamed creature entered whatever heaven she believed in.

CHAPTER 11

Scott struck chords on the remote toner, using dragon tone talk to transmit his message. "Pegleg toning the *Ark*. Come in, *Ark*."

Acknowledgment was immediate. "*Ark* here. Britt toning."

Scott strummed again. "Halfway point reached this noon. All well. How's with you?"

The receiver toned in a clean, harplike timbre. "All well. Repairs under way, forty percent complete. Rusty warming."

"Prosperity."

"Health."

Scott slipped the transmitter into its tanned hide case strapped to his backpack.

"What was that all about?" Sandra stirred the pot of soup with a shaved stick. "I know your handle and the sign-off cipher. But what did she mean by 'Rusty warming.' What is she doing, stirring him into a kettle of stew?"

Scott laughed and exchanged winks with his wife. "She's got her hooks into him, but he's putting up a good fight. That's why she didn't come on this safari. She's afraid his fingers will grow roots into his input terminal, and he'll become a talking computer link."

Sandra cocked an eyebrow. "She's got her work cut out for her. If she keeps the chlorophyll out of his diet and the calculus out of his sleep, she might have a chance."

The sun was a dull orange ball hovering a few degrees above the western horizon. The sky was only partially clear after yesterday's rainstorm. For Scott, the day cooped up under the tarps, keeping dry, had had its advantages: rest, recuperation of sore muscles, and time to share with his wife. Then, the entire People's Expeditionary Force spent the morning drying out moccasins, clothes, and the furred skins they used for blankets. But the rushed afternoon, double-timing through heavily forested terrain to reach the caves spotted by Nomad scouts, had tired him out even more. The breakneck pace was almost more than he could stand. He propped his footless leg atop the supply stash; as the blood drained out of it by the force of gravity, the pain induced by venous pressure eased off.

Jane dragged the travois farther into the protection of the sandstone overhang. It was loaded with wood she had collected while the others were setting up camp. She propped the logs and branches against the back wall for drying. When her chores were completed she pulled two small bundles of fluff out of her pack. Cradling them in her arms, she held them out where Sandra could see them. "Have you seen my new pets?"

"Hey. They're cute. What are they?" Sandra left the stick in the pot and took one of the furry animals. For a moment her upper lip curled. "Uh, they're not Pleistocene rats, are they?"

Jane laughed. "No. They are wolf pups."

"You mean, like one of those pack hounds that attacked us the other day?"

Jane nodded. "The mother was killed. Bold One found the litter nearby. He kept two, and gave two to me."

Sandra puckered her lips at the little critter, then nuzzled its soft, silky fur against her face. "What're you gonna call 'em?"

"Pete and Repeat if they're boys," said Scott. "Joyce and Rejoice if they're girls."

"Oh, you."

"One is male, the other is female." Jane knelt and let the pup sit in her lap. She ran her hands along its sleek fur.

"Okay. How about Jack and Jill?" Scott offered.

Doc entered the arena carrying a slab of meat the size of a man's torso. "My dear, do not tell me you are going to the wolves?"

Sandra looked up startled. "Pop, where did you get that steak?"

A plastic packing sheet lay by the fireside. Doc blew the dust off the top, then placed the massive hindquarter on the sheer surface. "It is more rightly called venison, I suppose, since it came from a kind of antelope with a great rack of horns. I strongly suspect it might be the famed Irish elk, although my biological studies of this time period are seriously lacking. Would you mind if I thickened your soup with it?"

"Mind?" yelled Scott. "Try to take it away."

"I rather expected that attitude from you, my boy. To answer your question, Sandra, the Nomads managed to drive three out of a small herd over this very precipice yesterday." He pointed upward, indicating the cliff above the overhang. He took a long-bladed knife out of the sheath strapped to his waist, and carved the meat into bite-sized bits. "It was when they climbed down to retrieve the flesh that they discovered this shelter. Instead of bringing the meat to us, they brought us to the meat."

"It's nice and cozy in here, I'll grant you that." Scott stabbed a chunk of meat with a screwdriver honed to a point and shoved it into the blue flame just above the red-hot embers. "With the fields and open plains right out in front, it would make a good permanent camp—if we needed one."

"Yes, the Nomads are of the same mind. They are quite enamored by the profusion of wildlife and the vitality of the soil. They see a land where food is plentiful, and there for the taking; quite different from what they are used to. Besides a boundless supply of animals to hunt, they imagine cultivated grain and rows of vegetables, even orchards of fruit trees."

Slender Petal climbed up the dirt embankment and stopped at the fire pit. She bent over in order to tear apart a leather bagful of small wild cabbages, and deposit them into the pot of steaming water. Her pitch-black hair was tied in a ponytail and hung down her back as far as her waist. She flashed even, white teeth. "Earth good. Grow much." Like all Nomads, she made her point without saying more than necessary.

Doc grimaced. "Yes, I just conveyed the same sentiment in ten times the wordage. I sometimes get carried away with my rhetoric."

Scott rotated the bite of venison on its makeshift spit. "What you call rhetoric, others call fustian."

"The point was made without such accuracy of definition."

Slender Petal pulled carrots out of her tunic pouch and pointed one at Sandra. "Wolf." She diced the cleaned roots into the pot with deft slashing motions of a slender knife. "Keep?"

"They belong to Jane." Sandra put hers on the ground. It swayed back and forth on wobbly legs. "Aren't they adorable?"

Doc plopped a double handful of meat in the pot, then tossed a slice of raw fat in front of the pup. "If we are going to feed them scraps, we will have to call them dogs."

Jane took a bit of meat and held it out for her pup. "You may keep one if you like, Sandra."

"Really?" Sandra scooped up the critter and held it in front of her face. "I guess if we killed your mama we'll have to take care of you. Little orphans like you won't last long alone in this country." She rubbed it against her cheek. "Jane, thank you. I'd love to have it."

Jane pointed to the travois. "I will carry him."

"Hey, I never knew being pregnant had so many perks. I don't have to carry a pack, or haul a travois, or hunt for food. Maybe I'll make a career out of having babies."

Slender Petal slowly shook her head. She picked up the shaved stick and stirred the brew. "Raise children much work. Break things. Make trouble. Run away. Death Wind bad boy. Never listen." She pointed to the wolf. "Easier to train pup."

"Yeah?" Sandra corraled her puppy. "Tell me more."

"Uh-oh. Wait till I tell Death Wind his mother's telling baby stories."

"Scott, you keep out of this." Sandra winked at Jane. "We'll talk about it later. In private." She stuck out her tongue at Scott. "Away from prying ears."

Sam and Helen, holding hands, wove a path through the campers to reach Sandra's fire pit. "What's this about prying ears?" Helen wanted to know.

"Mother, Slender Petal's got some delicious tidbits about Death Wind when he was a little boy. She's going to tell me all about him—later. When we get rid of the men."

"Sandra, you're becoming such a gossip."

Sam waved a hand to attract attention. "I hate to interrupt such an important discussion, but would anyone like to hear the news." He waited for a moment, scrutinizing each person's eyes, until he had their attention. "The dragon fortress has been spotted. Right where Rusty said it would be."

Scott forgot the pain in his leg and jumped up. "Wow, that's great. And I just got finished telling Rusty we were only halfway there."

Sam held up his hands. "Sorry. I didn't mean to give any false impressions. It's still pretty far off. Bold One and Death Wind and some of the other braves saw it from the top of the mountain. Ararat."

Scott remembered the near collision the *Ark* had had with the snowcapped peak. "I've been as close as I want to get to that place. What made them climb to the summit? I thought they were just going to scout around the base."

"You know these Nomads. Sorry, Slender Petal. I guess you do know them. Well, once they got close and saw the ridge in between, they figured if they got high enough it would save them having to make an actual reconnaissance on foot. You know, sort of seeing the lay of the land from up above? Well, sure enough, once they got up there they could see the glow of the TTS in the distance. They camped up there overnight. Sounded like pure hell, even with the insulated moccasins and musk ox blankets."

"Did I understand you correctly, Sam?" Doc asked. "They could see the focusing nodes coruscating? As if they were in use?"

"That's what they said. Well, I mean, that's the message they sent back. The runner just got in. The rest of them will meet us on the trail sometime tomorrow."

Doc rubbed his white beard thoughtfully. "That is very strange intelligence, indeed. If, as we supposed, the Pleistocene structure is the last stronghold of the dragons, when are they transporting to—or from? They have no past, the future is blocked, and they have nothing to gain by selecting another upstream destination when the geological record shows no evidence of dragon incursion."

Sam tilted his head questioningly. "I don't know, Henry. I'm just reporting the facts. Scott, get on the toner and tell Rusty what we've found. Maybe he can search the crystal and pick up something we missed. He told me the dragon menus are difficult to trace because they rely on key words he might be unfamiliar with."

Scott eased himself down by his pack. "I thought they just used this TTS as a receiving station. But if they're transporting elsewhen, we've got to be careful not to destroy any documentation about their whenabouts. Doc, I apologize. You were right about not coming in with guns blazing and obliterating the place."

"Yes, now more than ever we must proceed with caution."

"Not only that, we've got to be sure not to tip our hand about the ground assault. Granted the dragons may not be expecting us to waltz in among the glaciers, but if they've got observation posts surrounding the fort, we want to make damn sure that if the alarm is given we're ready to storm the place before they can mobilize."

"I've sent out a fresh runner and told her to get the boys back here on the double. I don't like having my troops spread out like this. Especially since Death Wind came so close to becoming cat food. I've issued orders that there's to be no more solo scouting. But you know that boy. He's got his own head."

Sandra smirked conspiratorially with Slender Petal and Jane. "Yes, so I'm told."

"And his father's just as bad. Between those two, I sometimes wonder if giving instructions does any good. They're going wild out there in the forest, as if they'd just gotten out of jail. Slender Petal, was Bold One always like this?"

Slender Petal nodded but once. "Always."

"Like father, like son," said Sandra.

"Yeah, well, they may be two of the best scouts in the world, but I'd like it a hell of a lot better if they'd follow the routine instead of their noses." Sam ran a hand through his hair and scratched his black beard. "This place can't be taken lightly. It's utterly different from anyplace—or anytime—in our experience. Sure, it's full of wildlife; but most of it's lethal. You've got to watch yourself every step of the way. It isn't like home. We didn't have wild animals to contend with. We never had to worry about anything but dragons, and we knew how to hide from them. But here you've got packs of bloodthirsty wolves, saber-toothed tigers, bears the size of a house. To say nothing of the swarms of smaller types that are constantly nipping at our heels. This is the Age of Mammals, all right—predatory mammals."

Slender Petal sat back on her haunches. "Much challenge."

Sam scowled. "I'm sure that's what the Nomads like the most about it. Well, to each his own. I just want to win this war and not have to fight anymore: with dragons or wild animals."

"Sam, I don't think you're being fair," said Helen. "You're not looking at what this world has to offer, only at how hard you have to work in order to earn its fruits." She gestured toward the savanna in a supplicatory manner. "Compared to this, our world is a barren wasteland. Up till now, the largest mammal I've ever seen is a rabbit—"

"And they're practically overrunning the Holocene forests."

"If we catch a glimpse of a raccoon or a chipmunk—"

"*They're* not even worth eating."

"—we ooh and ah because so few mammals survived the holocaust. How can you be so calloused in a world so alive, so full of the wonders of nature—the world the way it used to be before the coming of the dragons?"

"Okay, okay." Sam held his hands out in front of him, defensively. "I didn't mean to sound like a pessimist. I'm just saying that the world is a seductive pitfall. You've got to be on your toes all the time."

"Easy for you to say." Scott removed the browned venison from the flame and nibbled the edges.

"We've got to watch out for insects, snakes, and birds of prey. We've got half a dozen people down with fevers from stings and snake bites, one gal nearly lost her head when a teratornis mistook her hair for a nest and tried to fly off with it. Those wolves mauled two men before they were beaten off. Even a herd of herbivorous musk ox charged through the Fusiliers' formation and caused such a rout that they had to drop their packs and run for their lives. We were lucky not to have anyone trampled by those cloven hooves. Hell, one of the Nomad women was feeding a cardinal out of her palm and the thing pecked her face and almost took her eye out. We've got a dozen casualties, and we haven't even met the enemy yet."

"All of life is a risk," said Doc.

"Henry, this isn't the time for philosophy. We're at war. And I'm wondering if we'll have any soldiers in fighting trim when we reach the battlefront."

Scott swiped several more chunks of meat off Doc's makeshift cutting board, slid the metal point through them, and placed the miniature shish kebab over the fire. "There's a lot to what you say, Sam. Invasionary forces are always at the mercy of the elements, the terrain, and the unknown defenses of the enemy. But look at the brighter side. We've been able to live off the land with relatively little expenditure of time and resources. That means light loads, fast travel, and no supply line."

"And don't say that having pregnant women along slowed you down any," Sandra scolded. "We've all kept up the pace and managed the work load, without complaint."

"If it had been up to me, you'd have stayed with the *Ark* until we called in for reinforcements," said Sam.

"No way, Daddy. I go where my husband goes. If he wants to walk halfway around the world, I'll follow him."

"An admirable quality you get from your mother."

Helen nodded. "I seem to recall giving birth to Sandra on the trail. That was how we lived at the time. We were always on the go, trying to keep one move in front of the dragons. We hid in a rock shelter for the night and started out early the next morning with a papoose in a blanket tied to my breast."

"But that was necessity. It was either run or die. This is a planned military campaign, not a family outing."

Helen shrugged. "Conditions may change, perceptions may be different. But women are women, no matter what the age."

Sam flung his hands in the air. "I should know better than to argue with you. Or your daughter."

"*Our* daughter."

"Our daughter," Sam said grudgingly. "Sometimes I think I

should just let the Femme Fatales infiltrate the dragon stronghold and talk their ears off while we read all their crystals."

Scott said, "Lizards don't have auricles—"

"Don't you start," Sam cautioned, wagging a finger. "I've got enough trouble on my hands."

"And you may have more trouble—later." Helen put her hands on her shapely hips.

Sam feigned a scowl. "I never thought a general had to fight on so many fronts."

Scott removed the venison from the flame and blew on it to cool it off. "Try being a private."

CHAPTER 12

Bold One and Death Wind ran side by side, like split images of the same subject. Each wore hide jackets and leggings, each slung a bow and quiver of arrows over broad shoulders, each held a spear at the balance point. Their pace was fast, and one they could keep up for hours.

For the first time in his life, Death Wind felt free as the wind that blew the hair off his neck. The dragons were a minor nuisance, to be taken care of in due time. But for now he reveled in the thrill of the hunt, in the rush of the chase, in the longing for dominance over this primitive world. He and his tribe were the lords of this planet.

Bold One raised a hand to signal for attention, then bent his wrist and drew back three fingers so he was left pointing. Death Wind saw, and nodded in silent assent.

They separated, each veering off to opposite sides.

The ground was purified by a blanket of snow, clean and white. The crystals crunched under Death Wind's padded moccasins. Lofty evergreens wore a cream-colored blanket that wrapped around each tiny needle, that pressed down on each slender branch; the trees looked like veiled, mourning ladies. The sun was a muted ball struggling to shine through the overcast.

Death Wind jogged down the lower slopes of Mt. Ararat. The pitch was not as severe as it had been at the higher elevations; a series of long, gentle slopes alternated with flat, level plains. Far ahead a black dot moved, its size undiscernible because of the distance and lack of perspective. It might be a giant bear such as the one they had killed in the forest. Or it might be even larger.

There was no need for communication, for both father and son knew what to do, and knew what the other would do. Death Wind entered a stand of fir trees. The snow was deeper here because the tall sentinels captured it and prevented the wind from blowing it away. Waist-high drifts barred his path. Death Wind skirted the edge of the grove and slogged through snow that was only knee deep.

He slipped wraithlike around the trees, out of sight of the animal resting unsuspectingly in the frozen savanna. Many minutes later, when he reached a point as close to the creature as he could get without stepping out into the open, he uttered a sequence of hoots in imitation of a fat, nocturnal bird that Doc called an owl. A moment later came the twang of a jay: Bold One's response.

Neither Nomad moved. Death Wind observed the shaggy black mound with growing curiosity. If it was a bear, he did not want to disturb it. It had taken a dozen men and women of the Sintu tribe to corral and kill the other, and in retrospect they felt that good fortune in addition to their native skills prevented death or serious injury in the ensuing skirmish. Yet, they had proved that with only primitive weapons, coordinated effort, and ingenuity born of a lifetime of wilderness experience, they could conquer the beasts that inhabited this vestal, untamed land. Nomads could adapt.

The cold bit through his clothing. After an hour of astute observation, Death Wind used a trick to keep warm that he had learned since penetrating the frigid highlands. Without moving perceptibly or jumping in place, he vibrated his muscles in a controlled shiver. His entire body trembled, yet his clothing disclosed not a hint of movement. Several minutes of enforced muscular friction warmed him measurably.

Still, the sleeping animal lay quiescent.

Bold One took the initiative. He called like a jay, to let Death Wind know he was moving again. He had rubbed snow into the outer hide of his clothing, and held in front of him a snow-covered bush. Crouched low, he worked his way toward the monstrous, unknown creature. Death Wind held his place; he was upwind, and would surely be detected should he attempt the same tactic.

His father glided across the snowfield with infinite patience. He was a hundred yards away when the black mound shuddered. Death Wind could not tell head from tail. The beast was a giant mop of hair, a shaggy boulder caught in an earth tremor. It heaved upward, then settled back down into its crypt of snow.

Death Wind's gaze alternated between beast and bush. Bold One sank into the snow behind the white shrubbery. He lay there for many minutes, until the animal thrust up again. This time it rose out of the snow like a mythical titan, larger than any living creature Death Wind had seen in post-Cretaceous times. The huge bulk was covered with thatch that reached the ground.

The thick coat of hair disguised its shape. One end was lower than the other, like the stance of a bear, but the angle was such that Death Wind could not distinguish its facing direction. Then, after Death Wind thought the beast was already standing, it heaved once more, lifting the bulk of its body on four massive, columnar legs, like a house on stilts.

The animal rotated slowly. The tail waggled on a low-slung rump like a tassel on the end of a stick. The backbone inclined upward like a ski slope to broad, bulbous shoulder blades. The head alone was the size of a small bear. Then came a great, ear-shattering trumpet as a long, thick trunk pointed toward the sky, and the ivory tusks stabbed the air like curved pikes.

The woolly mammoth directed its gaze toward the hidden Nomad. Its large ears flapped, and its entire body swayed from side to side as it lifted first one huge forefoot, then the other. It seemed uncertain, as if its visual acuity were deceiving its olfactory sensitivity; as if what looked like a bush smelled like something it had never before experienced. It trumpeted its discomfort.

The mammoth approached Bold One warily. The Nomad made not a move. Once again the beast trumpeted, as if showing displeasure at uncertain circumstances, or issuing a final warning. Death Wind put his mind into the brain of the pachyderm, striving to think how it would think, to see what it saw, to interpret situations in light of the mammoth's experience, to deduce what its instinctive reactions might be. Death Wind clutched his spear tightly, knowing full well that the puny weapon was no defense against a creature of such size.

Less than a hundred feet separated the mammoth from the bush. The trumpeting resounded in the still, crisp air like the deep-throated rumble of a landslide. The tusks pointed forward, the trunk held high.

Bold One lunged out from behind the bush. He raised his spear in both hands and let out a war whoop that rang across the countryside. The mammoth hunched back indecisively, trumpeted, leaned forward, trumpeted, leaned back, trumpeted, and poised. If the Nomads knew how to read such behavior, they could have responded accordingly. But they had never before encountered such an animal—had in fact met very few mammals in their Holocene lifetimes, and those small ones.

Death Wind waited for the turn of events.

Bold One rushed the hesitant pachyderm. The mammoth

charged. Bold One skidded to a halt, spun around, and dashed for the protection of the distant fir trees.

Death Wind ran out from his own place of hiding, whooping and waving his arms at the distant pachyderm. The beast was amazingly fast and agile for one so huge; it galloped through the deep snow like a black steed racing across a field of grass. It rapidly closed the distance to the bounding Nomad.

To Death Wind, running through snow was like wading through water. He exerted every ounce of energy to reach his father's side. His angled course closed on a vector with the rampaging, madly trumpeting mammoth. He screamed at the top of his lungs. The gargantuan head swung his way, a dark eye the size of his fist glared at him. The mammoth slowed to a halt. Bold One stopped in his tracks and faced the woolly mammoth defiantly. The pachyderm pivoted its great tusks from one Nomad to the other. It was now forced to confront two opponents. The shaggy head swayed from one to the other.

Bold One feigned a lunge. His son followed suit. But Death Wind had no intention of getting any closer than he already was. He was not going to attack, but he could not let the mammoth know that. He merely wanted to hold it at bay until his father was safe. His heart pounding with excitement, Death Wind stared back at the mammoth. Part of him wanted to attack, to prove his manhood, to bring down the greatest mammal he had ever seen. But part of him knew that this was not a challenge for one brave, or even two. To kill such a beast would require stealth, planning, and collaboration. All he wanted for now was to leave in peace.

The mammoth leaned back again on its haunches. It trumpeted like a peal of thunder. Bold One and Death Wind acted aggressively, each whooping and taking a step forward with his spear poised.

The mammoth's charge turned into a rout. It rolled back on its hind legs, executed a low cartwheel, and took off across the plain.

Father and son exchanged startled glances. Then they whooped in delight and chased after the retreating mammoth. On and on they ran, screaming like banshees. The woolly mammoth outdistanced them with ease. But they ran for the sheer exhilaration of running, ran until their legs ached with pain, ran until their lungs gasped for air, ran until they had their fill of adrenaline and were happy to be alive in a land so full of life.

Then they stopped and watched the pachyderm galloping away,

watched until it was a small black speck on the horizon, until its shape blended with the dark trees. Without exchanging a single word, they nodded at each other and headed for camp.

Death Wind felt an ecstasy he had never felt before. And knew that it was a feeling he must experience again. There would be other days, other mammoths, and other hunts. That was the way of the Sintu.

He was awake behind the closed lids, but so groggy he could not open his eyes. He snuggled deeper into the warmth of the blanket, soaking in the deliciousness of sleep. Partly, too, he did not want to face the world of reality. Slumber land was so cozy. He dreamt of faraway places, of faraway times, of the infinity of space-times that stretched out before him like coarse hemp in which each strand split into myriads of branches, and out of each branch grew smaller offshoots, which branched out farther into slender filaments, which themselves consisted of even tinier—

He felt a soft touch on his forehead. He dragged his eyes open as if they were creaky barn doors. The suffused glow that filled the bridge was partially blocked by a familiar shape. Rusty forced a smile. "Did I oversleep?"

Britt shook her head. "You not sleep enough."

Rusty smiled more broadly. "I *do* not sleep enough," he corrected. His voice was cracked and weak.

"You *do* not sleep enough."

Rusty pushed himself up to a sitting position, tucking the blanket around him as he did so. "That's right, but without the accent."

She perched on the edge of the cot like a bird about to fly off. "Breakfast?"

For one crazy, fear-filled moment he was afraid she would scoot away and leave him alone. As he scrunched up against the bulkhead and pulled his legs under him, he grabbed her hand and held it in a way that he hoped was not obvious. "First let me get the cobwebs out of my eyes."

Britt leaned so close that Rusty could feel her breath upon his face; it reminded him of a warm spring breeze with the scent of flowers in the air. "Pretty eyes. But no cobwebs. I keep spiders off bridge."

Rusty could not stop from laughing. "That's just an expression, Britt. It means I'm still drowsy."

The smile never left her face. "I understand." She picked up a cup from the floor and held it out to him. "Tea?"

He patted her hand to complete the illusion of mere friendship. "Sure. Thank you." His eyes never left hers.

"Message come in. Say 'ice ahead.'"

Wearily, Rusty brought his mind into focus. He forced his memory to dump into the buffer of his brain the programs he was running. "Oh, that's great. They're making good time." He sipped his tea, flung his feet off the pad, slipped into his moccasins, and took two steps to the computer console. He used his free hand to actuate the screen. "How are they otherwise?"

"All well."

Rusty nodded, and continued sipping. He studied the equations highlighted on the monitor. He was hardly aware of Britt standing by his side. Reading spatiotemporal coordinates required extreme concentration. He had programmed the onboard computer to function on multilevel problems. Since the calculations he had started were still undergoing checking and evaluation, he let the computer do it off-screen. He booted the crystal format and began menu scanning where he had left off late last night.

With a touch of the controls, Britt pulled back the opaque canopy cover. The light that flooded the bridge was not the yellow beam of the sun, but a white scattering that cast no harsh shadows.

"Look, Rusty. It snows."

He cast his eyes upward. Large, flat flakes landed delicately on the clear plastic bubble, existing only a trice before melting into an obscure smear of water.

"I never see before."

Rusty stared at her numbly, part of his mind still on his computer scan. "Then, how do you know what it is?"

"Scott explain. During ori-en-tation. He talk about this world. About con-ditions. He is good teacher."

Rusty cast his eyes back at the screen. He allowed himself to smile. "That he is—among other things." He glanced at Britt for a moment. "He's a good person, a good friend." A dragon symbol caught his attention. He typed instructions on the keyboard that halted the scrolling data, backed up to a suspicious entry code, and stabbed the button for expansion. A submenu appeared. Still standing and sipping, he set the new list into motion. "There's got to be an answer here somewhere. Too many things don't add up."

Britt set a fried cake on the counter beside him. Rusty absently picked it up and shoved it into his mouth. He took another sip of tea.

"If I only knew what I was looking for."

CHAPTER 13

For the umpteenth time Scott pulled his stump out of the morass. The cylindrical leg extension continually sank into the soggy soil like a pointed stick into mud.

The rain forest was magnificent in the panoply of life it offered. Giant sequoias towered hundreds of feet above the lush, moss-covered, root-filled ground. The trunks of fallen trees lay like great monarchs throughout the forest, oftentimes larger in diameter than a person's height: a barrier that meant wide detour. Spanish moss hung in huge clots from the lower branches. Vines clung to bark like varicose veins. Mushrooms grew in great profusion, and added their distinct flavor to the evening stew.

Scott saw more species of animals in one hour than he had seen in his whole life. Everything from colorful slugs twice the size of his thumb, to immense Irish elks that ran through the brush with an uncanny knack considering the wide, palmate antlers they carried on their heads. The ground was alive with fox, raccoon, bobcat, hare, hog, and a wide variety of rodents.

"I don't care what you say, those birds sound to me like they're chirping *merrily*."

Doc chuckled to himself. "Whatever you say, my boy. If that is what you wish to believe."

"But those damn squirrels—" Scott shook a fist in the air. High overhead, fluffy-tailed tree rodents chattered incessantly. "They *have* to be aiming. I've been hit by three cones this morning, not counting the near misses. Nobody's going to make me believe they're not dropping them intentionally."

Doc was having the same trouble with his cane that Scott was having with his stump: it kept slicing into the soft earth. The makeshift basket of vine wrapped around the end helped quite a bit. "They are merely expressing an aggressive territorial instinct."

"Yeah, well, if we come back this way and I still have power in this thing—" Scott reached behind and rapped his knuckles on the side of the battery pack. "I can guarantee you that some of those rascals are going to get fried."

"Save your aggression for the dragons," Doc laughed.

"Believe me, right now I've got plenty to spare."

During the course of the afternoon they continually gained elevation. With the level, open savanna now far behind, and the rain forest yielding to fauna more adapted to the cold, the trees became shorter, the brush sparser, the ground rockier. Scott found himself getting out of breath as the climbing became steeper with each step. He paused more often, leaning forward at the waist with hands on hips, fighting the agony in his legs.

"Rather a tough climb," said Doc with a hint of a gasp. The older man did not carry a pack of any kind, but Scott still found it amazing that his stamina held him in such good stead. "We need the acclimatization. The worst is yet to come."

The newly trodden trail led to the top of a precipice that overlooked the valley below. Scott was enamored by the open vista. He stood on the very edge and gazed in awe; it was as if half the world were laid out beneath his foot. A glacier-fed, crystal-blue pond supplied water to a meandering creek that carved a deep gorge through the forest. Eagles with their wings spread wide rode the air currents with effortless ease. From a lower ledge, a furry marmot screamed at the human intrusion. Mountain sheep as white as snow bounded along the opposite cliff face.

Jane was suddenly by his side. "We camp ahead."

Scott kissed her hair. "Good. I'm about tuckered out. Doc, are you okay?"

He was breathing a little harder now. Leaning heavily on his cane, he stared out at the green, lowland pasture. "These weary bones are fatigued, my boy, and my stomach grumbles without compassion; but I suffer from nothing that a good rest and a grilled steak cannot cure. Lead on, Jane. I believe I detect the lovely fragrance of a campfire."

"I think if you tried Nomad dialogue it would save you a lot of breath."

Doc ran his fingers through his great shock of white hair, pulling out twigs and leaves. "There is undoubted truth in what you say. I shall give it some thought." He admired the view for another few seconds, then continued on his way before he lost his place in line. A Charon gal hauling a travois stopped to let him in front.

When he was out of earshot Scott shook his head. "He just never gives up."

Jane nuzzled her husband. "Neither do you."

They camped that night in the scrub pine; burning logs scented the air with their essence. Blackened pots hung over the fire pits; the boiling water was thickened with chopped herbs, tubers, and vegetables, collected during the day's march. Escaping steam added its aroma to that of the natural forest. Meat sizzled over the open flames.

The powwow began right after dinner, in the light of upheld fire brands.

"The way I see it is this." Sam scraped a spot flat and drew lines in the dirt with a stick. "Here we've got the stronghold, in the same location in terms of geological reference as Charon in the Holocene. The *Ark*'s glide path carried us over the mountain range into this valley. A good thing, too, because it puts us out of visual range from the stronghold. Right in front of us is the western flank of Ararat, which we can cross here." He drew a jagged line that described a switchback trail to the crest of the ridge and back down the other side. He pointed through the trees behind him. "That's just up ahead. Bold One, you want to brief us on that?"

The Nomad spoke in a deep monotone, like a base fiddle with only one string. "Very steep. Much snow. Wind on top. No game."

There followed a long pause punctuated by the crackling of embers. The warmth radiating from the fires compensated for the cold of night. The flickering, yellow glow tainted serious faces with a touch of jaundice, while casting dark shadows into the blackness beyond. Bold One made no further attempt to elucidate.

"Right. Well, that was pretty brief." Sam doodled with the stick. "Anyway, we've got plenty of provisions: more now than when we started. But it'll be snow and ice from here on: tough slogging, with no chance for hunting or gathering food. The worst part is we'll be out in the open. Now, we've got plenty of skins for protection from the elements, but what I'm worried about is being exposed on these snowfields. It doesn't look like the dragons have any flyers in this era, but we can't be sure. It might be parked in an under-ice hangar."

Helen raised her hand. Sam acknowledged her. "I've been studying the aerial photos taken on the way in. They're a little blurred because of the *Ark*'s speed, but they do show a lightening in color that extends throughout the glaciers surrounding the stronghold. If you'll look at your maps"—paper rustled throughout the moonlit clearing—"you'll see a cloverleaf effect around the central structure. Under magnification these teardrop-shaped arms appear to be interconnected by faint lines, as if the dragons have tunneled under the ice."

"Could they be living quarters?" Scott asked.

"If they are, there are an awful lot of dragons holing up inside that glacier." Helen placed the blowup where everyone could see it. She outlined the curved perimeter with a long fingernail. "Correlate your maps with the computer image. See how extensive these areas are in comparison with the central core, which I interpret as the reactor and TTS? There's either a fairly large community of slaves, or these are storage facilities."

"Storing what?" asked Sandra.

Helen shrugged. "More time transport equipment. Extra batteries. Arms and munitions. Food. Possibly four flyers that are being assembled this very minute."

Scott thought about making the comment that everything in the universe was happening at this very minute, but let it slide. He was not in the mood for levity, even his own. These were serious matters at hand.

"In that case we need to spread out during the approach march." Broderick was a small man who spoke with impeccable diction. He combed his hair short and trimmed his beard to the same length with a scalpel. "We can communicate by radio."

Sam nodded. "Yes, the Sintus will lead the charge and secure a beachhead. The Rangers and Fusiliers will take flanking positions during the crossing. Sandra, can your gals manage the cannon on that ice?"

"We're going to build a sledge for it." Sandra pointed her chin at her mother-in-law. "Slender Petal is in charge because she's done it before. We'll use the reins from the gun carriage like we've been doing. It shouldn't take any more than four of us to haul it across the snowfield. But when we have to take it uphill or down, we're going to need help from a few strapping men."

"Windy, Broderick, pick two men each and detail them to the Fatales. How much time will we need to make snowshoes?"

"One day," said Death Wind.

"Slender Petal, can the sledge be built in a day?"

"Yes."

"Good. Then we'll stay here tomorrow, rest up, and prepare for the trek across the snow. Bold One, have all the scouts returned? I don't want to tip our hand by having them spotted."

Without uttering a word the Nomad tilted his head.

Doc pulled the bear skin tighter over his shoulders. "No doubt the dragons anticipate an attack."

"But they don't know when, how, or from what quarter. I think a sneak ground assault is our best chance."

"Oh, I do not question your decisions concerning methods of attack. Clearly, the dragons are fully prepared to repel an aerial bombing raid. Nor can we afford to have the *Ark* irreparably damaged. It represents our only way out of the here and now. I merely want to emphasize—for everyone's benefit—that we must proceed with extreme caution—perhaps even trepidation. We know nothing about the dragons' motivations for setting up a base of operations in this time zone. We have so far surmised that the stronghold is nothing more than an escape mechanism, but there are indications that reasons more pervasive exist."

"Such as?"

Doc squeezed his long beard as one would wring out a damp washcloth. "Such as surface-to-air missiles. When the dragons constructed this stronghold and armed it for defense, I am sure they did not foresee an attack by one of their own aircraft. There are no political factions within dragon hierarchy, no competitive infrastructure. Yet they showed no compunction against shooting down a flyer obviously of dragon design and manufacture. There was no attempt at communication."

Long branches spread out from the central fire pit like spokes from the hub of a wheel. Doc snapped off the nearly burned-off tip and shoved the branch farther into the flames.

"I see what you're getting at," said Sam. "It almost seems as if they were expecting us."

Broderick added, "They knew exactly when, where, and how we'd be coming."

Doc shook his head. "No, the evidence does not warrant such conclusions. I am merely pointing out that the facts do not add up to any known quantity. Which is all the more reason to enter the stronghold clandestinely, to infiltrate rather than to destroy wantonly, to overthrow their leadership. I have a curious feeling about what we may encounter."

"Henry, it's already understood that we're gonna do as little damage as possible—"

Doc interrupted his son-in-law with an upraised palm. "Forgive me, Sam, but I must be more emphatic than that. We cannot allow *any* destruction of dragon equipment."

"Be reasonable, Henry. There's bound to be a few stray shots—"

"No demolition whatsoever. We must contain laser fire to perimeter sorties."

Sam's jaw dropped. His mouth opened wide enough to swallow an apple whole. "What the hell are we supposed to do? *Negotiate?* We didn't drag that cannon through hell and tarnation as a conversation piece. Or all these laser guns, either. If we don't blow the bastards off the face of the earth they'll be here to haunt us for the rest of our racial existence. I understand about not wanting to damage the controls to the reactor; we don't need to learn any more about plate tectonics. And we've gotta know what TZ they're sending to or receiving from, so we can't tamper with the TTS until we trace its activation memory circuits. And, well, I guess we don't want to interrupt power to the central computer. But—"

"Doesn't leave much, does it, Daddy?" Sandra sidled close to her husband. "Pop's right, as always. If we break a single circuit, it may shut down an automatic override or disconnect an important safety valve. The whole place may be sabotaged for self-destruction. Then we'll never know when they're coming or going."

"Hey, whose side are you on, anyway? You never side with your grandfather—or anybody else for that matter."

"I'm on the winning side, Daddy, and so are you." Sandra pulled her fur coat over her legs. The bulky beaver pelt hid her growing pregnancy. "You've been so caught up with planning this operation as a military campaign that you've lost sight of the final objective."

Sam threw his hands into the air. "Now I've heard everything."

In the short silence that followed, glowing embers crackled like scattered rifle shots. Green wood sizzled as sap oozed into the red-hot coals. A meteor streaked across the star-studded sky with soundless splendor. The tranquility of the night was broken only by the caterwauling of a wildcat seeking a mate and the stridulating of crickets in the trees.

Windy tossed pine needles into the fire as if they were darts. "'Pears to me she gots the right attitude, Gen'ral. I may be a blimp brain mosta the time, but I gotta 'gree wit' the young lady."

"I need to gain access to their systems program so Rusty can—" Scott started.

Sam held out his hands defensively. "Hold on a minute. Don't everybody gang up on me. I'm not protesting. I just don't quite know what our objective *is* anymore." Facing Doc, he said, "If you're trying to tell me we've got to tiptoe in there past armed guards without firing a shot, I won't stand for it. We'll lose too many people. Human wave attacks are for the birds—well, you know what I mean. Don't just tell me what I *can't* do, Henry. Tell me what I *can* do."

Doc took his time before answering. He beefed up the fire again and held his hands close to the flickering flames. "Sam, I have no intention of usurping your authority. You are in tactical command of this outfit, and you are doing a fine job of it. My position here is that of advisor."

"Then advise me," Sam said, raising his voice truculently.

Again Doc paused. He waited until the silence screamed to be broken. Then he spoke in his mellifluous, finely wrought baritone. "Rusty and I have given the matter of paradox as thorough an examination as philosophy will allow. In the dearth of empirical data we have come to separate conclusions that, while not mutually contradictory, are at best mildly antagonistic. The only thing we agree on is that the ramifications of time travel cannot damage the universe as an entity.

"But," Doc held up an index finger for accentuation. "The delicate balance between cause and effect can be upset the same as a precarious ridge of snow can be turned into an avalanche by the molecular vibration generated by a sharp clap. In a similar manner dragon technology has disturbed the fabric of local space-time with results that, as you all know, have had far-reaching effects on the continuance of life and on the geology of this planet. Such worldwide changes are the inherent danger of playing with time."

Sam chafed at Doc's lengthy discourse. He ran his hand through his hair and gritted his teeth at the ground.

"The dragons have started something that we must finish. We cannot take an ostrich posture in light of what we know. The dragons, and the horrible avalanche they have set in motion, must be stopped before humanity is engulfed in a temporal snowball. That is why we are here now. But we must be extremely careful not to trigger events that may cause our own dissolution. We do not want to overexert our leverage and tip the balance of nature.

"Sam, I must caution against the use of power weapons during the assault phase on the dragon stronghold. The cannon and back guns must be withheld. The Nomads can provide cover with bows and arrows while the rest of us go in with spears and knives. Hand-to-paw combat is the only means of attack that will give us the measure of control we need. If we break a link in the chain of events, the human race may end in the Pleistocene instead of originating here."

Sam exhaled so hard that his breath blew aside the flames of the fire in front of him. "Well, why not tie one hand behind my back, too."

"I understand your frustration. I feel it as well. I would prefer to bomb the glacial retreat and let matters fall where they may. But I cannot in good conscience take that chance when we may do irrevocable damage to the continuity of time. The renascence of the world depends upon conquering the dragons not just of this time zone, but throughout eternity in both directions. What we need now is knowledge, not a body count."

"Okay. Okay. I get the point. You make good sense. You always do. But I can't ask these people to attack the dragon stronghold under those restrictions. I want to win this war more than anybody. But there's still the human equation to figure."

"Son, you are learning that the lot of a military commander is a troubled one. Decisions that involve life and death are never easy to make. Unlike the doctor, the soldier has no Hippocratic oath to shape his judgment."

Sam shook his head. "You're a big help." Helen rubbed his back through the thick hide.

"Sintu agree." Everyone looked up at Bold One's intonation.

"Yeah, an' that goes fer the Rangers, too." Windy tossed a rock into the fire that stirred the embers and caused ashes to fly. "We ain't afeared to face them lizards with our bare hands. Get a stranglehold on 'em, we will."

Broderick spoke with quiet elocution. "The Fusiliers will do what is necessary to win this bloody war, with or without weapons."

"I'll speak for the Femme Fatales," said Sandra. "We'll back you all the way, Daddy, in a subordinate position if necessary. We came here to fight dragons, and if the best way to fight them is to do as Pop says, then that's the way we'll do it."

Sam looked from one to the other, mouth agape. A cheer went up around the fire, followed by the incantation of the Nomad code. Helen leaned hard against her husband's shoulder. Sam worked his jaw, but no sound came out until he cleared his throat.

"I guess—I guess I'm not—a very good soldier. I can't order troops into battle with the certainty that not all of them will survive."

Doc said, "If you cannot order them into battle, lead them. My only request is that I want to be by your side when you do."

CHAPTER 14

The snowshoes were a godsend to Scott. The flotation offered by the curved hickory sticks lashed together at the ends and strung across the middle with interlaced leather strips gave him the best support he had had since leaving the *Ark*. The long wooden tail helped in tracking by keeping the heel aligned with the direction of travel. Unfortunately, it made backing up impossible.

"Hey, Doc, this is great. With these things on I'm finally on equal footing with the rest of the gang."

"I noticed you were having no trouble keeping up." Doc lumbered along on his own snowshoes with very little difficulty. The snow was piled high in drifts that would have been exhausting to traverse without the Nomad footgear.

"And I can really get a foothold with the wooden spikes digging into the ice."

"Modified crampons. The Nomads know every trick in the book when it comes to outdoor living. I knew they would be indispensable."

The snowfield angled up a gentle slope that was just enough to keep Scott huffing and puffing. He and Doc were at the front of the Femme Fatales. Far to the left Scott saw the last of the First Fusiliers, while to his right a straggler from the Texas Rangers made his way sluggishly over the glistening crust. The Nomads were out of sight over the crest. Great yawning crevasses of unknown depth gouged the plateau like squiggly fingers.

"You know, I just had a crazy thought."

Once again Scott adjusted his snow goggles: the temples made his ears sore. He had started out with a pair of glasses made from laminations of shaded plastic. They fogged up so often from his breath condensing and freezing on the lenses that he soon switched to the Nomad variety: a thin sheet of bark lashed around the face with treated gut; pinholes poked in front of the eyes limited the amount of light allowed to penetrate.

"Not another one."

"Suppose the dragons perfect the time transfer device like

Rusty has: with infinite incremental verniers. Then they'd be able to go anywhen they wanted with exact precision."

"I think 'exact precision' is grammatically redundant, but I understand your meaning."

"Okay, so how about this scenario? Let's suppose this stronghold is a testing station. Now, we know that in the past the dragons built their time transfer structures way out in the boondocks in case their future experiments backfired on them; they didn't want to blow up the city, or the taxpayers. But suppose they were investigating new principles of space-time, with possible consequences so lethal they didn't want to take a chance on having something go wrong in their own time zone."

"An interesting speculation." Doc stopped at the top of the rise and leaned against the cane that had been converted into a ski pole by the addition of a woven basket. "So they establish a subdivision in the Pleistocene so that if the experiment goes awry, they forfeit only the laboratory and its contemporary environs."

"Exactly!"

Doc's face clouded over. "But they would still suffer the loss of highly trained personnel: the technicians and scientific team managing the project."

"Not if they transferred the high-echelon dragons a short way through time when the actual experiments were conducted. Time is a better safeguard than space, and you don't have to go very far: a few minutes will do."

Doc nodded thoughtfully. "But that presumes their discovery of a more finely tuned incremental transfer control."

"No, I was just using that as an example. They might have something else up their sleeves besides scales. Even with their million-year transfers, they could still time-warp the VIPs into the past or future."

"Which brings us back to why we must access their computer instead of destroying it."

"Not only that, it means we may be walking into a real hot potato."

"Hey, you ain't gonna get any hot potatoes till dinnertime, and then only if we can spare the wood." Sandra stood with her hands on her hips, her bulbous shape lost in the profusion of furs. "How about quitting your jabbering, and picking up the pace a bit."

Scott feigned a scowl and shook his head. "You are one tough lady, Sandra. I don't know how you can chug along like that with such a burden."

"Children are not a burden, they are a blessing."

"Uh-oh. Doc, she's been taking proverbial lessons from you."

Doc cocked a snowy white eyebrow. "I am beginning to understand how grating that can become to the senses."

"I've been telling you that for millions of years—" The radio crackled, interrupting Scott's train of thought. "Hold on." He slung the backpack off his shoulders and set it upright on the snow; it sank in the soft surface slush melted by the rays of the sun. He pulled the transmitter out of the leather pouch and plucked away at the keyboard. The tones wafted melodiously across the snowfield like the tinkling of ice crystals on a cold winter's morn.

Jane topped the rise and kept walking until she found a level spot on which to park the travois. The runners were greased with animal fat and slid along the glazed surface at the slightest exertion. "We rest?"

Sandra squinted in the glare. The sun turned the snowfield into a mirrorlike sheet. "Let's get everyone onto level ground, over there by that first crevasse. Those guys with the cannon are so far ahead I can't even see them."

"White make them invisible." Jane reached down and gathered a handful of snow and rubbed it on the back of Sandra's fur coat. The snow did not melt because the body heat did not penetrate the thick hide. The white covering camouflaged the platoon like snow tigers.

Scott toned away on the transmitter.

"Yeah, well, I guess it works. If I can't see them, neither will the dragons when we sneak into their burg. Hey, Scott, that's a pun. Get it? Burg? Berg?"

Listening to Britt's reply on the toner, Scott waved her off.

"How come they're only funny when you make 'em? Huhn? Huhn?"

Jane suddenly froze. She removed her homemade goggles and stared ahead with eyes pinched.

Scott saw the look on her face, turned with the toner still up to his ear, and saw a bright speck of light rising in the sky.

"What the hell—" Sandra started.

"I do not like the looks of this," said Doc.

The long stream of light ascended fast at first, then appeared to slow down and diminish in brightness.

Scott was totally disoriented by the glowing apparition. He thought that the Nomads must have fired a flaming arrow into the air, but could not understand how they could have launched it to such a height. "Doc, what kind of signal—" Scott slowly let the still-twanging toner slip away as his hand dropped to his side.

"It rose from far away," Jane offered. "From other side of crest."

"It is difficult to judge size and distance without perspective. It is either a small object close by, or a large object far away. Despite the optical illusion, I would say there is a fair chance that it is a dragon missile headed our way."

The beam exhaust was partially hidden by the nose cone as the missile reached the peak of its trajectory and angled over toward the ground. The blue thrusters were occulted from Scott's point of view the same as the sun during a solar eclipse.

"It's coming right toward us!"

"Run for cover!" Sandra turned and ran back down the slope toward her platoon.

Scott saw the lip of a crevasse directly in front of him. "Doc! Jane! In here!" Without looking to see if they were following his direction, he leaped toward the opening in the snow. The crevasse was barely wider than his shoulders, with the snow built up like a ramp leading down into the darkness. "Come on!"

He jumped down onto a platform four feet below the surface, sinking past his knees into the powdery drift. He lost his balance and plummeted forward. When his chest hit the snow the edge of the platform broke away like a cornice; he plunged face first onto an ice glaze and slid down in a tumble to the bottom of the crevasse.

Facing up he saw a slender finger of blue sky punctuated by a few sparse clouds, saw Doc's face peer into the corner of the opening, watched him roll over the edge onto the platform, heard the Dopplering whine of the descending missile, saw Jane leap practically on top of Doc, noticed the fine detail in the mesh of her snowshoes as she did an accidental somersault over the venerable doctor and slid feetfirst down the slope, saw a blue-purple streak arc across the top of the crevasse, heard the deafening roar of an explosion, felt the concussion that was transmitted to his body through the hard-packed snow, saw a blinding flash of light followed immediately by a pure white sheet being drawn over the opening, felt pain in his ears as a torrent of snow funneled into the crevasse and pressurized the air, screamed, gulped in a hasty breath, felt the stinging cold hit his face, and reveled in the final, utter blackness that dropped over him like a pall.

Silence ensued.

Scott could neither see, nor hear, nor feel, nor breathe. He was in dark limbo: a place where there was neither pleasure or pain, hope or heartache, cheer or sorrow, life or death. There was only endless continuance, without meaning.

Sometime in another place, in another time, the essence that was Scott felt the urge to take on new life.

His new body needed air. He opened his mouth to draw in the initial breath of the newborn, but found his throat stunned by cold and clogged with snow. He forced himself to cough with whatever air remained in his starving lungs. Out come a clot of ice, and for a moment a narrow passage existed in the center of his throat. He inhaled hard. The sudden pressure collapsed the tunnel. Frigid snow was sucked into his lungs, he choked. He coughed again, gasped, coughed and gasped, coughed and—

Something rasped across his face, brushed vehemently over his mouth. Then warm lips pressed against his, and a breath of hot air was forced into his throat. He inhaled instinctively. As soon as he exhaled, another breath was blown into him. It happened again, and again. Then he went into spasms, gagging on chunks of ice. He spit them out and was able to breathe on his own.

"I can't see."

The goggles were suddenly whipped off his head. In the faint glimmer of light he saw Jane's importunate face only inches away from his own. Her blue eyes were undimmed by the gloom.

"You okay?"

Scott coughed a few more times before he could speak again. "Yes. I'm— No. I feel funny." Then he realized where they were, what their predicament was. He struggled for a moment, then screamed, "Doc?"

"Over here, my boy." The doctor sat up dusting white fluff off his parka. When he shook his head snow flew off his hood. "I am unhurt, but we are in a bit of a bind."

"I—can't—move." Scott strained against invisible bonds. Try as he might he could not move any part of his body. He felt no pain, just a curious paralysis that struck him from the neck down. Shivers of fear coursed along his spine. But if he could feel that—

Jane scrabbled at the snow. Scott could feel her hands beating against his right arm. Then she shoved back on his shoulder, reached down and located his hand, and pulled it up out of the snow. "You are stuck."

In a few moments she had his upper body uncovered. With both hands free he helped her scoop out the compacted snow. Several blocks of ice lay on his lap, pinning his legs under their combined weight. Together they shoved them aside. Scott arched his back and got his hips clear. His snowshoes acted like anchors; it was quite a while before they managed to dig out the foot gear enough for him to roll free.

"Whew." Scott lay gasping from the exertion. Despite the cold of the snow, he was sweating profusely inside his furs. "Does that feel good."

"If you two have succeeded in disinterring each other, I could use a little help in excavation." Doc was buried up to the waist. When he brushed the soft fluff off what Scott thought must be his lap, it became obvious that he was standing upright. His goggles lay askew on his cheeks; he pulled them up onto his broad forehead. "But please be careful. These walls are undoubtedly less than stable. We do not want to start a cave-in."

It took them five minutes of hard work to extricate Doc from the drift. Then they all lay on the snow-covered floor of the crevasse, breathing hard. The arched ceiling towered more than twenty feet overhead. An eerie, gray glow suffused through the ice cap.

"We were lucky to have rolled away from the entrance," said Doc, after he caught his breath.

"So we can suffer a slow death rather than a fast one."

"Please do not be so negative, my boy."

"Life means hope," said Jane.

"Oh, no. Another convert. Doc, are you giving these gals lessons in platitudes?"

"I like to refer to it as positive fluxion philosophy."

"That's great. But it'll take more than phraseology to get us out of here. I don't know how much air can filter through the snow, but I'll bet we can convert oxygen to carbon dioxide faster than natural circulation can replenish it."

"Have no fear. Those topside will soon know exactly where we are." Doc reached into the ample folds of his overlapping furs and pulled out a tin bowl and a soup spoon. When he clanged them together the sound reverberated throughout the chamber. He beat a staccato tune that was grating to the ears. "We will not be entombed for long."

Ten minutes later a tent pole was thrust down through the ice bridge. Doc altered the beat. Several more poles poked through the thick crust; one pole fell all the way through.

Scott yelled, "Hey, watch out. You almost hit me with that stick."

"If you guys are finished playing hide and seek, we'll widen the hole and drop a rope down to you." Sandra's voice was muffled by several feet of intervening snow. "Or would you rather stay for lunch?"

Scott made two fists and thumped his thighs. "I hate it when she has the upper hand."

CHAPTER 15

Rusty's hair had not been cut in ages; his curly locks had grown to such lengths that they framed his face like a ragged mop. He stood behind his computer console with a mug in one hand and a printout in the other. He placed the vellum sheets on the reader, punched a few function keys, and gazed intently at the monitor as calculations scrolled across the screen.

He absently took a sip of tea, frowned when he rediscovered for the tenth time that the mug was empty, and lowered his arm to the bent elbow position.

Britt appeared by his side with a fresh pot of brew. "More?" She never poured without asking, because more than once she had begun to refill his mug and ended up spilling most of it on the floor because he was so preoccupied that he had no awareness of her presence and walked away after she had tipped the teapot.

He stared at her blankly. Fully five seconds later his hand jerked upward. "Oh. Sure. That would be great."

She filled his cup with the steaming brown liquid. "Do you have time yet?"

"Time? Time for what?"

Britt pointed to the computer screen. "Time to transport?"

Rusty shook his head. "Oh, you mean, have I figured out the short-cut formula for calculating the infinity variable? Well, almost, I think. It's mostly a matter of reducing a temporal asymptote to a real-time figure with enough precision that I can insert coordinates on the time axis in relation to an arbitrary prime."

Raised eyebrows implied perplexity.

"Okay. Remember when I showed you the meridians on the globe, and how one was selected to be the prime meridian from which all others were calculated?"

Britt nodded as she put down the teapot.

"Okay, we call that the space axis. Now, I've done the same thing on the time axis by choosing an instantaneity from which all upstream and downstream determinants can be computed. But right now it takes an epoch and a half—sorry, I'm exaggerating. It's what we call hyperbole. Anyway, it takes a lot of computer time to run through the mathematics program. Once I derive the formula that accounts for all the variables, I'll be able to tell the computer when I want to go based on an arbitrary prime temporal meridian. It'll make the computations automatically and immediately, relay the data to the time transfer verniers, and we're then."

"You are very smart." Britt smiled. She reached out for Rusty and ran her hand up and down his slender forearm.

Rusty reacted galvanically to the tingles Britt caused in him. His face turned a shade of red that rivaled the color of his hair. He backed away and took a perfunctory swallow of tea. The brew was still so hot that it burned his lips; he jerked the mug away from his mouth.

"If I were so smart I'd taste the tea before I scalded myself with a mouthful of it." He put the mug on a work space.

"You hurt?" Britt placed a tender finger on his lip.

Rusty backed away so fast he slammed his elbow into a stanchion and nearly tripped over the copilot's seat. "No. I'm okay. It's just that—I guess my mind was on the next set of equations to be input." He quickly thought of something to say. "Do you remember the conveyor belt analogy?"

Britt cocked her head and flashed white, even teeth. "Tell me again. I am not your smart."

"Well, you see," Rusty rushed on. "When you calculate temporal distances on a small scale you don't have to take universal influence into account. At least, not in the proximity of large gravitational bodies, like planets. A mass the size of the Earth forms its own energy well in the space-time continuum. Temporal interaction with the rest of the universe exists to the same degree as gravitational interaction. It's immeasurable in the proportions we're dealing with. We can treat the Earth essentially as an isolated quantity. Are you with me so far?"

"I am with you."

"Okay. If we measure the distance between the two of us, and neither of us moves in relation to the ground, we will always be the same distance apart." Rusty put his hands on Britt's shoulders and made sure she did not come closer. Even at that range he could smell the fragrance of her hair. "That is, throughout the brief span of individual human existence. Understand?"

She pursed her lips. "I understand."

Rusty dropped his hands. "But, even though we can't perceive it with our senses, the ground is in motion all the time. The continents move in a process called plate tectonics. You remember that?"

"I remember."

"Well, these plates slide across the molten core of the Earth like leaves on a pond, and they carry us with them. So, if I calculate the distance between Africa and South America, the quantum result is correct only for a short while—geologically speaking—both upstream and down. But you and I are anchored to the same spot by the product of temporal and gravitational interference. We cannot move in the spatial dimension while moving in the temporal dimension."

Britt stepped forward quickly so that her bust brushed up against Rusty's belly. She looked up at him. "Like this?"

With the chair behind him Rusty could not retreat. He held his ground, but sucked in his stomach in order to break body contact. "Exactly," he said, without relaxing his abdominal muscles. "We are carried along as if the surface of the Earth were a giant conveyor belt."

Britt placed her hands on Rusty's sides. "Now comes the part about the iceberg?"

Due to temperature control within the *Ark*, Rusty wore only shorts, T-shirt, and sandals. Goose bumps rose instantly on his skin. "That's right. You do remember. If I were floating across the sea on an iceberg the distance and bearing to land would change constantly on a scale I could measure. Well, calculating the distance between two points in time is the same thing. It's impossible to get off the temporal conveyor belt; we must move through time—we must flow from one point to another—because that is what gives length to our existence. Or, tautologically, without time flow our bodies could not exist. Any more than our minds can exist without the physical structure of the brain in which to store the sensory inputs that are the essence of our being."

"You are cute when you get flustered."

"So this temporal forward motion has to be taken into account when calculating the time delay to a specific destination, because we're moving all the time, and a calculation that's good right for now would be way off if I initiated the transfer five minutes from now, because of the geometric progression of time, and the further we want to go from our temporal position the larger the chance is for error, and if we wanted to define a specific arrival time within the span of days, or even minutes, we'd have to perform the calculations way in advance based on a later departure time, but the dragons don't have to worry about this because they have no variable control and every transfer they make is preset according to their original placement on the temporal conveyor belt so they always arrive the same amount of time after the last transfer, thus avoiding a paradox—"

Rusty fell into the seat with a loud whoosh of air.

Britt plopped onto his lap. "I remember all that. Let us talk about something new."

His Adam's apple bobbed like a cork in a creek. "Do we have to?"

Britt nodded seriously. "No more calculations. I learn fast. I think it is time for *us* to flow on our own."

Rusty gulped. He opened his mouth to protest, but Britt covered his lips with hers.

Gale-force winds whipped across the ridge line, tossing particles of ice into Death Wind's face. The bark goggles protected his eyes, the fur-lined parka hood was pulled down over his forehead, and a scarf was drawn tightly across his mouth.

"There!" shouted Bold One, his voice barely audible over the shrill blasts of wind. He held out one arm and pointed with the four-finger pocket of his mitten.

They had been trudging through deep snow for hours. Death Wind hunched over with the blizzard at his back. In the near-total whiteout he had to blink several times before his eyes cleared; due to the dry air it was difficult to keep his eyes moistened. He squinted, but there was nothing on which to focus but swirling snow clouds. "No see."

Somewhere up ahead should be the col that showed in the aerial photos. They hung back from the edge that could be a cornice; if the unstable snow bridge broke under their feet, they could plummet thousands of feet down the steep, ice-covered rock face.

"Wait." Bold One dropped his arm.

Nothing was visible but white fog. Father and son stood shoulder to shoulder in the freezing air, waiting for a temporary dissipation in the clouds. The spectral aura of the sun faded in and out of existence like a white globe dim enough to look at directly. Uneven gusts buffeted Death Wind from all sides, knocking him about. He clung to his father for support.

Bold One thrust out his arm again. "There!"

Death Wind saw a faint purple glimmer in the valley below. The dragon stronghold's time transfer equipment coruscated in the near distance. The sky cleared for a moment, affording a fine view not only of the alien structure in the middle of the glacier, but of the lower levels of the saw-toothed ridge.

One deeply carved notch dipped down to only a few hundred feet above the lateral moraine of the glacier in which the stronghold was situated. Both sides sloped gently enough to make an easy traverse for an army carrying weapons and supplies in shoulder packs and hauling travois.

"Good passage. We check." Bold One led the way down the precipitous ridge tooth. He slammed his feet down hard, gouging big imprints with his snowshoes that compressed the snow into a level platform.

Death Wind followed in his father's tracks. They sideslipped slowly down the mountain, at a pace geared to ensure the stability of each step. The barren higher altitudes soon yielded to snow-capped scrub pine, most of whose limbs and trunks were covered with snow. They made a wide detour around the trees, for the lower branches often concealed hollows gouged by the wind and which acted as traps for one unwary enough to get too close.

A large, white rabbit scampered into a snow hole at the Nomads' approach. Death Wind marveled at the proliferation of life even at this altitude and in these severe climatic conditions. Mice were seldom seen, but not rare; their prints abounded. The large pads of mountain lions and bobcats, or some ancestor of theirs, followed the smaller spoor. Glossy black hawks, oblivious to the frigidity of the upper atmosphere, soared on air currents that swept up the mountainside.

Bold One and Death Wind dropped a thousand feet with relative ease. Below the tree line the wind died out. The snow was piled deep on the gentle slope, and even in snowshoes the Nomads sank a foot or two into the soft fluff. With long, sweeping steps they charged through the stunted woods with savage exhilaration.

Great ice falls hung over granite cliffs like frozen tapestries. Death Wind broke off a slender icicle half his height in length, and sucked on it gratefully. The water was tainted with the flavor of surface minerals. He paid it no mind, as long as it coated his splitting lips and quenched his thirst. He did not worry about lowering his body core temperature because under the furs he was overheated by the exertion of travel.

They took a long circular route behind a rocky outcrop,

eventually emerging from the miniature forest on a bluff over-looking the col. Now that they had discovered a pass through the mountain range, they could take a more direct route back to where their companions struggled with their burdens over the snow-fields.

"There." Death Wind pointed to a speck in the snow that glistened in the light of the sun. He moved to a position where the reflection did not shine directly into his eyes. The silvery glaze took on a dull orange color. "Stay."

Bold One crouched while his son scampered down the deeply piled snow to the base of the col. The wind was funneled through the depression by the high walls on either side. The rock was swept bare in spots. Pools of frosted ice collected in the lee of large boulders.

Death Wind slipped his knee-length moccasins out of the snowshoe bindings and got down on all fours. Slowly, cautiously, he approached the orange ball. It had recently been buried, but the shifting winds had swept away the covering of snow and created a huge drift a few feet away. It was clearly a manufactured object: a plastic globe whose surface was smooth and unbroken. Wires protruded from opposite sides, angled down into the ice, and disappeared into the snow.

The Nomad made no attempt to touch the ball. His gaze followed the direction of the wires. The prevailing wind ripped at his back, forcing its way up under his furs. Death Wind tucked the parka flap between his legs now that he was not trying to dispose of body heat.

He saw nothing else suspicious. Careful not to knock loose rocks about or cause vibration of any kind, he backed away from the plastic globe. He waved to his father. A few minutes later they stood together.

Death Wind shook his head in silent communication.

Bold One nodded.

As one they turned and took a course that would take them back by the shortest route to the band of warriors. They had discovered something of greater importance than a way across the mountains to the dragon stronghold.

CHAPTER 16

"This stuff smells *awful*."

Scott shoved another log onto the fire. "Quit complaining, and just think about how nice it'll make you feel the next time we get caught in a blizzard."

"That's hard to do when my body's this close to the fire and my nose is stuck in the fumes." Sandra stirred the malodorous brew in the cooking pot. "We have to eat out of this pot, too, you know."

Scott ladled out a portion of the viscous tallow and poured it into a plastic bowl. He tested the temperature with the tip of his finger. "Just right." He rolled up his sleeves, exposing white skin that was flaking from prolonged exposure to the dry, frigid ice-age conditions. He shivered involuntarily in the draft. "Whatever we don't use will grease the pan for dinner."

Slender Petal cut slivers of bear fat off a thick slab and placed them in the soot-blackened pot. "Inside, outside. Warm."

"Yeah, well, I'm not too keen on wearing this stuff, much less eating it." Sandra wrinkled her nose, and leaned back as far as she could and still keep the spoon moving. "Besides, I've put on too much weight already."

"My dear, you should not be concerned about obesity. It is normal for a woman in your condition to increase her body mass. It is Nature's way of providing extra warmth during gestation."

"Thanks for the vote of confidence, Pop."

"I say that as your doctor, not as your grandfather. It is also natural for people living in colder climates to retain a higher percentage of body fat, most of it superficial and subcutaneous. Parturition, continued exercise, and a return to milder temperatures will bring about the return to your previous weight." Doc took a handful of fat, opened his fur coat, and rubbed the greasy glob over his midriff. He let out a groan of ecstasy. "Aaahh, once you put it on you will never want to take it off."

"Don't kid yourself." Sandra continued stirring the pot. "Scott, take my mind off this stinky concoction. What's all this talk about preelimination. And what's bootstrapping?"

113

Scott followed Doc's example and coated the rest of his body with grease. "It's another one of my theoretical brainstorms, this one based on the premise that the dragons didn't come to the Ice Age just to freeze their tails off. Everything they do has a perfectly logical reason within the parameters of their cold-blooded, reptilian intellect. Therefore, they chose this time zone with a specific purpose in mind."

Sandra shrugged. "Makes sense."

"With all the time in the world at their disposal, they can't possibly want to live here. Therefore, there must be something strategic about either the place or the time."

"The middle of a glacier doesn't sound very strategic. Not for a creature that's so lethargic in the cold they can't move a muscle without thinking about it for a day and a half."

"Exactly. So we rule that out—at least on the count of probability. Unless, of course, there's some rationale for *desiring* arctic conditions. But we have no evidence for such speculation. So, even though we know the gradations of their time transport equipment are not fine enough to be more selective with respect to temporal displacement—that is, allowing them to land *between* ice ages instead of in the middle of one—why didn't they just go back another million years? The extra energy required to generate that much more time transmittal for what it would gain them in terms of a more suitable climate would appear to be worthwhile in the long run."

Sandra tilted her head and eyed Scott warily. "Okay, you're still making sense. What're your conclusions?"

"Deductions, not conclusions." Scott buttoned his fur coat, wiped greasy hands on his pants legs, and ticked off his fingers. "One, we know the dragons are here now. Two, since their TTS was observed in use, we surmise they're also somewhen else. Three, there's an overriding motive in everything they do, one that is beneficial to them. Four, their presence in the Pleistocene is not accidental. Five, they have not yet accomplished whatever it is they came here to do—"

"How do we know that?"

"Because they're still here. If they finished their mission, I bet they'd waste no time hightailing it to tropical shores." Scott switched hands. "Six, they don't have air or ground transport—because we haven't seen any. They'd come after us in a flyer if they had one available. Seven, if they don't have spatial transport they don't intend to stay in this time zone and emigrate to warmer weather. From which we deduce eight—that they will use time transport to find a better climate. Which means nine, the stronghold is a temporary advance base that will be abandoned when they accomplish their goal."

"If you don't get to the point soon you'll be taking off your moccasins."

"One of them, anyway. I've never had cold feet before, now it's halfway impossible."

Sandra grimaced. "Okay, the dragons didn't come here for a winter vacation. Then why?"

Scott held out both hands, palms outward and all ten fingers extended, and waved. "To liquidate us."

Pinched eyes glanced from Scott to Doc and back to Scott again. "The cold must have pierced your sinuses and frozen your brain. *They* aren't following *us*, *we* came here after *them*."

Scott wagged an index finger at her. "That's when you're wrong. You're still thinking in a straight line. When you're dealing with time travel the arrangement of events is variable, depending on your point of view. The end may come before the beginning, and the beginning may come after the end."

"Doc, see if he's got a fever. He's having hallucinations."

"If he is, we both are." Doc finished greasing himself, buttoned his coat, crossed his legs, and let himself down onto his fur bedroll by sliding down his cane as if it were a fire pole. He tucked the extra material under his buttocks as insulation from the ice floor. "I think you should hear him out. If nothing else, he has an imaginative sense of the macabre."

Scott said, "Is that a vote of confidence, or castigation?"

"To one who is secure in mind the former is not necessary, and the latter ignorable."

Scott opened his mouth to rebut, then thought better of it. "Right."

The fire roared. Ice melting off the ceiling dripped like slow rain. Slender Petal continued to add chunks of frozen bear fat to the pot.

Sandra stirred the offensive brew. "The only thing that'll be liquidated in the near future is this ice cave. So get back to your story while we still have a roof over our heads. You were somewhere in the middle, between the beginning and the end, and going both ways at once."

Scott shuffled on his knees closer to the burning logs. "Okay, what do you think about this? Since the dragons failed to kill us off in the future, what better plan could they have than to annihilate us in the past?"

"Huhn?" Sandra did another double take between Scott and Doc. "Scott, we wouldn't even *be* here if the dragons hadn't come here first. If they were going to lure us into a trap, even a lizard mentality could find a simpler and more creative way of doing it."

"But suppose they came here to slaughter the Cro-Magnons—our direct ancestors—in order to prevent their propagation? And our genesis?"

Sandra's jaw dropped. "Could—could they do that?"

"Why not?"

"Well, because, we exist. That's a fact. They know it, and we know it. You're talking in loops and circles. Where would we have come from if the Cro-Magnons became extinct? I mean, that's proof already that if that *is* their scheme it's already failed. You can't escape the truth, even with time travel."

"I'm not talking about escaping the truth, I'm talking about changing it."

"You can't change the truth," Sandra protested, raising her voice in a mild, high-pitched whine. "Truth is what is."

"No. Truth is what we perceive it to be. Suppose, in a straightforward flow of time, the dragons sent here were hatched after the destruction of their Cretaceous ancestors, and were raised without any knowledge of past and future events. They'd have no preconceived notions about the reality of the future, if indeed there is such a thing as a future. Remember that time can be juggled about just like any other physical quantity."

"Don't be ridiculous. You're saying that what we don't perceive, isn't true. That's like saying that what you don't know, can't hurt you. We're not gods. Or cartoon characters, who don't fall until they realize they've walked off the edge of a cliff. Our perceptions can't change reality."

"I'm not saying they can. But maybe our perception of the flow of events is all wrong. Maybe our entire concept of the universe is based solely on the way our senses perceive reality. Like me looking at your back and having no idea how well built you are from the front. My point of view doesn't alter your shape."

Sandra stabbed a finger at him. "It may get you in trouble, though."

Scott remained serious. "If we accept the fact that finite minds cannot fathom an infinite universe, why can't we accept the fact that neither can we comprehend the workings of time within the framework of that universe? Infinity applies to time as well as to space. So what we see of it is limited by our senses. Which means that looked at from a different perspective, time may have variables of which we are unaware—of which we cannot *be* aware. So, when I talk about making changes in events that we think have been established by observation, I'm not suggesting that the events themselves can be changed, only that the continuity of those events can be perceived in other ways. In other words, there's no such thing as predetermination, postdetermination, or *any* determination. Everything in space and time is relative."

Doc hugged his knees to his chest. "I think you are obfuscating logic with tautology."

"And I think he's talking through his hat." Sandra banged the carved wooden spoon on the edge of the pot, placed it on the ground cloth, and backed away from the smoke. "I confess naivety to relativity, but I damn sure can't believe you can go around warping reality to fit your notions, whether they're preconceived, postconceived, or ill conceived. Maybe you think you can change the world, but sooner or later you're gonna come up against an incontrovertible truth."

Scott said, "If I recognize it when I see it, I'll fight it with polemics."

Doc sighed. "In that case I fear for the truth, because once you and Rusty put your heads together the fate of the world is at risk."

Scott tilted his head, thinking over Doc's statement. "Right."

"But, I suppose that is the price one pays for leadership."

"I don't care what the price is, I'm not buying it." Sandra pulled her hood over her head because so much water was dripping from the roof of the ice cave that her hair was getting soaked. "But just for the sake of argument, let's say I believe your crazy conjectures. Whether the dragons know it or not, we're here to save the world. And whether they like it or not, we will."

"That's what I like: a positive attitude."

Sandra brushed him off with a wave of her hand. "What I don't get is how the dragons're gonna bump off the Cro-Magnons when nobody can find 'em." She cocked an eyebrow at Scott. "Or have they already exterminated 'em?"

Scott shrugged. "I don't think so. Or should I say, I don't believe it, therefore it's not true."

"Forget the fancy philosophy. Let's stick to visible facts. Without transportation the dragons can't gun down the Cro-Magnons. So whadda they expect 'em to do, commit suicide? Or come running into their paws pleading for execution? For that matter, where the hell *are* the Cro-Magnons? We haven't seen hide nor hair of 'em anywhere, and we passed plenty of cozy caves along the way. They should have been out there in the savanna where the Neanderthals were."

Scott shrugged again. "It's a big world. And they may be shy people. They could have run and hid whenever they saw us coming. But I'm sure they're here, because future anthropology says they have to be."

"Now you are contradicting your own ratiocination," said Doc. "You are joining cause and effect when in the universe you postulate there may be no such connection."

"Here we go again," Sandra scowled. "I wish you two would stop chasing your tails. It's so confusing."

"It is impossible to argue syllogistically about notions that have no foundation in human perception, and that operate beyond the rules of human logic."

"Well, as far as I'm concerned, what you see is what you get. You wanna make anything more out of it, you gotta prove it to me. I'm gonna wait till we get to the stronghold and see what gives before I make up my mind about all this time travel business. But if I see a Cro-Magnon on the way, I'm gonna tell 'im to watch out for crack-brained clods from the future who might *think* 'im right out of existence."

Scott laughed out loud, his voice echoing off the chamber walls. People huddled by neighboring fires turned at the outburst. Scott shrank into his parka in a sudden surge of self-consciousness. After the baleful stares melted away, he said in a low voice, "If it were that easy, I'd wake up from this dream and leave the dragons in distant memory. Then I'd pull them out of the past whenever I wanted to frighten little children into doing what they're told."

"Legendary legerdemain," said Doc with a grin.

"Whatever you call it, you better not scare *my* kids with any of your bogeyman stories. Life is scary enough as it is without making up any—DW!" Sandra jumped to her feet at her husband's approach. With him were Bold One, Sam and Helen, and Jane with the two furry pups on leashes. "When'd you get back?"

"I am back."

Sandra threw her arms around him. "Don't start talking in Nomad monosyllables again. Speak English."

"I'm gonna speak some language to both of 'em that you ladies might not wanna hear." The expression on Sam's face was anything but pleasant. "You know what these jokers went and did?"

Helen held firmly on to Sam's arm. "Now, Sam, you'd better curb your tongue and act with decorum."

"I'm gonna act like a general and give these two the dressing down they deserve. I *told* 'em not to go near the stronghold, just find a path and we would take it from—what am I telling you for?" Sam faced the two Nomads, who nonchalantly crowded close to the fire, hands outstretched over the flames, and stabbed a gloved index finger in the air. "You should have reported to me immediately when you saw the obvious approaches were mined. Suppose you had gotten blown away? We'd never have known what hap—"

"They found mines?" Scott said incredulously.

Sam turned in frustration at the interruption. "Yes. Land mines. The dragons seeded 'em across all the easiest routes and buried 'em in the snow. Oh, these lizards are smart cookies, I'll give 'em that. They don't miss a trick. But these two—"

"I have done a bit of mine laying myself in the past—or rather, in the future. That is, in my past, but the Earth's future. Although, if we assume that universal synchronicity is a human convenience, I do not know that subjective tense has any communication value."

"Henry, what the *hell* are you talking about?"

Doc did not bother to stand; he huddled a little closer to the fire and looked up at the confused general. "The mine is a useful weapon in the arsenal of guerrilla warfare. I have slain more than one unsuspecting dragon with just such a device." Casting his gaze upon Bold One, he said, "Were these contact mines, or command detonated?"

Bold One crouched and threw an arm around Slender Petal's shoulder. He drew her close. "Wire from one to another."

"Hmmmn. Trip wires?"

"Insulated," offered Death Wind.

"Then that infers an electrically triggered mechanism. Sam, I fully concur. We have underestimated the dragons once too often in the past. Or was that the future? I guess it depends upon your temporal position relative to the event. In any case, this is a discovery of mammoth proportions. My congratulations to both of you for your perspicacity. The question that naturally arises is whether the mines were sowed as a purely protective measure, or whether the dragons are anticipating an assault."

Sam stood with his mouth agape.

Rubbing his beard thoughtfully, Doc went on, "Either way, prudence must be pursued."

"Henry, you're missing the point entirely—"

"No, Sam, I am missing nothing. These two braves have brought valuable intelligence that will guide us in a more forceful prosecution of the war against dragon domination. For that they should be praised."

"But I told them not to—"

"Sam, Sam, Sam. Hold back your anger." Doc rolled onto his side and pushed himself up to his feet. He leaned heavily against his cane. "Sam, you are doing a fine job leading this rabble across the Pleistocene wastelands, fraught with the dangers of natural catastrophe and untamed beasts, and filled with the incertitude of reptilian attack from unknown quarters. We have had our casualties along the way: none fatal—"

"And I intend to keep it that way."

"—but none unexpected considering the hostilities that have confronted us. Against that remarkable record there can be no slander. Nevertheless, you have become intractable. Your rank has altered your sensitivity to purpose."

"I didn't aspire to this commission, I was elected to it. But I took the office in good faith. I was given a duty to perform. And if I'm going to conduct this army in a military manner, I need the cooperation of every volunteer soldier under my command. I expect my orders to be obeyed."

"No one has ever questioned your authority."

"No one answers to it, either. I'm trying to keep this outfit together for mutual protection. I don't want the loss of good people on my head. But when these—scouts—take it upon themselves to exceed their orders—"

"The wise leader never stifles individual initiative."

"—they jeopardize the success of the entire operation, as well as endangering their own lives. I can't plan a campaign of surprise attack if someone is spotted. And we all agreed right at the beginning that this was to be a clandestine operation. When my best men are insubordinate, how is it going to affect the morale of the rest of the troops?"

"Sam, you are taking too strong a stand on administration and losing sight of the objective: to wage war. That means taking chances, it means sometimes yielding control to the soldiers in the field who have a closer view of the battle than you have from the rear, and it also means incurring fatalities: that is the grimmer but truer side of war. Some things cannot be changed."

Doc held his hands out to the two Nomads. "I love these men as my brothers. We have been together through much sorrow and suffering. We have fought shoulder to shoulder. And someday, each of us, in his own way, must die—perhaps for the cause that has banded us together. That is the chance that each soldier takes. He hopes, though, that his death will serve a greater purpose than he could have achieved by living. The swift stroke of mercy is the only justice a soldier can hope to receive."

Sam, flustered by Doc's fustian, pulled off his mittens and ran his hands through his dark hair. "I know what you're doing, Henry. You're using elocution to cloud the issue."

"Not at all. I am merely adding temperance to your temper."

"That doesn't change the fact that my scouts keep forging ahead and taking chances."

"Henry, that is what scouts are supposed to do. That is the definition of a scout: one who reconnoiters enemy territory. If the entire company blundered into that mine field, the results would be disastrous."

Sam held up his hands defensively. "I have no problem with that. But they should have turned back immediately and told me what we were up against. Instead, they went out across the glacier by an alternate route and explored ways to the stronghold. And that's where they could have given us away."

Doc looked dumbfounded. He threw up his hands. "It had to be done sooner or later."

"But I would like to have had the army in reserve, so we could press forward an attack if they had gotten caught. Losing shock value is one thing, but completely giving up the element of surprise we can't afford to do—not when we don't know what we're up against."

When Doc shook his head, his great white mane waved like a broaching sea. "I still attach more importance to what they found than how they found it." Addressing Bold One, he said, "Did you also discover a way to the stronghold?"

Bold One nodded.

The faint glimmer of a smile touched Doc's lips. "Then there is a way over the ice despite the presence of deep crevasses in the glacier."

Bold One moved his head once to the left and once to the right. "Under."

CHAPTER 17

The alarms in Rusty's dream clanged incessantly. He tried to shut them off, but his dreams were always uncontrollable. The only way to silence the clamor was to wake up. Since he had been up half the night, that option was not the most desirable.

When he moved under the covers he felt a weight across his upper chest, and a warmth that was not all his own. He wanted to sink back into the delicious pleasure of dreamland, but the loud ringing would not let him. It was not until he opened his eyes that he realized that the alarm was not in his head, but on the bridge.

He flung aside the covers, slipped out from under Britt's arm, and leaped across her to the annunciator control board. He fanned a switch; the awful pealing stopped immediately.

Now fully awake, Rusty activated the intercom and toned for input. The singsong notes of a harp played a brief message: someone coming. Rusty toned back: acknowledged.

Nothing out of the ordinary was visible on the viewscreens. That meant that a sentry on all-night observation post must have relayed the approach call on a remote toner. Rusty opened the bubble shade; bright yellow sunshine flooded the bridge. Britt was standing in the golden rays, unappareled except for a quixotic smile, soaking in the radiant energy like a flower about to bloom.

It was not until he stood watching her for several seconds that Rusty remembered his own state of undress. He turned aside quickly and fumbled in the bedding for his shorts. He slipped his feet into moccasins.

"I'd better go see what it is."

Britt made no effort to cover her body. "I wait at console."

Nervously, Rusty pecked her cheek as a chicken might peck at a kernel of corn. "Bring the reactor power up to full emergency mode."

"Aye, aye, Skipper."

Rusty was totally disarmed by her charming, carefree manner. He managed a smile and winked at her as he pulled a shirt over his head on the way down the ramp. "And get ready for liftoff, just in case."

The lower decks were a flurry of activity as the crew scrambled to general quarters. Rusty ran down the entrance ramp behind a squad of heavy gunners hauling a dismounted gatling gun out of the ship; they headed for a prepared bunker that was left unarmed in case it became imperative to move the *Ark* instead of standing and fighting.

"What is it, Ned?"

"There's a runner coming in. I hit the siren 'cause I didn't know if anyone—or any*thing*—was chasing her. But now I got word she's bringing a message from the front."

Despite the early-morning chill, Rusty wiped sweat off his brow. "Whew, I'm glad of that. I just hope it's good news. It's been four days since their last communication."

"Could be mechanical breakdown."

"Four radios, all at the same time?"

"Mountains in between."

"We were picking them up fine till they missed a call." Rusty strode out beyond the undercarriage, into the full light of the sun. He turned and waved at the overhead camera lens. Britt waved back from the clear plastic bridge canopy. "How long?"

"Perimeter guard picked her up and is escorting her in. They should be here—"

An owl hooted from the tree line at the edge of the grove.

The clatter of weapons melded with the pounding of feet on the trampled grass as backup troops tumbled into position behind makeshift bulwarks. Slowly, the muffled racket faded until nothing stirred but a few insects buzzing in the air and the livestock in the corrals. Goats, pigs, and large, wild birds seemed not to notice the tension in the air.

When the militia was fully mobilized, a guard chirped from the hidden safety of a bunker.

The owl hooted again. Two people stepped through the thick layer of brush: a tall man who looked like a scarecrow with most of his straw plucked out by crows, and a young woman who would have had to wear more than a loincloth and halter top to weigh over a hundred pounds. The woman's long black, braided hair and reddish skin branded her a Nomad. Her narrow chest heaved slightly from the exertion of her marathon run. Rusty remembered her as Swift Fox.

"Greetings," she said.

"Greetings," Rusty replied.

"Men stick together, it is code."

"It is code."

"All are safe."

Rusty felt his entire body go limp. He had not even realized how tense he was. The release from fear that his companions had been massacred filled him with renewed energy, and took from him the awesome responsibility that he had made the wrong decision by sticking to the original plan not to lift ship until he had proof that the invasionary force had failed its mission.

"You bring good news, Swift Fox."

The Nomad acknowledged with a faint nod of her head.

A host of questions wanted to roll off Rusty's tongue all at once. He curbed his excitement. With forced resolve he framed his thoughts toward obtaining the most pertinent intelligence first. "Why did Scott stop transmitting?"

"Radio waves bring dragon death from sky."

"What death? I thought you said everyone was okay?"

Swift Fox repeated patiently. "All are safe. Dragon death come on wings of flame, like spear that burst. But all are safe."

Rusty did not talk down to Swift Fox in simulated Nomad dialect. "You mean, the dragons fired a missile that exploded without killing anyone?"

Swift Fox nodded. "Get to cover."

"What makes you think the radio brought it?"

"Destroy radio after tone talk. Doc say no use again. Bring more."

"Damn!" Rusty ran his hands through curly locks that had long since passed the description of shaggy. "The dragons must have triangulated their position after the first transmission within range of the stronghold."

"Never underestimate a dragon," said Ned. "The problem now is how're we gonna coordinate an attack without fast and firm communication? We can't synchronize timers if we have to wait for days between messages."

Swift Fox replied, "Sam say first objective is to stop dragon sky death. Call when safe."

Rusty pursed his lips. "I don't like it. Negative communication leaves too much chance for error."

"On the other hand, if we go in there with guns blazing we're likely to get blown to pieces as soon as they get a fix on us. And who knows, they may have a ground radar warning network."

Ned addressed the Nomad runner. "Swift Fox, how close were they to the stronghold when you left?"

"Two, three days."

"Hell, they could be there already." Turning to Rusty, he said, "Maybe we oughta sneak a little closer with the *Ark*. At least that would shorten the supply line."

"No. Sam said to stay put until further orders."

"And Doc said to use your own initiative."

"He meant if they got into trouble and there was no other way to stop the dragons. He said most definitely not to be influenced by their plight. You know Doc."

"Yeah, but I ain't gonna stand by and let 'em get slaughtered without going in after 'em, no matter what he says."

"And I'm not going to take a chance on losing the *Ark*. She's too valuable." Rusty covered his mouth with his hand and squeezed his lips between his fingers. "She's our only way out of here and now."

"How about if we pull in our sentries so we're ready to fly at a moment's notice?"

"Do it." Rusty faced an external microphone. "Britt, are you getting all this?"

Britt replied on the toner.

"Good. Get the *Ark* shipshape. I'll help out here. Ned, let's get the livestock loaded."

"Want it butchered first?"

"No, we'll keep them fresh."

"How 'bout that pliohippus the Nomads've been training to haul the carts."

Rusty was on his way across the clearing to give orders to the men and women in the bunkers. "Sure, bring the whole herd. Horsepower is something we never have enough of."

Scott was having a difficult time picking his way up the boulder-strewn ravine. Rock slabs that had sheared off the vertical walls lay at awkward angles that were impossible to climb, and whose sharpened edges barked his shins more than once.

"You never did explain about bootstrapping," Sandra insisted.

Breathing hard, Scott struggled to keep up with her. Being pregnant and near the end of her term did not slow her down at all. What was worse, the gals hauling the travois were way ahead; they had doubled their loads, left half the travois behind, and put two gals in the traces of the remaining reins. Only the cannon was behind.

"Yes, well, I was interrupted at the height of my revelations."

"So tell me now. You got something better to do?"

Scott's stump slipped on the wet rocks. "All this moss makes it hard to get a foothold."

"Yeah, I know what you mean. I've bounced off my belly more than once. Don't be surprised if I have an early labor."

"That's all we need." Scott leaped across a trickle of water to firmer ground. Beside him a noisy cascade of glacial runoff splashed into the cold air. "You could have stayed behind."

"What? And miss all the fun? Not a chance. Besides, I've got a sling all rigged up. After the kid is born I'll just carry 'im on my back like the Nomads do. Having babies doesn't mean dropping out of life, you know."

"I know. It's just that this is pretty tough terrain." Scott got down on all fours as he scrambled up the side of a rounded, house-sized boulder. "If Jane were as far into her term as you are, I wouldn't want her taking a chance of losing the baby."

"That's life in the wilderness, Scott. And I have to give you credit. You're doing okay for a guy with one leg."

There was little enthusiasm in Scott's voice. "Thanks."

"No, I mean it. I think you're fantastic." Sandra stopped for a break. She plopped down on a dry slab where the stream bubbled quietly underneath. "You could have stayed with the *Ark* and nobody would have thought you were wimping out."

Scott untied the sleeves of his parka from around his waist, laid the fur out on the rock, and settled down beside her, grateful for the rest. He never would have made it up the rocky creekbed with the heavy laser gun; he was glad it had been disintegrated by the dragon missile. "You know how I am: always trying to prove something to myself."

"You've proved it to me." Sandra took a plastic cup from her knapsack and dipped it in the stream where the current kept it fresh. "I think you're quite a guy."

Scott's scowl turned into a frown. He accepted the cup and took a long draft of the clear, cold water before speaking. "Did Jane put you up to this?"

"Up to what?"

"You know. Feeding my ego. I've heard more kind words from you in the past hour than in all the time I've known you."

Sandra took back the cup and scooped another drink of water

from the glacier-fed stream. "Are you counting all the way back to the Cretaceous?"

With the lack of physical activity, it did not take long for Scott to feel the numbing chill. He pulled the parka over his shoulders; it was long enough to still pad his seat. "I guess I have been feeling underfoot lately." He tapped his stump on the ground. "I just can't help it."

"Scott, I know how difficult it must be dealing with your—loss. But that doesn't change who you are—or what you've accomplished. Your true self is no different, only your self-image. Let yourself go, and be what you can be with what you have."

"Footloose and fancy free, huhn?"

Sandra stabbed him with a finger. "See, you can joke about it."

"I know. But that's just a front for the pain I'm keeping inside. It's the kind of thing I don't want to talk about because—well, partly because it hurts so much." Scott absently chucked stones in the stream. He watched the splashes that were quickly carried away by the current. "Partly because I'm afraid of imposing sentiment on people with other things on their minds."

"Scott, we started this venture together—a long time ago, it seems, although the events have yet to happen in the continuity of this world. And I don't understand any of that stuff. But you do; you're brilliant. I know I've been pretty hard on you in the past—and in the future. But I've grown up since then. I'm a different person now. And I love you. Uh, you know what I mean."

Scott patted her thigh in a brotherly fashion. "I know what you mean."

"So, don't shut me out. Whenever you have a problem, I'm here. Whenever you want to talk about something, my time is your time."

"When you have a time machine, your time is everyone's time."

Sandra slapped his leg playfully. "Stop being silly. I'm trying to be serious."

"Sorry. But as long as we're making up, do we get to kiss?"

She slapped him again. "You never let up, do you?"

Scott cocked an eyebrow. "Should I?"

"No. I guess it's part of your charm." She leaned close to give him a smack on the cheek. Scott spun his head quickly and caught the kiss on the lips. Sandra jerked back as if she had been electrocuted. Slowly, her look of astonishment changed to one of amusement. "Okay, you got me that time. But that's the Scott I like to see."

"Want to try it again?"

"Sometimes I wonder whether you're a guerrilla—or a gorilla."

"Just keep in mind that wherever or whenever you are, you're the gorilla my dreams." The clatter of the gun carriage echoed up the ravine. Four men pulled the traces while two women pushed the cannon from behind. Scott pushed himself up off the rock. "Well, I guess it's time to go." He held out his hand. "My lady?"

Sandra allowed herself to be helped up. "You've always got some trick afoot, don't you?"

"Touché."

They hopped boulders adjacent to the stream, they angled away from a raging waterfall that spewed droplets in the air that soaked their outer clothing. They scrambled up a steep embankment to an isolated patch of earth on which grew a grove of trees—an island in the middle of the gorge. People congregating ahead indicated that they were close to the headwaters.

"You still haven't told me about bootstrapping," Sandra insisted.

Scott walked more slowly, stopping every few steps to catch his breath. "That's because it's more fancy than fact. But I'll lay it on you. Suppose the dragons refined their time travel technique to the point when they could travel short spans—say, on the order of minutes, or seconds. If they played their paw straight, they could create an army of infinite size by looping their soldiers through time."

"Huhn?"

A fine mist hugged the ground, carrying with it a biting cold. Scott snugged his parka around his chest and pulled up his hood.

"Take a sample soldier who's going into battle. Before the attack you send him back through time, say, an hour. Then, he joins his former self on the battlefield. Now you've got two soldiers standing side by side, one who an hour later will go back through time to become the other."

"But I thought you and Rusty said you couldn't meet yourself without causing some kind of cosmic disorder—or dissolution."

"We don't *know* that, we just can't conceive a cause and effect relationship that would account for it. Anyway, now you take soldier B and send *him* back through time. He then becomes soldier C. Do it again, and you have soldier D. Eventually you can build an entire army from a solitary soldier."

"No, you can't, because when soldier B goes into the time machine you've lost him into the past. He's no longer around to fight."

"Okay, so you wait until after the battle and send back one of the survivors. Then, you don't let him fight until he duplicates himself a few more times."

"But, if you keep sending them back through time, when do they get to fight?"

"Well, you stretch your time span over a couple days instead of an hour. Then you have them go into combat after they've all been looped."

"But, what if one of them gets killed?"

"That's the beauty of it. They're impossible to kill because all but the last one have gone through time to create the successive downstream versions. The continued existence of the army is predetermined."

"Now wait a minute. You keep arguing that predestination is a godlike conceit that can't happen in the real world."

"What is real? What you see, or what you get?"

Sandra tilted her head, wincing with one eye. "Didn't I already state my position on that?"

"The circumstances were different. The question in this case is, how many soldiers do you have to fight if a hundred of them are facing you, despite the fact that they're all downstream versions of the same soldier?"

"Well . . ."

"Accordingly, you can kill only one—the last one to go through time. And you still have to face ninety-nine more. If they were smart, they'd put the final version in a safe place where he would be protected. The only way you could destroy the army would be to knock off the soldiers one by one—in the proper order from last to first."

Sandra was silent for a moment. "Oh, yeah? What if you attack from the rear and knock off the original soldier? Then the rest would instantly disappear because he would not be alive to go through the time machine in order to create all the rest."

"Are you sure?"

"Hell, no. I'm not sure about anything anymore."

"Want to give it a try?"

"No!" she whined. "One of me is enough for this world. Besides, I don't think it'd work because the first me would have preknowledge of what was going to happen because I'd suddenly

ind myself surrounded by all my subsequent versions—which is
a way of preordaining what I was—or am—going to do. Then, if
changed my mind—"

"As women are wont to do."

"—or didn't do it out of spite, I'd really get the world in trouble
because my inaction would alter reality."

"You can't alter reality by going through time any more than
you can change the world by crossing space. It's all a matter of
perception."

They stopped a hundred yards from the base of a thousand-
foot-tall cliff of ice. Scott had been so intent on his footing that he
failed to look ahead until he stepped into the penumbra. He looked
up and saw blocks of ice the size of buildings lying in a gargantuan
tumbled heap.

A torrent of water spewed from the base of the terminal
moraine. The icy river charged over a cataract, spuming and
thunderous. The people standing at the base of the glacier were
dwarfed by the ten-mile-wide flow of ice.

"Scott, you're crazy."

"That, too, is a matter of perception."

Chapter 18

"Glaciers do form creeks and rivers, but usually not of such immensity. The normal rise in global temperature would occur slowly—over thousands of years—causing glaciers to shrink by a reduction of accumulating snowfall. Even during the age of overall glacial recession I doubt that tunnels like this were carved by natural erosion."

Doc stood on the broad bank of solid ice just inside the cavern mouth. The glacier's terminal moraine was unstable; constantly calving blocks of ice that weighed many tons. No one stood in its shadow for fear of being crushed. Those approaching the entrance did so hastily.

"But in this case the process of thawing has been aided by the dragons' need to melt out a stronghold. The heat generators are probably a by-product of their nuclear fission reactor plant. Very efficient, really, since the ice undoubtedly helps cool the core."

"If you're finished admiring dragon techniques and technology, and can shelve your scientific curiosity, we can get on with the final briefing."

"Pardon me, Sam." Doc tore his gaze from the vaulting, icebound grotto, and joined the war council encircling the general. "It is true that I sometimes tend to babble over imponderables, but in this case I think that my observations will augment those of Bold One and Death Wind. They may have explored a mile or so up this glacial ice cave, but I have explored much further with my mind."

The ceiling arched fifty feet overhead and curved down to the floor with walls glazed to a smooth, scintillating finish. The river lay at the bottom of a deep, narrow gorge. The upper level was wide enough on each side for several armies to spread out their cooking fires. The cave was contoured much like a mushroom, with the river flowing along the base of the stem, and the upper floor pasted to the frilled underside of the umbrella-shaped cap.

Sam gritted his teeth. "Sorry, Henry. You didn't deserve that.

133

I'm just anxious. Small-time skirmishes I've lived with all my life; I'm just not cut out to be a general."

"No one is. And you have every right to be jittery. We are facing what is likely to be the biggest skirmish of all time."

Sam inhaled deeply. "Then let's get it over with so I can give up the commission. I just want to be a farmer and grow vegetables. Now, what point were you trying to make?"

"Simply that I am fairly certain that this highway under the glacier will take us unopposed all the way to the dragon stronghold. Apparently, this horizontal plateau was formed when the dragons melted out a hollow where their time transport structure first appeared in this time zone. The initial flood of hot water thawed the ice and created this broad, domed cavern. After the major excavation was completed, the continued flow of melt water gouged this deeper, threadlike notch. I suppose it is not a particularly astute observation, but it should put our minds at ease about the viability of our method of infiltration."

Sam cast his eyes down at the frozen floor. "Thanks, Henry. That's important to know."

"I'll say it's important!" shouted Sandra. "Most of our attack plans revolve around what to do if we run up against an ice wall. I say let's take his word for it. If there's anything in our way, we can melt or chop through it. And we got enough rope to bridge the Grand Canyon."

"Okay. Okay." Sam held up his hands, palms outward. "I agree. Let's just take a count of supplies and pick the rear guard."

Scott wolfed down the last of a bison steak as he hitched himself to the reins of Jane's travois. "This is where the pregnant women stay behind." He wiped his mouth on his furred sleeve.

"Wisht I had one ta leave behind." Windy snugged the laser nozzle in its holster and shouldered the battery pack. His face was nearly the same color as his parka, making him practically invisible inside his upraised hood. "I think ma philanderin' days're over. After this I'm gonna settle down permanent like."

Broderick scoffed. "I will believe that when I see it." He formed the First Fusiliers into ranks and counted them off his slate. Windy did the same for the Texas Rangers.

When the outfit was ready to depart, Jane hugged her husband and kissed him longingly. "Take care, Scott. I love you."

"I love you, too, honey." He cinched the straps across his chest. "You keep that radio handy. As soon as we're in the clear

I'll give you a tone. Then we'll get Rusty to bring the magic carpet and fly you to the front. Okay?"

"Okay."

Scott tightened the leather thongs that held the makeshift crampons to his moccasins. The flat wooden boards armed with sharpened plastic spikes offered perfect traction on the slippery ice. The moccasins' padded soles and uppers not only kept his feet warm, but prevented the stoppage of circulation from the laces.

They kissed again. Scott leaned against the traces, amazed at how easily the runners slid over the smooth ice. It took very little effort. He passed Death Wind and Sandra, still locked in a full body embrace.

"Hey, cut it out, or you'll melt the walls down on top of us."

Sandra stuck out her tongue at him, then went back to hugging Death Wind. They talked softly to each other. Scott crunched on ahead to get out of hearing range. The tiniest sound was magnified by the strange acoustical qualities of the ice cave. Helen and Slender Petal trudged off together, fifty feet in front of him.

"The dragons will hear us five miles off," Scott whispered as he caught up to Doc. The cave reverberated the crunching of crampons on ice; it sounded like the tearing of a hundred sheets of paper of unending length.

"I doubt that even a supersensitive seismograph can pick up our vibrations. Although they appear to be stationary, glaciers are in a constant state of flow: they are, in fact, extremely slow-moving rivers of ice. The constant crackling of internal stress produces much more sound than we could possibly make."

"Doc, you're always so reassuring. You have an answer for everything."

"One of my finer qualities, my boy. Knowledge is often its own reward, for it soothes the pain of ignorance."

The strange procession advanced along the tubular ice cave like a cabal of witch hunters. Flaming brands, made from stripped branches lashed together and dipped in tallow, flickered eerily in the gathering darkness. The crystalline structure of the ice reflected the yellow glow like a magnificent, multifaceted jewel.

"Then you must be the most pain-free person in the world."

Somewhere up ahead, an electric beam powered by a battery pack stabbed out with the intensity of an aircraft landing beacon. The laser gun nozzles were removable, and a variety of accessories such as lights, heaters, and power tools were designed to operate off the stored amperage. Each attachment came with its own transformer. The light bounced off the ceiling, swung down into the deep gorge, and glinted off the rippling surface of the river, then switched off.

"Perhaps. Although too much knowledge can sometimes be a bane. Take this cavern for example." Doc pointed his cane, with its tip now honed to needle sharpness, in a sweeping arc in front of him. "It has certainly not escaped you that such a cavity cannot have been sculpted overnight. Unaided geological activity would have taken eons, no doubt, to carve such an immensity. And while I indicated the unnatural building process that created this intraglacial boulevard, I did not expound upon the span of time necessary to gouge such a tunnel."

Scott hardly noticed the slight upgrade. "If you're trying to make a point, get to it before the Ice Age is over."

Doc chuckled. His deep-throated titter resonated hollowly in the ice cavern. "Quite right, my boy. Quite right. The gist of the idea is that this twenty-mile-long tube is not a recent development. The dragons must have been here much longer than we heretofore suspected."

"Are you saying that they didn't come here as a last resort, but sometime contemporaneous to their other temporal invasions?"

"Precisely."

The silence was broken only by the crunching of crampons on ice.

"Well, go on."

"Oh, I have no inferences to make. It is merely an interesting observation."

"But, doesn't that bother you? That the construction of the stronghold was—premeditated?"

"As opposed to being precipitated by our actions against them? No, it does not worry me. But it does make me curious as to its original purpose. If not as an escape mechanism, what?"

Scott chewed on that for a while. Neither he nor Doc carried a light. So much illumination was reflected by the floor, walls, and ceiling, from the torches of others, that none was necessary. They trudged along in the wake of the brigade. The foundation of ice was flat and featureless, without dents or moguls.

"I see what you mean. About too much knowledge, that is."

"No matter how many answers you have, there is always another question to lead you on."

"I'm learning that. I'm also beginning to see that the dragons are a lot more devious than I ever gave them credit for, and their machinations more insidious."

"We have underestimated their resourcefulness nearly as often as they have underestimated ours. In the final analysis, it is not he who is better armed who turns the tide of war, but he who is more imaginative."

Scott grimaced in the dark. "If that's the case, I've shown the imagination of a potato. You know, when I think back on everything we've seen and done, I realize that the script for this entire intertemporal war was written in the geological strata, if only we'd known how to interpret the clues. The Great Dying, plate tectonics—inscribed in stone for all to read, if only you have the key. Up till now."

"By 'now' do you mean the Pleistocene, or our placement along the stream of universal events?"

"Anymore, Doc, I don't know *what* I mean." Scott loosened the shoulder straps and tightened the waist straps, in order to change the stress points and relieve pinched muscles. He was not comforted by the fact that Jane had hauled the heavy load for weeks without complaint. "But it scares me that, knowing now what I know about the past—the straight-line objective past of the Earth—that I don't recognize anything in the stratigraphic record that gives a clue to which side conquers in Armageddon."

"Evidence is sometimes circumstantial, conspicuous by its absence."

"Meaning?"

"Meaning that a word-for-word rendering does not always offer the best translation. The language of the rocks is as idiomatic as human speech. Call it geological syntax, if you will. By reading what is *not* written, I have my suspicions about the final turn of events."

"Well, let me have it between the eyes. Both barrels."

There was a long pause before Doc spoke again. "I think for now—the circuitous, subjective now of my personal life line—I will keep my own council. Predictions are so self-indulgent."

"Come on, Doc. You've never been wrong in your life." Scott danced ahead and tapped his truncated leg on the ice. "Granted, you've got two feet to stick into your mouth instead of one, but that's never stopped you before from speaking your mind. You're self-indulgent to the point of exasperation."

"Thank you, Scott. I suspect I have had that coming for a long time."

"Half a dozen epochs, at least."

Doc paused again, longer. "Let us just say that our very existence presupposes that we are the masters of our own fate."

"You're talking in riddles."

Doc planted his cane in the ice and shoved off against it as if it were a ski pole. His limping gait and rhythmical cane crunching gave the sound of his passage an offbeat three-quarter cadence. "Such is life."

CHAPTER 19

The shock troops camped that night under a crevasse. In the morning, sunbeams stabbed through the opening like golden spears.

Scott awoke well rested despite the difficulties of travel late in the day. The initial tractable, smooth floor had soon given way to cracks and upthrusts that required caution and hard work to traverse. Even so, they had eaten up the miles of rough ice with the staunchness of will with which they tackled the snowfields in the rage of a gale.

Slender Petal crouched by a fire. The cooking pot held stew, and a kettle steamed with hot water. "Hungry?"

It seemed strange to be hundreds of feet beneath the ice and still be able to see the sky. Scott had fallen asleep under a strip of stars that sped across the narrow opening like a parade in review. Now he lay in the reflected light of the sun; it bore no heat other than that felt in the heart. "I'm always hungry."

Slender Petal smiled with her eyes.

Scott thrust aside his fur coverings and spent several minutes doing calisthenics before dipping his mug into the kettle and drawing out his allotment of tea. The muscular friction of exercise coupled with the hot, spiced liquid gave him a delicious glow of warmth. By the time he was ready for something more solid in his stomach, Bold One and Death Wind were returning from the part of the crevasse that extended below the level of the flood plain.

"Any problem?" Scott said.

Bold One shook his head.

"Make bridge," Death Wind explained. "Travois."

Scott nodded. He could hear the sounds of hammering. "With all the ice fractures we've been encountering, it's probably a good idea to not bother reassembling the travois, and carry the timber as trestle material."

"My thoughts exactly." Doc sat up in his bedding, wincing as he stretched his arms over his head. "But if we bring our bridges with us, it means that we can no longer send back runners. This will be our last communication with the outside world."

Scott glanced around at the cooking fires scattered across the ice cave. Most people were already packing their meager belongings for the day's march. He saw Sam calling orders down the crevasse, while Helen played an electric light on the road crew.

As soon as everyone had eaten his fill, the fires were damped and the utensils loaded. Crossing the fissure required time and cooperation. A path had been hacked in the ice down to a ledge where the logs spanned the bottomless rift. Each person tied a rope around his waist before tramping across the logs; the safety line was belayed from both sides. Crampons jammed into the wood coupled with the taut ropes made an otherwise precarious crossing routine. Getting the equipment across took more effort, but was effected with the same procedure.

"You know, Doc, suppose this whole thing is a trick?"

"What thing is that?"

Because of the rough terrain and Scott's difficulties with loss of footing, he had been relieved of his towing job. He had nothing to bear but his thoughts. "Well, maybe the dragons deployed those mines in order to steer us into a trap."

"That is food for thought." Doc mulled it over in silence. He let Scott pull him up a pressure ridge and help him down the other side. "The possibilities are endless if we want to play intellectual games of who is outsmarting whom."

"That's what worries me. I always wonder if we're one step ahead of them, or one step behind. When you have only one step it becomes a precious commodity."

They passed under another gap in the ceiling. Tortured chips of ice hailed down in the frigid draft. The stark sunlight illuminated the way for hundreds of yards on either side of the opening. Far ahead, Scott saw another open shaft; and beyond that, another. He came to a deep furrow that broiled with water. The troops were taking turns leaping the gap. A Fusilier stood safety by the jumping-off point, using his battery light to shine the way as each person hopped over the crevice.

Scott stood on his good leg and swung his other back and forth as he prepared for the spring. "I'm about a foot from serious trouble." He vaulted into the air, scissored his legs in midstride, and came down on his real foot. He turned and held out his hand. "Come on, Doc. You can make it."

Doc did not hesitate, but made a limping, running jump that

carried him clear across the void and into Scott's waiting arms. Crampons bit deep into the ice, pinioning Doc to the smooth surface like a weighted schmo doll. "These legs have not lost *all* their elasticity."

Scott had to pull Doc's feet out one at a time. "You never cease to amaze me."

They climbed up the ice embankment and forged ahead.

By midafternoon, Scott was forced to remove his heavy furred parka. "Is it me, or is it getting warm in here?"

"I can feel the temperature changes whenever we pass under a surface vent." Doc unbuttoned his coat and tied it around his waist by the arms. His great shock of white hair billowed above his head. "Do you feel the breeze? A siphon effect is caused by the mass of warm air escaping down the tunnel and out through interstitial flues."

"The river's falling, too," Scott observed. "Or else the channel is broader here. Maybe the hot water has hollowed out a big under-ice grotto."

The cave was also filling with fog. As warm water contacted the cold tunnel walls, evaporation took place on the surface. White streamers of mist rose off the river like dancing wraiths.

"I suggest we stay away from the edge. There is likely to be undercutting and collapse."

"Good idea. I'll pass the word along." Scott dashed ahead to a Femme Fatale, a former Charon resident, and gave her the message. He waited for Doc. "Let's veer toward the wall."

Where the ceiling curved down at the cave's edge, dripping ice formations created a fairyland spectacle of stalactites, stalagmites, and joined columns. Several Rangers were exploring the crystalline city; their lights shone through the vertical maze in breathtaking wonder. Icicles sparkled like diamonds. The magic was made more dazzling by the constant wavering of flaming brands and the crisscrossing beams of electric torches.

Scott broke off a shaft of ice as long and thin as a pencil, and sucked the water off the sharpened tip. "Good." He bit off the end, then chewed the ice like candy. "It must still be below freezing in here."

Doc snapped off a piece of ice and stuck it between his teeth. "Just barely. Only the sheer mass of the floe prevents the glacier from melting away completely. It serves as its own insulation."

"Watch your head, Doc. These things'll pierce your skull like a needle though sackcloth." Heeding his own warning, Scott

backed away from the wonderful landscape, breaking off stalagmites with his feet. "And you could impale yourself easily on
these ice spears."

Doc scooped a delicate fragment off the floor and held it up in
front of his eyes. "Beauty is often deceiving." He tested the point
with a gnarled finger. "Such treacherous elegance."

Farther on they came across columns as fat as trees, and as
many as a forest. Their ribbed exteriors glimmered with melted
wetness. Flat, faceted leaves of ice, each with a pattern as
distinctive as that of a snowflake, curled off the trunks of ice like
peeling bark. The floor was damp and strewn with puddles.

Moisture-laden air rose from the river gorge, curled along the
icy ceiling, and dripped down in a constant drizzle driven by the
ever-increasing draft. Wind racing along the wave tops whipped
the seas to an icy froth; foam flecked the edge of the plateau.

The floor tilted downward, its surface solid and without
fractures or folds. Great ripples, each the size of a humpback
whale, were planted permanently in the ice. Torch-bearing troop-
ers in staggered disarray looked like fireflies flitting across a
milky, moonlit savanna. In the limited illumination the frozen
cascade could have been a surrealistic impression of the descent
into purgatory.

Far, far away, seen dimly through the clinging haze, a glowing
purple dot hovered in an indistinct, horizonless void.

"Somehow, I expected to see more," said Scott.

"You will," said Doc, and after a pause, he added, "after
sunrise."

Dawn was slow in coming.

Not even the Nomads, master scouts that they were, dared
venture into the nebulous realm of the dragon stronghold until
the visibility cleared. The sun was an amorphous, dull-white
globe that drifted in and out of sight as the morning mists burned
off. The ethereal landscape glimpsed through the overcast reminded Scott of Charon at nearly full scale.

"I never grasped the size of it from the snapshots." Scott sat on
his haunches on a high bluff of ice that overlooked the stronghold;
he felt like an eagle in its aerie. "I thought it was nothing more
than a way station, or at most a city in miniature. It looks like a
well-developed community."

"There is no traffic yet, although it is a bit early in the morning
to expect dragons to be up and about." Doc sat on his furs with his

legs stretched out before him and his chin resting on his cane. He wore only long-sleeved underclothing. "They must move with extreme sluggishness under these conditions."

"I think it's kind of temperate."

Despite the solid ice underfoot, the atmosphere was warm and muggy. Water ran in rivulets over frozen hummocks to the edge of a sheer precipice, then cascaded several hundred feet into a clear lake.

Death Wind munched on a blackened steak. "We will soon see dragons."

"That is a prediction I acquiesce to," said Doc.

The entire guerrilla company stood on alert, like sports fans in the bleachers of a stadium. They watched and waited.

As the fog lifted, the evanescent purple glow resolved itself into a time transport structure that occupied the center of the hollow. From rim to rim the haze-filled basin was five miles across. The melt water that formed the central river flowed around the TTS, creating a moat that was crossed by a drawbridge on either side.

The stronghold complex was bisected by the rampaging watercourse; each side was a mirror image of the other. There were duplicate nuclear reactor plants, transmission stations, workshops, and living quarters, all intermingled with lush jungle growth, grainfields, and dinosaur pens. Four squat, multilevel tenements, constructed of orange plastic and lined with windows, dominated the hidden sanctuary; they occupied the four diagonal corners, and beyond each lay a yawning hole that tunneled through the base of the continental glacier.

Steam pipes radiated from the generating stations like giant spider webs; the conduits were buried under plastic roadbeds, and were discernible only by the coiling wreaths of vapor that were discharged into the air to fight off the severe cold of the natural climate. The hot air rising to meet the cold caused a chronic condensation layer hundreds of feet above the artificial valley; the light drizzle never ceased, nor did the air ever fully clear.

Most of the dragon stronghold was permanently cloaked in a thick, miasmal distillate.

"Here they come!" Scott pointed to the nearest tunnel entrance, practically underneath him.

Wisps of steam intermittently obscured the scene, but during spells of clearing he saw dragon slaves shuffling along the orangetop. They were clothed in loose-fitting, reflective garments that left the limbs and tail exposed. None strayed far from the vapor vents.

"With all this smoke I don't think we'll see much about how this place operates."

"Do you recognize anything that could be a missile silo?" Doc wanted to know.

"There's too much ground cover. Any of those tall buildings could hide a launching pad."

"Death Wind, you've got the sharpest eyes here. Can you see any signs of defense armament, gun emplacements, guard shacks?"

The Nomad slowly shook his head.

"I don't like it, Doc. It looks too simple, like we could prance right in. It's not like a dragon to go undefended."

"Perhaps they never expected to have enemies in the Pleistocene."

Scott detected the sarcasm in his voice. "You don't believe that."

"No, but it is still a possibility. Although you would think that since they detected our arrival in this time zone, they would have prepared for an eventual attack."

Scott squeezed his lips with greasy fingers. "I still don't like it. No matter how many land mines they've got topside, I'd expect some kind of home guard like they had in the Cretaceous. I'm not about to walk into another ambush."

"I quite agree, my boy. I quite agree." Doc scrounged in his knapsack for a bit of food. "Let us not jump to any conclusions. As Sam prescribed, we will rest here for the day and see what we can see."

Death Wind suddenly sat bolt upright. He cupped a hand over his brow.

"What is it, lad? What do you see?"

The Nomad pointed down at the nearby tunnel entrance. "People."

CHAPTER 20

With ropes and rigging they let themselves down the ice wall.

The huge, hollowed bowl sported impregnable ramparts hundreds of feet high. As the glacier flowed into the steamy area of dragon occupation it was continually melted away. The resultant river carved a channel through the stronghold and created a cold-water lake at the downstream end that then formed the tunnel that ran under the glacier.

"Okay, let me go." Scott glanced over his shoulder. A hundred feet below him the waves lapped at the irregular shore. He dug his crampons into the ice, leaned out so that his body was perpendicular to the wall, and walked backward with crunching steps as he let his hands slide along the smooth texture of the rope. A safety line wrapped around his chest was held by Windy who himself was tied to an ice anchor; he kept the rope taut, letting go just enough slack to allow Scott to proceed. If Scott lost his grip, the safety line would prevent him from falling more than a couple of feet.

Scott made sure to jam all ten points into the ice before pulling out his other crampon and taking the next downward step. He climbed in the sequence of pull, lower, jam, pull, lower, jam, until he reached the midway plateau where two Fusiliers stood by. He rested a moment, then proceeded the rest of the way to the bottom.

"If we weren't on such an important mission I'd say that was fun." Scott let a Fatale untie the belaying line. He loosened the harness so it could be pulled up for the next climber.

"I thought it was rather exciting myself," said Doc.

A couple dozen men and women were already hard at work knocking down the travois and reassembling the lumber into rafts. In the gathering darkness the opposite shore was a mere silhouette of tall trees that grew down to the water's edge. The mist peeling off the sparkling blue water lent a haunting aura to the scene.

"Wow, that's cold." Scott pulled his hand out of the lake and blew on numb fingers. "I thought it would at least be tepid."

Doc took Scott by the sleeve and pulled him away from the rope fall; a Ranger was on his way down the line. "Although it is colder than you would like, it is warmer than you think. You are feeling the difference between air and water temperatures."

"I'll have to put my furs on before I go swimming."

Doc held out a handful of milk-colored grease. "You had better smear on another layer of bear fat, too."

Scott did not hesitate in complying. "I guess thawing this stuff is out of the question."

All the cooking pots were being used to float essential equipment across the lake.

"When we announce our presence with fire it should at least be with laser fire."

"Only kidding." Scott removed his crampons and tossed them aboard a raft. By the time he was greased and dressed, the last of the commandos had descended the ice wall. Scott was sweltering in his thick furs; the atmosphere was thick and humid. "Okay, I'm ready for the big plunge."

Two women were already in the water, holding onto opposite sides of a raft. They floated high on the buoyancy of their furs. Scott slipped into the water and joined them. His furred trousers and parka were pulled close around his skin, the cuffs tied tight with line. The water that leaked in through the seams felt like icy fingers kneading raw muscles. The freezing lake was bearable until he stepped into a hole and went in up to his neck. His vital organs reacted violently to the cold-water incursion. He did his best not to scream.

Doc joined him a moment later and quickly swam to the after end of the raft. His parka hood was thrown back; his hair remained dry and bushy, but his beard dipped beneath the surface and came out looking like bleached, wet hemp. He inhaled sharply. "I do hope this is my last scouting mission. These old bones have seen better days."

Windy and Death Wind joined their raft. Windy's dark hair and beard blended with the fringe fur of his hood. "Ain't so good fer us younguns, neither, Doc."

Death Wind made no complaint.

They kicked with their feet under the water. The flotilla scudded across the lake without splashing or churning. The main current bisecting the lake created a mild backwash that propelled them along the bank in a counterclockwise motion that would eventually bring them to the opposite shore.

Scott chilled down quickly; very shortly he wished he could suffer again the sweating he had only moments before repined. By keeping his arms up on the end of the raft he prevented water from running down his sleeves. His moccasin was already soaked through from walking through melt puddles; his foot soon became as numb as the prosthesis on his stump. In order to reduce the lowering of his body core, he pulled his chest partway out of the water.

He kicked furiously. His one foot did not add much propulsion, but the exertion slowed down body heat loss.

Several rafts floated past, each attended by half a dozen bobbing heads that stretched out of the water like a gaggle of geese. Scott heard teeth chattering so loud that they sounded like repeating rifles in concert. He bit his tongue, finding it strange that his body could be so cold and his face so warm; the air that lay on the surface of the lake carried residual heat from the steam vents.

It seemed like hours before he saw the shoreline approaching. Then he realized that he had not even been looking for it. He was concentrating so hard on fighting off the cold that his awareness extended no further than the physical anguish hammering at his brain. Through their combined efforts the six propellers swung the raft around and pointed it toward the icy beach.

Scott was glad he was behind the raft, because by that time his muscles were too numb to climb up the blunt embankment. The two-foot-high, rounded ice lip was as slippery as silk. Scott kept kicking as much to keep warm as to keep the raft butted against the shore. Death Wind was unable to climb straight up the bank; he first had to climb onto the raft, then jump to shore. He carried the painter inland and lashed it to an exposed rock.

With the effortless, fluid motion of water moccasins the two Femme Fatales glided up the side of the raft and onto the ice. Scott gratefully accepted a feminine hand. He kicked hard against the water with his good foot as she yanked on his arms. Once aground he lay there like a beached whale, gasping for air, until he had to crawl away to make room for Doc. All along the beachhead commandos clambered ashore and pulled up their rafts.

Windy climbed out last. He chafed his body to get his circulation going. "Can't recall when I liked anythin' less. I was better off as a prisoner than a free man. I ain't never suffered like this at the paws o' the dragons."

"But the advantage of free will," Doc chattered through

clenched teeth, "is that you can choose the method of your suffering."

"Ain't no consolation to a freezin' man."

On hands and knees Scott waddled through the puddles of warm water until he reached bare rock. The heated air washing out from the jungle soon warmed his body. He stood up on the slick ice, carefully made his way back to the raft, and took a load that was handed to him.

He was just putting down the battery pack when a deafening discharge rent the air; he was blinded by a white flash as bright as a thousand suns. He dropped instinctively and clung to the rock like a limpet. The retinal pattern burned into his eyes showed the outline of a human figure surrounded by a ball of flame. As the image faded Scott realized he had just seen someone incinerated. A moment later he smelled the nauseating odor of burnt flesh.

True to their trade, not a soul made a sound. Half a dozen laser guns were whipped out of holsters, but the Rangers and the Fusiliers held their fire; there was no visible target.

Scott scampered on hands and knees to the smoldering corpse. It was burnt to a crisp. When he pulled back the furred hood, the person's face came away with it. Scott turned and retched.

He felt a hand on his shoulder. "Who is it?" Broderick said in his perfect diction.

Scott fought hard to find his voice. "I can't tell." Out of the corner of his eye he saw someone else sneaking toward the trees. "*Get away from there!* It's booby-trapped."

The female Nomad froze in her tracks, a drawn bow aimed at the tree line. She glanced at Scott.

"It's electrified."

Doc and Sam, the two resident doctors, knelt by the inert body. Doc perfunctorily slid up a sleeve and felt for a pulse. He shook his head in silence.

Sam peered into the blackened orbs. "Can't tell. We'll have to take a head count. It's a male—"

Something big and heavy thundered out of the trees. In the near darkness Scott saw what looked like a small house on moving pillars. Crisscrossing laser beams blasted its flank in unison. The arrows that arced through the air disintegrated in sheets of flame as they passed through the electrified zone. The hulk in motion stood up on huge hind legs. The air whined with recharging capacitors. Another broadside brought the creature down in concordant flashes of stimulated radiation, illuminating the beast .

in the bright discharges. It fell with a thud that shook the ground and knocked over a tree.

Doc said, "I believe we have just killed a triceratops."

Scott did his best to put out of mind the still-mocking cadaver that but a moment before had been a living human being. He scuttled toward the danger zone as delineated by scorched rock and the sparks of burning debris, but maintained a safe margin in case the discharge was static: direct current could leap incredible distances. He lay flat on his belly, looking for some indication of the cause of such a violent, all-consuming chemical reaction.

A moment later Doc lay by his side. "Any ideas?"

"I smell oxygen." With his visual purple destroyed by the blast of light, his night vision was gone. It would be a while before his eye produced enough of the chemical for him to see adequately in the dark. He hissed, "Hey, bring me a light."

After a few moments of scuffling, Windy slithered to his side wearing a battery pack with the laser nozzle replaced by a lamp. He switched it on to low power. "Where you want it?"

Scott took the electric torch and stretched out the cable. He played the light along the ground. At the danger line lay a copper tubing punctured every eighteen inches with venturis. Just inside it a thick, insulated electrical cable ran along the surface; it was only partially covered by dirt and grass. "Doesn't look as if they tried to hide it very well."

"Dinosaurs are not known for keenness of eyesight," said Doc.

"Huhn? What do you mean?"

"I mean that this barrier is more likely intended to keep dinosaurs in, not intruders out. The dragons would not want their livestock falling into the lake and drowning."

"You gotta be right, Doc," Windy said enthusiastically. "Hell, we could yank out these wires and rip apart this tubing lickety-split. Look-a here. It runs right over the rocks."

Scott shone the light on the copper tubing under Windy's hand. He traced the thin conduit to the water's edge, where it dipped through the ice. "There must be a submerged electrolysis unit that's breaking down water into oxygen and hydrogen, then piping the oxygen up here. In addition to aerating the atmosphere inside the glacial dead zone, where there's very little natural circulation, some of it's used to intensify the oxidizing effect of this—force field."

Doc said in admiration, "Customary dragon genius."

"That lizard genius jus' fried one of our men," chafed Windy.

All three backed away from the invisible fence.

Sam shoved a boulder inside the dead man's parka, buttoned the front, and nodded to the attendees. He turned his gaze on Doc. "His name is—his name was Reynolds. One of Broderick's men. He's got a wife back on the *Ark*. What the hell am I supposed to tell her? That I let her husband become a goddamn firebrand? I should have taken the lead. I should have been in front instead of giving orders from the rear."

Helen placed her arms around his shoulders. "No. No recriminations, Sam. It wasn't your fault."

Sam shrugged her off. He paced a few steps, staring futilely as four pallbearers carried Reynolds by the arms and legs to the water's edge. They laid him down on the ice bank.

Broderick knelt by his friend's side. "He was a good man. But at least he died for a worthy cause."

Doc bowed his head to deliver the eulogy. His voice was soft and solemn. "Casualties are a sad fact of war, not a general's shortcoming. While we put our brave warrior to rest we must remember that hearts are never separated, nor does love ever end. His spirit is kept alive by the continuance of thought. Only when the last member of the human race dies will his essence be lost. It is our task to see that his memory is carried on forever. We fight now not just for Reynolds, but for every human soul that ever existed, or ever will exist, in whatever universal plane or temporal zone is occupied by this great gestalt that we call humanity."

Stifling his tears, Broderick shoved the body into the water. The weight of the rocks carried it straight to the bottom. "So long, chum. You were a good mate."

The commandos mourned their loss, but were more than ever ready for battle. They could not allow themselves to yield to the emotion of the moment. They had a higher cause than revenge. They were fighting for the survival of the species.

CHAPTER 21

The rafts were unloaded, broken up, and tossed back into the lake. The lumber drifted with the current, to be taken eventually into the under-ice passage up which it had so carefully been dragged. The fur garments followed. They were taking no chances on stashing their clothes only to have them discovered by a dragon perimeter patrol. The commandos donned their packs and weapons.

Another triceratops lumbered out of the forest.

"Don't shoot!" Scott shouted.

The three-horned beast nudged its fallen comrade with the tip of its central horn. The thick, bony plate that protected its neck was laced with copper-tinted wires. As the triceratops neared the buried cable the wires glowed; the beast immediately backed up.

"Amazing," said Doc. "The animal is wearing a proximity shock device. Do you know what this means?"

"You were right. It's a corral utilizing a sophisticated electronic fence instead of the poured plastic bulkheads they used at the Outpost."

"Of course I am right, but that is not the point. Scott, it means that dinosaurs have the intelligence to grasp the concept of learned association: in this case, pain with place. It means they are trainable."

The triceratops stared myopically at the human onlookers. Its thick tail flicked, and its massive hindquarters swung back and forth like a cat about to strike. It let out a low, caterwauling moan.

"That's great, Henry. That's just great." Sam flung his hands in the air. "Let's save the scientific discourses for later. Right now I need to know how to proceed. You're my advisor. Advise."

Doc said simply, "Oh."

Scott was more informative. "As far as I can tell the fence isn't rigged with a discharge sensor. Even if it was, a dragon watchman couldn't tell whether it was tripped by an intruder or a blundering dinosaur. I think we're undetected. Now, I can probably cut the power leads, but that'd be a dead giveaway. My advice is, instead of taking the triceratops by the horns, walk around."

Sam mulled that over for a moment. "Doc?"

The doctor pursed his lips and tugged on his damp beard. "I quite agree. As long as the dinosaurs are penned in, the coastal route is the best one to follow."

"Okay." Sam pulled a crinkled sketch map out of his pants pocket. The diagrams he had drawn during daylight observation, at times of temporary clearing, showed the general outline of the stronghold. "If we follow the lake away from the river it'll take us right to the tunnel entrance in the southeast quadrant. We've got to know what those excavations are used for before we assault the stronghold. If they're full of dragons, I don't want them counter-attacking from the rear."

The triceratops bleated as it turned and disappeared into the jungle.

"We must watch for other pitfalls," cautioned Doc.

Bold One produced a long spear that he held out in front of him like a lance. "I lead." He strode off without waiting for acknowl-edgment. Slender Petal marched half a step behind.

Sam opened his mouth to protest, stopped with his jaw down, then clamped his teeth together. "Okay, people, let's go." The commandos followed the shoreline in single file, staying on the rocks just inshore of the overhanging lip of ice. "Don't bunch up."

Despite Sam's admonition, Doc closed ranks with him. "Sam, please accept my apology for becoming momentarily side-tracked."

"Exchanged for mine for being so uptight. It's a big relief not having to prance through a jungle full of dinosaurs. I've had the heebie-jeebies all day long. Now we know why they weren't roaming the streets. And if this fence goes all the way to the highway we won't have to worry about crossing swords with those oversized horned toads."

As the coolness of the night settled in, the fog, produced by the generated steam mixing with the cold glacial air, slowly evapo-rated. Heat inversions caused the stars to twinkle. The moisture-laden air was clammy, the wet rocks slippery. More than once Scott's artificial leg skidded across smooth granite.

The jungle was a cacophony of chirps, wheezes, honks, and grunts. Scott found it disconcerting that fifty feet away dinosaurs as large as bungalows prowled surreptitiously, browsing and grazing. The intangible barrier gave him very little comfort; the safety it offered was an intellectual exercise in belief in the unseen.

"You want weapon?"

Scott practically jumped out of his moccasin at Death Wind's sudden approach. "Whew, I didn't realize how much on edge I was." Scott felt his heart thumping. He placed a hand on his chest and let out a deep breath. "I guess I've got dragons on my mind."

"How foot?"

"Better than your English. Death Wind, your language skills are retrogressing."

The Nomad shrugged. "Not need. All understand."

Scott humphed. He thought about it before saying, "There's some truth to that. The purpose of language is to communicate ideas. I guess as long as you accomplish that I shouldn't complain. Still, I'd like to see a compromise between your speech patterns and Doc's. Sometimes he's so long-winded that by the time he winds up his narration I've forgotten what the point was."

"He smart. Very deep."

"Oh, I'll give him that. And I'd sure miss his affectations if he changed." Scott paused, lost in thought. "You know, I've missed you on this mission, too. It's not like the old days when we were always together. Now you're out in front and I'm in the rear. It's good to be side by side again."

Death Wind was silent for so long that Scott thought he must have lost his tongue. Finally, the Nomad tapped the long hair that covered his temple. "You think farther than I see. You have much wisdom."

Scott's impulse was to object. But when he reflected on his friend's remark he knew that it was not intended to bolster his ego. Nomads did not suffer from egotism, and therefore did not feed the egos of others. Neither did their makeup contain false modesty. Nomad feelings were primitive in the sense of uncomplicated.

"That is my role, just as yours is to scout."

Death Wind had doffed the constricting, long-sleeved garments. He wore only a G-string, moccasins, and a quiver. He unhitched the belt at his waist and handed it to Scott. "Take knife."

Scott reached out automatically before he realized what the Nomad was offering him. "But, your father gave this to you."

"You need."

As long as Death Wind had been a brave, that knife had left his side only when drawn and held in his hand. If Nomad psychology allowed for sentimentality, this knife would be Death Wind's most prized possession.

Scott swallowed hard and tried not to falter his speech. In imitation Nomad terseness, he said, "Thanks." He tied the belt around his waist and adjusted the sheath so it lay easily against his hip. He rolled his sleeves past his elbows; he had an unobstructed path to the knife, and could draw it quickly and smoothly.

The word to halt was passed back from person to person.

"Scott!"

At Sam's beckoning call Scott dashed to the front of the line, where the general crouched with Doc, Helen, Bold One, and Slender Petal.

Sam pointed to a plastic conduit that stretched across their path of travel. Beyond it lay a grove of shrubbery too thick to see through. "Check it out, but be careful."

On hands and knees Scott approached the pipe. At three-foot intervals mushroomlike caps protruded upward; the opposite facing was scooped out. "Get Windy up here," he hissed.

A moment later the Texas Ranger lay by his side. He pulled out the flexible cable and handed the light nozzle to Scott. "Better use low power. Don't know what's on t'other side o' them bushes."

Scott cupped a hand over the light as he played it along the tubing. He inspected one of the caps, then followed the pipe to a plastic junction box. "You hear that?"

"A kinda whirring sound?"

"Yes." Scott snapped a branch off a nearby bush, shortened it to the length of a pencil, placed one end against the box, then tilted and lowered his head until the other end of the stick slid into his ear. The vibration was transmitted through the solid material of the wood, and magnified. "It's an electrical device of some sort: a motor or a contactor."

When he illuminated the top of the box he saw a dragon claw switch, the kind that was inset and that required the sharp point of a talon to actuate. He gave the torch back to Windy. "Hold it like that." He removed his newly acquired knife from its sheath and used the keen steel edge to hone the stick to a fine point.

As he worked the carved needle into the hole, Windy's strong hand clamped down on his own. "Are you sure you wanna do that?"

"No." Scott stared at Windy's wiry beard and cragged features. "But I have to do something."

"Suppose it blows up?"

Scott wriggled his fingers and worked the stick into a position where he could jam it into the switch. The tiny click was followed by a loud snap and a gushing sound. Windy gasped and shuddered; his eyes rolled into his head. Then his face and Scott's were splattered with water that fell in great droplets from the sky.

"Bombs don't have manual set-off switches." Scott pressed the wooden needle into the hole once more, and the rain ceased. He leaned back on his knees, but his hand was still pinioned to the junction box. Gently he pulled Windy upright. He called out over his shoulder, "It's okay. It's just a sprinkler system."

Sam's shoulders dropped half a foot; from twenty feet away Scott heard the sigh of relief. "Thanks, Scott."

"No problem."

Sam pulled out the map again and tilted it so he could read it by starlight. "The road leading into the tunnel should be on the other side of this bush barrier."

The troops ranged along the hedgerow looking for a way through. Slender Petal found a disguised wicket near the water's edge. Scott checked it for booby traps, gave the all-clear sign, and led the way along a narrow path that terminated at the shoulder of a poured-plastic roadbed. The orangetop was faintly illuminated by ground-mounted nightlights.

"Okay, since everything's going according to schedule, we'll stick with our prearranged plan. Helen, you stay here with the Fatales and guard the supplies." Sandra had relinquished control of her platoon to her mother. "The Sintu will scout inward—but I don't want you straying too far. You got that, Bold One? Death Wind? I mean it. I don't want to get spread too thin, and I don't want to show our hand."

Both Nomads nodded wordlessly.

"Henry, Scott, you're with me. And the Rangers, too. Broderick, leave some of the Fusiliers with the Fatales, then take the rest and look for a place to hole up for the day. Any questions?" No one made a sound. "Henry, any advice or observations?"

Doc looked both ways along the road. Hundred-foot-tall trees lined both sides of the plastic passageway; upper branches intermingled to create a leafy parasol. Steam vents along the curb issued thin streams of vapor: a permanent, haunting fog. The street surface glistened with condensation; water ran in rivulets down the grooved edged and into a culvert. Inward lay the urban area of the stronghold; outward was a heavily constructed mole that cut through the solid wall of the glacier.

He winked at Scott. "Not to be long-winded, I would like to say that even though we saw very little activity today we do not know whether the traffic was typical, how heavily the inner sanctum is garrisoned, or what light we may find at the end of the tunnel. And while I agree that our initial directive is to proceed by stealth, we must not fall prey to subdued belligerence. We came here to fight, and fight we will. If discovered prematurely we must each take the initiative to accomplish our goal despite our losses." Doc paused dramatically, casting his gaze over the surrounding troops. "I bid fond farewell to those I may not see again. But one thing I guarantee—better times are coming."

There were muttered choruses of "Here, here."

"Thanks, Henry," said Sam. "Your words are an inspiration to us all."

As the commandos settled into their assigned positions there was a short period of hugging and handshaking. These people had traveled together through space and time, thousands of miles and a million years, some to die an untimely death on foreign shores. Some would not return to their homeland, or to their hometime. But all would live on in spirit.

"Okay, let's get moving. We don't have long before sunrise."

Steam vents along the top of the mole spewed heat into the air. It was along this very road that early that morning they had spotted human slaves hauling covered wagons, like draft animals pulling Conestogas. The swirling mists prevented an accurate count, but Scott was sure that several dozen had been employed in the task. More might be living in the stronghold—or in the hollowed grotto at the tunnel's end.

The band of guerrillas loped quickly across the exposed mole. The sidewalls were taller than a man, but short enough for a long-necked dragon to see over. The twin rows of nightlights extended straight as a Nomad's arrow as far as the eye could see, into the dark maw of the tunnel, until they converged in the distance through optical illusion.

Scott peered into the tunnel opening. It was like looking down the wrong end of a telescope. "It shouldn't be more than a couple miles long." At the end of the mole a blast of frigid air mixed with the warmed atmosphere of the inner stronghold, forming a fog bank that ascended with the updraft. He rubbed his bare arms. "I don't think we should have thrown away our furs."

Doc studied the towering ice wall. "Glaciers are in constant motion. I wonder how they keep the ice from destroying the tunnel. Certainly a power that moves mountains cannot be stopped by dragonfactured bulkheads."

"Henry, don't even think about going off on a scientific quest."

"Mere speculation, Sam, and idle curiosity. Nothing more."

They stopped at the tunnel entrance. The black maw was a curved arch fifty feet across. The floor lights seemed hardly adequate for a passageway of such mammoth dimensions.

"It's getting colder." Scott reluctantly rolled down his sleeves.

"Hey, looky over here. In the alcove." Windy stepped into a shadowed opening. His voice became distant and muted. "They got a heater in here. And insulated duds."

As Scott neared the doorway he became aware of a suffused red glow that emanated from the ceiling, as if it were on fire. The heat was a welcome relief; his goose bumps subsided. "It's infrared."

The walls were rubbery and resilient, and seemed to absorb sound.

Windy pulled an odd-looking jumpsuit off a wall rack and tried it on for size. "Made for a dragon." The sleeves were padded, the leggings adjustable, and the tail opening as low as the floor. An attached dickie extended from the neck to accommodate the long dragon neck.

"Not exactly tailor-made, but warm as toast." Scott slipped into a jumpsuit and pranced around the dressing room like a June bride. "But if we hack off the bottoms it'll do the job." The racks were triple-tiered, and extended all across the back wall. "They'll never miss them."

Everyone donned the one-piece uniforms, made quick, slashing alterations, and stashed the scraps in a waste receptacle. The oversized, padded booties were the hardest things to refit.

"I certainly hope it gets cold enough to warrant such clothing," Doc said.

"It must be here for a reason."

Doc's face was flushed under the infrared lamps, and sweat gushed down his face and forehead. "I must get out of here at once."

Scott followed him into the corridor, glad for once for the cold. "Doc, this isn't normal ice temperature. The tunnel is being refrigerated."

When the commandos were all together they continued their march along the under-ice passageway. They advanced in double columns, weapons drawn; Sam and Doc led the way. The bulkhead was constructed of extruded plastic, like so many items of dragon manufacture. Removable panels were spaced at hundred-foot intervals.

"Sam, I think we should have a look behind these doors."

The Gentleman General looked askance. "Henry, this isn't just a trick to study the workings, is it?"

Doc shook his head. "Serendipitously, perhaps, but my main concern is to ensure that the façade does not conceal guns, guard stations, or warning devices."

Sam thought for only a moment. "Okay, but make it snappy."

Scott and Windy removed the panel and set it aside. Windy detached his laser nozzle from the connecting cable, attached the light, and played the beam inside as Doc directed. The glacial ice wall lay exposed; except for a thin veneer of dripping water, it appeared solid. The crawl space was crammed with power lines, plumbing pipes, refrigeration coils, and motors and transformers.

"Ah, I see how it is done." Doc stepped back and let Scott and Windy replace the panel. He nodded to Sam. "It's a mechanical raceway."

The dimly lit corridor was hauntingly quiet; there was no echo effect as one might suspect. To Scott it appeared that the end was no closer now than when they had started. The floor-mounted nightlights stretched out seemingly forever. They marched on warily.

Scott whispered to Doc, "Did you see the alignment of the heat pumps?"

Doc nodded. "The freezer coils create the abnormally low temperature in the tunnel, while the exhaust heat is used to melt the encroaching glacier. The melt water is channeled under the floor. I suspect that if we were to look behind the right side bulkhead we would see nothing but solid ice. The dragons have ingeniously permitted the glacier to flow around the tunnel without going through it."

"You have to give them credit for mechanical marvels." They passed by a nightlight. Doc's whiskered features were momentarily illuminated. "Doc! Your face."

The doctor's skin was chalky; it matched his beard and great mane in whiteness. "You are looking a bit peaked, too. Almost as if—" He halted in midstride and touched his nose with his finger. "That is strange."

"Hey, I can't feel my skin."

"Sam," Doc called out. "The incredible insulating qualities of these wraps prevent us from feeling the extreme cold on exposed flesh. I am afraid that we are suffering from frostbite."

Scott rubbed his face vigorously to restore circulation.

"Okay, at each light I want everyone to stop and check the

person behind you." He added in aside, "What the hell are the dragons trying to do, add fuel to the Ice Age?"

As the yards dragged on the cold became more intense. Ice crystals grew on the plastic walls like hoarfrost, and snapped and crunched underfoot. The guerrilla army sounded like a centipede wearing clackers. The walls sparkled kaleidoscopically as rime ice refracted the light through its frozen facets. The air was so dry that Scott had to constantly moisten his lips with his tongue. His breath condensed and froze on the hairs of his upper lip. When he looked over Doc's face at the next light station, the older man's beard was frozen solid.

"Doc, you look like a snowman. Even your eyebrows are covered with frost."

His lashes were so thickly coated with ice that they hung at half mast. He paid Scott no mind. Under half-opened lids he stared straight ahead. "I believe we are about to get some answers."

The tunnel flared outward like the end of a trumpet, except that the floor remained even. The huge, high-ceilinged dome was filled with vertical glasslike cases, much like the interior of a colossal beehive except that the prism faces were rectangular. A thick growth of frost made the fronts opaque. Each case was eight feet tall and four feet wide, and separated from its neighbor by an airspace partially clogged with ice. Long icicles grew out of the junctions where four cases met.

"Unbelievable," Scott muttered.

"But not unanticipated."

"They must be thousands of 'em," breathed Windy. "Millions."

"Times four," added Doc.

The dome was still and silent. The floor lights were brighter and spaced closer; additional lamps climbed plastic columns that supported the roof. The cases were stacked from floor to ceiling, and placed back to back in long rows with separations every hundred feet.

As far as Scott could see there was no end of them. "It's a giant warehouse."

The rest of the troops bunched up in the bottleneck where the leaders had stopped.

"But storing what?" Sam wanted to know.

Scott did not realize that his mouth was agape until he felt the intense cold on his tongue. He clamped his jaw shut and did his best to salivate. "What would they need to freeze—" The awful truth hit him as hard as a block of ice.

"If my suspicions are correct—" Doc approached the first row of cases. The dragon mitts were floppy potholders on his gnarled hands. He wiped his fists across the front of the lowest storage container. Ice tinkled to the floor with the sound of miniature bells.

Scott joined him. He pounded the prism with padded knuckles. "It's solid." He pressed his face close to the glasslike front.

"Careful, my boy. At these temperatures your skin may adhere to the surface."

With his eyes only inches away from the scraped-off surface, Scott saw a clear, unblemished plastic sidewall an inch thick. The case appeared to be full of ice; fine, weblike cracks obscured a dark, brownish shape that loomed overhead.

"There's something in there."

Scott brushed a wide swath as far up as he could reach. As the frost fell away he peered in at the long, squat form that took shape like a child's connect-the-dots drawing. "Aaagh." He jumped back two steps when he recognized the reptilian face leering down at him. He had not seen a dragon since—the Cretaceous.

"Just as I thought," said Doc calmly. "Although why—"

"Hey, there's another one in here," shouted Windy.

Sam brushed his sleeve over another casket farther down the aisle. "And here."

Momentarily out of control, the commandos spread into the intersecting corridors. All reports were the same. Frozen lizard corpses were everywhere. The ice dome was a dragon mausoleum.

"Doc!" Scott screamed suddenly, his voice echoing in the tomblike silence. "They're not dead, are they? They're frozen. They're alive. They're an army of slaves waiting to be thawed out."

"Alive I am sure. Slaves I doubt. It seems more likely—"

"*Doc!* Over here!" Windy stood on the other side of the corridor, fiercely wiping frost off a storage case. "We got people!"

Everyone gathered around the platoon leader and helped him to brush off the adjacent cases. It was difficult to see clearly through the maze of tiny cracks. The bodies were naked and upright, and for the most part hairless.

Sam winced at the entombed humans. "Maybe this is what became of the Cro-Mag—"

Scott screamed again. He clamped his hand to his mouth; his eyes bulged. He uttered low, guttural sounds like the cough of a wounded animal choking on its own blood. Enough of one female was exposed to show a cadaverous face and a head of long blond hair.

Doc rushed to his side. "My boy, what is it?"

Scott wanted to scream again, but his throat was paralyzed. He desperately wanted to cry. He could only raise his mitted hand and point.

"You look as if you have seen a ghost."

Scott felt himself go weak. The strength left his legs so quickly that he fell back into Doc's arms. Sam rushed to help. Together they eased him down to the frost-covered floor. Scott closed his eyes as his head lolled back on a rubber neck.

Doc pulled up an eyelid and glazed into the dilated pupil.

Scott was aware of his surroundings, but everything was moving in extreme slow motion. He squeezed his eyes shut, then opened them quickly. He glanced up at the figure in the crystal coffin. It was no dream. The girl was really there. She looked so peaceful. She was tall and lean and shapely. Her eyes were closed, as if she were merely taking a short nap.

In a halting, high-pitched voice, Scott finally blurted, "She's—my—sister."

CHAPTER 22

Ned appeared breathless at the top of the ramp. "I was out checking the perimeter. I came as fast as I could." Chest heaving, he paused to suck in some air before going on. "You got a message?"

Rusty shook his head. "Not a tone."

"But Britt said you wanted to prepare the ship for flight. I've got everybody loading up."

"That's right. We're leaving. But we don't have to rush. We can take as long as we want."

Ned used his sleeve to wipe sweat off his forehead. "I don't get it. Where are we going?"

"To the dragon stronghold. We'll be there in no time."

"But the missiles."

Rusty grinned enigmatically. "By the time we get there they won't be able to get us. We'll be out of range."

Ned was breathing easier now. He approached the computer console with his head cocked and an eyebrow raised; he looked at Rusty askance. "Okay, Rusty, take it easy, and let's talk this out. Now, I know you've been under a lot of strain lately—"

Rusty laughed raucously. "I'm not crazy, Ned. You just don't understand what kind of morning I've had." Rusty wiped off his grin and replaced it with a half-serious mien that could not hide the excitement he felt. "Not only have my infinite-time calculations been resolved into a short-order formula, but I've broken a dragon access code I didn't even know existed. Ned, I know exactly when the dragons went, and why. And I can go then at a moment's notice."

Ned was still standing glassy-eyed when Britt appeared on the bridge. "Almost ready."

"Good. We'll take off as soon as Ned gives us the okay."

Britt sidled past Ned and tucked herself under Rusty's arm. He gave her a peck on the cheek.

Ned's eyes roved from one to the other. "You're serious, aren't you?"

"That's why I'm not in a rush. It doesn't matter when we leave, we'll get there at the time I choose. I just program the *Ark*'s time transfer equipment to launch us through the space-time continuum in accordance with the computer's present calculations. It's easy when you have a timely formula."

Ned nodded slowly. "Britt, does he have both oars in the water, or are we gonna be rowing around in circles?"

"I cannot follow. I do not have the mathematics. But Rusty knows. I trust him. If he goes through time, I go with him."

The long silence was finally broken by a toned message from below decks. The troops were aboard, the ship was sealed, battle stations were secured. Ned stood by the bridge toner. He hesitated with his fingers on the keyboard.

"I sure hope you know what the hell you're doing." He gave the signal for acknowledgment, then toned for the backup bridge watch to come up. The trainees could handle the secondary controls while Rusty, Britt, and Ned piloted the ship. "Because I hate the idea of leaving our friends in a time of need."

Rusty smiled again. "Don't worry. When we finish our future business we'll come back to this exact point in time. No one will know we were gone."

Britt disentangled herself from Rusty's arms. She checked the reactor readings. Her fingers flew over the control board; the monitor responded to her commands with scrolled data that she read at a glance. "Power up."

The trainees piled onto the bridge. Rusty directed them to their posts. "Okay, midshippeople, this is the real thing." Rusty took his seat in front of the big screen. He typed instructions into the computer. "We may as well get moving. Once I've set the space-time coordinates we'll have a strict timetable to attend."

"Okay, but I wanna know what's goin' on."

"Let's get off he ground, first. Taking the continuum as a whole, time is objective. But we, limited by finite references within that continuum, must stick to a subjective sequence of events."

Ned sat in the copilot's seat. He stared at the control board and the vast array of annunciator lights. "You're gonna hafta coach me on this, Rusty. Doing simulations isn't the same as flying."

"Sure it is. The only difference is that instead of just lighting up a screen with the correct responses, your input will have a real-time effect on the *Ark*."

"That's what I'm afraid of."

"Don't worry, Ned. I've programmed a computer module to handle the time transfer automatically. Manual control is a thing of the past. Uh, figuratively speaking. You get us there, she'll get us then."

Britt said, "All systems are go, Rusty."

"Let's hit it." The *Ark* lifted smoothly off the ground. When she reached treetop level Rusty tapped acceleration vernier buttons until she reached horizontal cruising speed. "I want to get out of stronghold radar range before we take on altitude." Rusty relinquished the controls. "Okay, Ned, she's all yours."

Ned licked his lips nervously. His fingers were glued to the keyboard as his eyes flashed from screen to screen.

Rusty lounged in his seat. "Would you like to know when we're going, and why the dragons went then?"

"Well, uh—"

"The dragons' overall survival plan was more complicated than we thought. It was shrewdly conceived, adroitly constructed, and almost perfectly carried out. The dragons' only shortcoming was in their failure to comprehend the interrelationship between space and time: not as disparate quanta each with its own set of equations, but both together as observable and interchangeable points of reference within the unalterable reality of the spatiotemporal continuum."

"Rusty, I'm trying to concentrate on—"

"Okay. To put it simply, they charged into time travel in the same straightforward manner they would use to attack a tyrannosaur: head on, and with lots of power. Dragons are blind to subtleties and incapable of understanding abstractions. It's not their fault. That's the way the lizard brain functions. Its capacity for creative thought is limited by its physical design.

"To the dragons time travel was not a discovery: it was an invention; perhaps their crowning technological achievement. And because they did not take the time to understand the ramifications of tampering with the fabric of space-time, it became their downfall. It's like building a skyscraper, then adding ten more stories to the top floor without bothering to see if the foundations could support the extra weight. Eventually, the structure has to topple."

"Rusty, I—" Ned was paler than Rusty had ever seen him. He handled the controls crudely; the *Ark* groaned with the strain. "Maybe you should—"

"No, you're doing just fine." Rusty did his best to look

nonchalant, but he glanced at the monitors whenever Ned was not looking his way. "Anyway, unlike mankind's skyrocketing evolution, the dragons had a history of plodding advance. Most of their Cretaceous city was thousands of years old. They progressed slowly—until they stumbled over the loophole in the time barrier. Their first jump—to a time zone a million years into their own future—proved to be their downfall. When they saw that their civilization no longer existed, they reacted according to the instincts of their kind: ruthlessly, murderously, cold-bloodedly, and, to one who understands dragon psychology, predictably. Without carefully studying the situation, they made immediate plans to ensure racial survival. The way dragons respond to threat is in keeping with the world in which they evolved: they destroy."

"How far do you want to go before—"

"You can start gaining altitude now." Rusty stood up and perambulated around the command center. He checked the readouts at each trainee's console. "Britt, make sure the radarscope is on extreme scale."

"Roger, Rusty. I activated proximity warning sensors."

He ruffled her hair. "Good gal."

Ned looked a little more at ease. "You can't feel the bumps on the simulator module."

"You're doing fine. Take her straight to the top."

Ned applied full power to vertical thrust. The external cameras picked up the purple radiance of the lifting cones.

"Where was I? Oh, yes, the dragons' inability to perceive the intricacies of time travel, the complications of paradox. That's all philosophical conjecture on my part, but the rest is taken right off Jane's engagement crystal: data that was so deeply imbedded under menu codes that I didn't know how to call it up."

Still pacing the bridge, Rusty soliloquized, "So the dragons rushed future events without adequate forethought. A million years after the end of the Cretaceous, mammals already ruled the Earth: the warm-bloods who'd been around for more than a hundred million years, coexisting with the dinosaurs in a subservient role, needed only to have the thunder lizards out of their way so they could expand into the niches previously denied them. The dragons hadn't developed the death bomb yet, so there was time to explore further downstream. Lo and behold, they discovered almost at the limit of their transfer equipment a period of glacial advance. Then, it didn't make sense to restart their global rule knowing that down the line an ice age might wipe them out."

Ned relaxed. There was nothing to do now but wait for the *Ark* to reach her ceiling.

"Now comes the real ingenuity. The development of the death bomb gave them the power to purge the Earth of dominant life forms in order to entrench their own. That's what they did to us, in the Holocene. Then they built Charon and the Outpost to sow the seeds carried forward from the Cretaceous. Eventually, they would have planted farms on the other continents as well.

"But the upper echelon, the dragon elite, didn't want to live in a barren, inhospitable world—one that would take hundreds of thousands of years to re-form into the image of the one they grew up in. They wanted to move immediately into a world that had been created just for them. And that's where the stronghold comes in."

Rusty felt it was time to unwind. He reversed his course and paced clockwise around the command center. All eyes were upon him, and necks craned as he walked behind people hanging on his every word. He stared up through the clear plastic bubble into the infinity of space.

"They couldn't go any further downstream—the Holocene, which began at the end of the Ice Age, represented the time limit of their equipment. They couldn't start their seeding farms one notch back—in the Pleistocene—because none of what they wanted to plant would grow in the oncoming cold." Rusty stabbed a finger into the air. "But they could use the Pleistocene as a leapfrogging post to enable them to travel further downstream.

"The stronghold is a way station—not a terminal, but a transfer depot for points downstream, beyond the reach of Cretaceous-based equipment. It's from now that they intend to repopulate the future with their own kind.

"In the hierarchy of dragon leaders it was the lower classes that were sent to do the dirty work in the Holocene, to oversee that plants and animals from the hometime were cultivated across the world. The most powerful dragons would enjoy the fruits of the labor by suddenly appearing another million years downstream—at a time when the Earth would be converted completely to Cretaceous conditions."

Rusty returned to his seat. He fingered the time transfer controls. "That is when we are going. And we are going in time to prevent the dragons from reclaiming a world they once threw away. You only go through this world once: the dragons had their chance, and they muffed it. Now they want to take away ours."

The *Ark* reached her highest attainable altitude. The air outside was too thin for her lifting cones to push her any higher. But that same thinness would let her time transfer circuits send her through the fabric of space-time with a minimum of expenditure of energy.

"And I'll be damned if I'm going to let them get away with it." Rusty pressed the button.

CHAPTER 23

"The dragon hibernation treatment is quite effective, not only in healing wounds and curing sickness, but in arresting, perhaps even reversing, the aging process. It was never used for slaves and soldiers because they could be too easily replaced: from egg to adult they grew with amazing swiftness."

"Doc, that there's nice to know, but—"

"An organism replaces worn-out cells throughout its lifetime. The adult human being contains not a single cell with which he was born: he is completely renewed every decade. As the original genetic code is passed down from cell to cell, seemingly minor imperfections accumulate until the coding sequence becomes unreadable. Later generations of cells no longer function exactly the way they were intended. Eventually, the organism loses its integrity. It's a process we call aging."

"But what's that got to do with—"

"Dragons did not excel in the biological sciences, but they knew that with proper treatment time heals all wounds. These people—" Doc swept his arms across the plastic facade. Scott's sister stood in quiet repose, like a perfectly sculpted mannequin. "—are not frozen in the strictest sense of the word. Their body temperatures have been significantly lowered, and they lie immobilized in a crystalline structure whose solid state is maintained by refrigeration, but they are actually bathed in an epidermal revivifying fluid that has the capacity to prevent growth and aging while rejuvenating the internal tissues."

Windy snugged the loose-fitting folds of the dragon cold-weather garb close to his chest. "Are you tryin' to say this here's a hospital?"

Doc opened his mouth, cupped his hand over it, then ran his fingers down over his frosted beard. "I was not. But given the evidence of observation, that is as good an explanation as any."

"What I wanna know is, can we wake 'em the hell up?" With paper and pencil in hand, Sam wrote furiously as people returned from the far corners of the dome with information about its contents. He was tabulating a body count on both dragons and humans; the subtotal had already reached the thousands.

"Undoubtedly. These individuals were hibernated with just that purpose. But as you know, the thawing procedure is a slow one. Remember how long it took us to revive Helen and the others."

"I'm not talking about length of time, but practicality. Helen was submerged in a coagulated gelatin, like a supercooled amniotic fluid, not a semisolid crystal lattice. This smacks of permanency."

Doc shrugged. "The dragons have a remedy for it, no doubt. Perhaps the indissoluble casing is merely physical protection for long-term patients—or prisoners. At least we know why they chose to bury them inside a glacier. The energy requirements necessary to sustain the congealing temperature of the solution is largely supplied by natural ice-age conditions. It is very efficient, when you think about it."

Sam stabbed the pencil point dangerously close to Doc's face. "Henry, I'm tired of you admiring dragon science and technology all the time. Whenever they come up with some new gimmick you've got nothing but praise for it. Now, why don't you go over there and talk to Scott. Reassure him. Get him out of his funk. The kid's practically as comatose as these—" He looked at the shapely feminine form. "Well, you know what I mean."

"Of course. That is a valuable suggestion." Unruffled, Doc left Sam and Windy to coordinate the explorers and collect data. He ambled to where Scott leaned with his back against a plastic bulkhead, staring at the domed ceiling.

Scott made no notice of Doc's approach. His mitted hands were tucked into the folds of his jumpsuit. Frozen tears clung to his cheeks like opalescent beads. Blond hair framed the stern features of his face. The resemblance between him and his sister was startling, except that Scott's countenance showed life while his sister's was more like that of a painted, porcelain cherub, or a stillborn fetus.

"Rather an unexpected turn of events, I would say."

Scott did not respond.

Doc ran his tongue over lips that were chapped from the cold. "I had a family at one time. A mother and a father, and"—he thought for a few seconds—"and three sisters: Heather, Betsy, and Pam. Pam died when she was still a baby—natural causes. Cute as a button, she was. Heather was killed in a building collapse when we were teenagers. Betsy, the last I knew, was still alive." He paused reflectively. "But that was many years ago. Both parents were killed by dragons—in a flyer attack. I guess that's when I left home, when I went out into the world to fight back. I was full of pain in those days: angry, aggressive, even vengeful. It was a long time before I learned that the pain of violent emotion was more debilitating than the pain of my loved ones' loss."

Shivering from the cold, Doc walked in slow semicircles in front of Scott. "The pain you feel at a time of loss is one that no one else can appreciate. It is a very private pain. The depth of emotional impact is measured by the closeness of a bond that only you can feel. Of course, life goes on; but it never goes on as well.

"You never get over the crying. Years afterward, for some unknown reason, an image will pop up in your mind—and you will experience a silent moment of remorse. Those moments are very important, so you can remember how much you once loved that person, and so you can remember how much you *can* love. There is no love without pain; and that pain is what makes us human. It is a small price to pay when you consider the alternative."

Scott cleared his throat. He blinked away more tears, unmindful that they froze barely halfway down his cheek. "Do you mean—" His voice faltered. He choked. He cleared his throat again and uttered in a froglike voice, "Are you saying that you always have these feelings?"

"Yes, I still have the feelings; but after a while the feelings no longer hurt. The pain becomes a dull ache—and I enjoy that ache, because it reminds me of the love I still harbor within."

Scott cleared his throat again. He looked down at the frost-covered floor and wiped his eyes with padded mitts. "She's still alive."

"I do not suspect otherwise."

"And the others, too. Mom, and Dad, and—" Scott cleared his throat once more. "We can't see them, but they're probably all here."

"It seems like a logical conclusion."

Scott's eyes grappled with Doc's. "Then why are you making this pitch? Why are you being so negative? That isn't like you. What are you trying to tell me?"

Doc inhaled deeply. The air had a bite that singed his lungs. "I was not even aware of an ulterior motive until you pointed it out to me."

The mausoleum was a strange dichotomy of dark shadows and

bright, silvery hoarfrost. The nightlights did not flicker; the cold, steady beams knifed through the frigid air like white spears. Mild air currents, set in motion by the heat of living bodies rising and mixing with the cold air descending, scraped frost off the ceiling; it fell like fine, granular snow, each crystal twisting and rotating, and sparkling in ever-changing nuance.

Doc's voice was soft but vibrant, his words cut crisply. "Life is as fragile as the petal of a rose. It can be snuffed out with infinite ease. That is why you must make of life what you can, while you can. Life is too short, and too uncertain, to do otherwise."

He cupped his palms in front of his mouth, breathed hard, and let the warm air wash over his face. "Scott, I do not want to raise any false hopes. I do not know if I can save them."

Scott inhaled sharply, his eyes reflecting disquietude.

Doc rushed on. "I know I have done it before. I studied the crystal texts and familiarized myself with the procedure. But I know nothing about the unsolidification process that in this case must precede dehibernation. I do not know what effect long-term homeostasis has on resuscitation. Dragon doctors possess tools and training that I do not."

"Doc, you can do anything," Scott said, imploring. "I've seen you in action."

The doctor maintained solemnity. "I am a man, Scott, with all the doubts and frailties any man has."

"So what am I supposed to do?" Scott exploded. "Forget my family is alive just a few feet away? Make believe they don't exist?"

Doc spoke slowly and carefully. "How did you deal with their deaths before?"

"Well, I—I—I don't know. I just didn't think about it much. It was a part of the past I wanted to forget, so I put it out of my mind. And I had to stay alive. I even looked forward to seeing the world, and finding out what it was really like. But now—"

"Nothing has changed, Scott, only the perception of your beliefs."

"A lot has changed," he screamed, blue eyes glaring. "Before I didn't *know* they were alive, now I do. I can't forget that."

"I am not suggesting that you do. I am merely pointing out that tranquility is a state of mind that you control. It has nothing to do with reality. Once you accept that, you can deal with any disaster, overcome any sorrow. That is how you mitigated the loss of your foot. You have the strength, Scott. Use it.

"We must take over this stronghold, we must gain access to the computer complex. We must go about it in an aggressive but methodical manner. That is the only way to salvation of the souls residing in this Pleistocene purgatory. But I warn you that despite our best efforts, we may fail. You must understand that the dead do not always rise from their graves. Their condition of finality may already be beyond our command.

"The intricacies of this spatiotemporal battle we are waging are progressing geometrically. I do not care to predict what paradoxes may occur should we tamper too much with the fabric of space-time. I see another broken thread in every complication. If the tear gets too big we may not be able to stitch it back together."

"Doc, what's that have to do with—with anything?"

Doc shivered, as much from consternation as from the cold. "I am not sure. The dichotomous reality of our predicament is difficult to grasp in straight-line terms. In one space-time the Maccam City residents are deceased; in another they cling tenaciously to unconscious afterlife. Were they ever truly dead? Are they now really alive? What happens if we tip the scales away from preconceived truth?"

"Doc, you're not making any sense."

"There is no sense in time travel, only interpretation of events. You yourself admit that Maccam City was destroyed by a corrosive gas—"

"No, Doc, that's what I *think*. That's *my* interpretation of what happened. But it's purely subjective, and subject to change. Even if I had actually seen them killed I'd have to believe the later evidence of my own eyes."

"Would you?"

"Well, of course."

Bushy eyebrows, coated with ice, arched into a wrinkled forehead. "Interesting. The question then arises, how did they survive? Or, in another frame of reference, *did* they survive. Perhaps, for some frightful, unfathomable reason your people are not in stasis; perhaps the dragons collected their corpses for some diabolical experiments—" Doc stopped with his mouth ajar. "Uh, I apologize, Scott. I did not intend to speak so crudely about your loved ones. But I wonder . . ."

"Yes, I wonder, too. And I'm beginning to see what you're getting at. Life is more than a chemical reaction, it's a state of mind. At least, intelligent life is. Once we add consciousness to the space-time equation we have to incorporate the relativity principle: reality then depends on the observer's point of view."

"I believe that is the speculation that was coalescing in my brain."

Scott was on a roll. "So, if I perceived them as dead, they are dead—that is, in a subjective approach."

"Out of sight, out of mind, out of existence."

"But if I say they are alive, then, in my heart, they are alive."

"The philosophy of solipsism."

"What you really mean, though, is that torment and internal conflict are the result of a conscious decision."

"Or a subconscious decision. Peace of mind is a mental exercise that takes great effort to control. As long as you keep a memory living inside you, its objective position is independent of perspective."

"But doesn't there have to be an absolute reality, unaffected by the way I think about it?"

"I say yes. Rusty says no. He ascribes to the theory of variability, or subsequent coincidental coexistence. That is why he exhibits such audacity while cavorting through time. He does not believe that anything we do can affect the architecture of the universe. The harmony of the spheres, he insists, cannot be untuned by human intervention. I am skeptical."

"Forget it, Doc. I'm totally confused." Scott shook his head. He held his mitts against his face, melted the frozen saline droplets, and wiped them away. "But, at least I'm not as distraught as I was."

"And that, of course, was the purpose of this conversation." Doc offered Scott a bright smile. "I admit confusion about the overall objectivity of space-time. But I submit that human perception affects its own conduct. You must believe that whether or not your folks are alive, at this time and in this place, you can equivocate your feelings according to chosen subjective precepts. That is the way to equanimity."

Doc placed a loving hand on Scott's shoulder. The chill of the room was offset by the warmth that passed between them. "We will do our best to bring them back to life. But should we fail to succeed, we can always sustain their lives from within. That is the great and awesome power of human emotion. It is truly infinite and unbounded."

CHAPTER 24

"Run for it! Run for it!"

The Fusilier who ran screaming around the corner fell headlong on the deck. He landed with a thump that was padded by dragon clothing, but the battery pack he wore clattered and scraped across the rime-covered plastic. He slid for twenty feet before his pack crashed into an encapsulated dragon. He made no attempt to draw his weapon.

"Come on! Come on!"

Although her arms swung in wild contortions, the woman rounding the corner maintained her balance. Her laser pistol was still snugged in its holster. "Where's Dan?"

"He's down. I saw him faint like the others."

Scott was galvanized into action. He rushed past Doc, skidded in his haste on the ice, and crashed into Sam and Windy, nearly knocking them down. "What's happening?"

Sam ignored him, other than to use his shoulder to lean against while he regained his equilibrium. He blew retreat on his whistle.

Windy crouched and drew his gun. He stood poised with the nozzle aimed along the darkened corridor. "I don't see nuthin'."

The shrill blast of the whistle brought commandos running and slipping from all sides. Hal, the man who lay on the floor at the far end of the corridor, was helped up by his partner, Lynn. They ran as fast as they could on the frosted deck.

"Why the hell ain't they shootin' at nuthin'?" Windy spat, covering for the runaway pair.

The intersection Hal and Lynn were retreating from exploded silently with a harsh, white light. Despite the weight of the backpack on her slender frame, Lynn quickly outdistanced her companion. In his panic Hal's feet kept slipping out from under him.

"I still don't see—" Although they were several hundred feet away, Scott expected to discern among the shadows some threat of dragon pursuit. Yet, there was no movement but the scampering duo.

Fifty feet overhead, another white light flashed on. Hal slumped to the deck without a word. Lynn spun around, fell, climbed to her feet using a crystal sarcophagus for support, started to go to his aid, stopped, then turned and ran.

Sam kept tooting his whistle. Most of the men and women under his command were pouring out of side passageways into the main corridor of the huge dome. Those farther afield had not yet appeared.

"Doc!" Scott looked to the doctor for aid.

The older man ambled along the frosty deck. "Without more information—"

Several people joined Lynn in her madcap scramble along the central corridor. Another ceiling globe shed light on the deck and on the frosted prism faces. Lynn screamed. Except for the row of incandescent bulbs lighting up behind her, Scott saw nothing untoward. If anything was chasing her, it was invisible.

"Get back!" Lynn screamed. "The lights—"

Every gun was drawn. The troops were agitated, but no one knew who or what the enemy was, or how to fight it.

Sam stopped blowing the whistle as the frightened gal skimmed to a halt on ice-capped moccasins. "What is it—"

"I don't know," she gasped. "Something—I couldn't see. It just—puts you to sleep. The light—a warning—"

Even as she spoke another globe burst into full brilliance. Windy discharged his laser gun at it. It was over a hundred feet away, but his aim was true. The bulb blew apart as the searing flash of raw energy drilled a hole through it and destroyed a sizable portion of the ceiling.

"Do not bother killing the messenger," Doc said hastily. "It may be our only indication of impending disaster."

"But what—" Sam started.

"A narcotic gas, I suspect, against which we are defenseless. I suggest a propitious retreat." Doc did not wait to see if his recommendation was being heeded. He turned on his heel and shuffled as fast as he could across the slippery floor. For added support he pushed his cane across the deck.

Scott made no comment about Doc's choice of words, but followed his lead.

It took two seconds for Sam to blow the signal to charge. A few stragglers scurrying to join the group found themselves the only ones left in the dome. In complete rout the erstwhile commandos poured into the tunnel connecting the dome with the melted basin. There were no ranks and files, but a disjointed, shuffling mob.

When Scott had prowled the tunnel on the way into the dome, traction had not been a problem. But in the rush of withdrawal his plastic stump was a major hindrance. He gained extra support by working his hands along the frosted bulkheads. The ceiling-mounted annunciator lights popping on behind him lent wings to his foot.

"The lights ain't comin' on no more," shouted Windy.

"Don't slack off," Sam called out. "It could be a ruse."

No one wanted to be last in line. The race along the tunnel was a controlled sprint in which the competitors struggled to maintain footing as well as placement.

Halfway along the tunnel, with no more globes indicating the presence of gas, and with everyone slowing down from fatigue, Sam managed to gasp, "Got any comments, Henry?"

"None that you care to hear."

Finally, out of sheer exhaustion, the commandos slowed to a fast shuffle.

Sam yelled angrily, "Come on, people, get some distance. You're bunched up like grapes."

With the adrenaline flushed from his body, Scott lagged behind.

"Could be a death gas," Sam continued.

"Unlikely." Still catching his breath, Doc spoke in terse terms. "Too much inherent danger—to the home guard—collecting in pockets—before dissipation."

"How do we get our people out of there?" Sam wanted to know. "How can we ever know it's safe?"

The jogging gait was a torturous one for Scott. His stump hit the deck like a pogo stick without a spring. Without muscles to absorb the shock, the pounding of his stump sent painful vibrations up his leg.

"We must capture the stronghold in order to learn its operations."

"Oh, we're gonna do that, all right. I'm missing five people back there, and I intend to get every one of 'em out."

Scott thought briefly about the others who were in the dome, frozen in time. He shook his head in order to clear his mind of such abstractions. He must be strong, he must exercise control. The universe was a crazy, contorted, complicated continuum: a space-time full of interchangeable parts: multidimensional orbits of infinite lengths, crisscrossing like wet strands in a pot full of boiled spaghetti.

From his personal pinpoint perspective, the future fluctuated according to what occurred in the past. But, as he had learned, the past was as malleable as the future. If past and future events interacted, then neither could claim to be the cause or effect of the other. Conversely, if a change in the past could affect the future, could a change in the future affect the past? The direction of time flow was not an absolute, but a point of view. In the grand picture, all moments of time occurred simultaneously; what he interpreted as flow was how he moved with respect to events: that was what gave life continuity.

Scott shrank mentally. According to Scott's placement along the stream of consciousness, he had already suffered the loss of his family: he had experienced that pain, and recovered from it. They died a million years ago, in his past but in this world's future. That torment was behind him. But if he were to lose Jane—

"What was that?"

Lost in reverie, Scott had only a subconscious impression of a flash of light. He squinted. Another beam lanced across the mouth of the tunnel. "It must be a fight—"

"Damn!" Sam gritted his teeth. The whites of his eyes glowed in the dimness of the tunnel. "We must have triggered a sensor—"

"We better hurry." Windy drew his pistol. He made wide sweeping motions with his arms in order to clear the folds of his jumpsuit. "Sounds like things're hot 'n heavy out there."

The crackling of laser guns was clearly audible. Muffled shouts attested to a staunch defense. A commando silhouetted in the predawn light ducked into the dressing room chased by searing lightning bolts. Scott suddenly realized how exposed their position was in the smooth-walled tunnel. Unless they reached the dressing room before—

A wheeled truck rolled to a halt at the mouth of the tunnel, blocking the entrance. The vehicle carried no guns, but a squad of armed soldiers dismounted behind armored flaps. The Rangers hit the deck as laser beams arced overhead. Scott felt naked without a gun.

"Fire at will!" Sam shouted over the tumult.

The front rank let loose bolts of lightning at the truck. The armor soaked up the energy like a sponge. Stragglers in the after ranks rose up on their knees to fire over the heads of their comrades. The return fire was slow and methodical and not very accurate. Blobs of hot plastic that were gouged out of the floor spattered the troops with telling effect, almost like the blast of a grenade. Commandos squirmed away from the molten showers like noontime worms on a hot macadam road.

"Get firepower on 'em!"

Without cover, the only tactic that would save them was to keep the heads of the enemy where they could not see. The dragons did not show themselves, but poked their guns through portals in the armored flaps and fired randomly. It was a temporary standoff, with the commandos at the disadvantage.

Out of the dressing room flew an insulated jumpsuit. It landed in front of the truck almost touching the armor belt. Another jumpsuit sailed in the air completely over the ten-foot-high flaps behind which the dragon soldiers hid. Then came another, this one landing on the roof.

A high-pitched voice shouted, "Flame it."

Several seconds passed before someone got the idea. A grounded trooper fired, cycled, fired again, and caught the padded material with a laser beam. The jumpsuit smoldered in the freezing air, then caught fire. The cold-weather uniforms kept flying out of the cloak room, laying a blanket of combustibles for the pinned commandos to ignite. Soon smoke and flame hid the truck behind a pall. The soldiers may not have been in danger of burning, but the effect was at least as good as that of a smudge pot.

"Cover me!" Scott leaped up and charged for a wall panel. He was fully exposed. He peered through the black haze for signs of movement while his fingers groped along the darkened bulkhead. He quickly located the exposed latches; in a moment he had the access panel off. He flung it aside and tumbled into the crawl space amid a network of cables, conduits, and junction boxes. If he had not been wearing the thick jumpsuit he would have been gouged by corners and sharp edges.

"Come on!" Scott ordered.

Windy climbed in right behind Scott, then turned and helped Doc over the raised lip. "Get in here, ever'body!"

One by one the commandos charged into the confines of the crawl space, while others laid down a suppressing fire. One dragon soldier lumbered toward the dressing room; as soon as it left the protection of the armored flaps it was caught in the combined beams of three laser guns. The dragon's breast and bulbous body were drilled through; it lurched over on its side, legs

kicking ineffectually in the air. The jumpsuits kept coming and
feeding the blaze.

"Let's flank them," Scott said. He squeezed along the crawl
space with his hands out in front of him, feeling his way in the
dark. A pipe rack served as a highway. He did not pick up his feet,
but slid his thick booties along the raceway so as not to lose
contact with it. He heard people clattering through the wires
behind him.

A light flashed on and cast its beam over his shoulder. Windy
said, "Kin ya see where yer goin'?"

"Hold it a little higher. But don't drop the gun nozzle; if it falls
through the grate we'll never find it again." Below the raceway
lay several tiers of pipes, open trays of insulated wires, and plastic
structural supports. "Shine it straight ahead."

There was not far to go before the tunnel gave way to the bridge
across the melt moat. In the stark white beam Scott saw that the
maze of pipes and wires converged through a watertight gland.
"End of the line."

From behind Windy, Doc called out, "All this piping must go
through the abnormally thick balustrades along the bridge."

"That's great, Doc. Windy, shine the light on the outside wall."

The beam jogged in a crazy arc that ended up illuminating the
grate. "Tripped over my own two feet."

There was enough side glow for Scott to see the inside of the
latch mechanisms. "Never mind. Screw on the laser nozzle."
The crawl space was not intended to be used as a hallway, and the
access panels were not designed to be opened from the interior.
"We're going to have to blast our way out."

"How're we gonna see where to shoot onct I take off the light?"
The crawl space went dark.

Through the plastic bulkhead Scott heard the muted sounds of
battle. "We'll do it by feel."

Doc's voice was crisp and clear. "Be careful, my boy. An arm
is not as easily replaced as a leg. Why don't you let me guide the
beam."

"I'm ready," Windy announced.

"No chance, Doc. Now, Windy, I've got both hands on the cam
locks. Hold onto my right hand, aim the nozzle, memorize the
position, and we'll both clear the spot. Then give her the gun."

"Gotcha."

Torches bobbed in the background as the rest of the platoon.

shuffled along the crawl space; the lights were too fleeting to be of any use.

Scott felt Windy's mitt feel its way over his. Windy squeezed twice, then let go. Scott withdrew his hand. "All clear."

He was looking right at the spot as the laser beam burst through the cam and blew out the mechanism. He was temporarily blinded.

Windy's mitt covered his other hand, squeezed, and withdrew. "Okay?"

"Go for it."

The lightning bolt struck again. Several tiny drops of molten plastic stung Scott's face. His eyes were still recovering from the first brilliant flash as he leaned back, stood on his good leg, and kicked out with his rigid prosthesis. The panel crashed into the tunnel, and Scott wasted no time tumbling out after it. He hit the deck in a roll that took him ten feet from the wall.

He was aghast to see the truck backing up, its front in flames. The dragon guards were retreating behind their armor. A hundred feet away the last of the Rangers was chased into the crawl space by stabbing laser beams. One dragon turned slowly, looked at Scott on the floor and Windy climbing out the opening, and swung its gun. The lizard hissed a warning to its comrades in arms.

Doc let out a blast on his whistle that attracted the dragon's attention. Windy got clear just as it fired its weapon. The beam narrowly missed the Ranger, and nearly parted Doc's hair as the electric discharge entered the opening and melted a batch of cables. The high-voltage short circuit exploded into a ball of brilliant white light that burned the insulation off neighboring cables.

"Aaagh," Doc screamed as he fell out of the opening with his back ablaze.

Without thinking about his exposed position, Scott leaped on the elderly doctor and smothered the flames with his own body. When he rolled up on to his knees, smoke was pouring off the front of his jumpsuit. He whipped it off and hurled it at the dragon that had fired at them. By this time the others had turned and were leveling their guns.

Windy scored a direct hit through the brainpan of the nearest. Scott grabbed Doc and pulled him to his feet. Quick action saved them all, for the laser blasts hit where the quick-witted humans had just been. Windy could not roll because of the battery pack on his back, but he scrambled on all fours across the tunnel, drawing off some of the fire.

Scott and Doc rounded the corner of the tunnel entrance just as another series of laser blasts seared the deck at their feet. They huddled on a narrow parapet that led down to the water's edge. The glacier wall at Scott's back was a monstrous barrier of ice that soared upward for hundreds of feet. Long, lancelike icicles dripped down the melting face. Cold air radiating off the surface mixed with generated heat pulsing out from the stronghold.

Scott dared a peek around the edge and was quickly met with half a dozen lightning bolts that burned through the block of ice like hot knives through soft butter. "They're still backing up."

"A rather uncomfortable southern exposure." Doc pulled the folds of his jumpsuit around so he could see the hole burned in the seat. Then he removed what was left of the material.

"Right now I'm more concerned about our northern exposure." Scott lay flat and ventured a look into the tunnel. Two more wall panels were kicked out as commandos fought their way out of the crawl space that was now a raging inferno. They were slightly in front of the slowly backing vehicle, and faced with the flames from the burning jumpsuits that clung to its forward armor belt.

Windy bolted to the opposite bulkhead faster than the dragons could track him. He fired on the fly, recording one body hit, then skidded onto the other parapet. He turned to pick off the dragons whose backs were exposed, but got off only one wild shot before he had to duck the concentrated enfilade from the dragon squad.

Laser blasts fired by the commandos who were back in the tunnel exploded against the side of the truck. Two more dragons went down before the armored flaps were folded back to create a cocoon. The flanking maneuver was only partially successful.

"Doc, we're in trouble." There was no place to hide unless they dove into the water and stayed submerged until the truck passed the short expanse between the tunnel and the bridge. Scott pulled out his only weapon, Death Wind's knife.

"So it would appear."

A dragon detached itself from the truck and waddled straight toward them. The rest kept up their fire at the commandos. Windy got off a shot, but nearly lost his head in the process. One dragon was detailed to watch his position and kept its laser pistol firing at the corner. As its weapon recycled, the gun burnt holes through the rim of ice. Windy was forced back by the onslaught.

Doc's jumpsuit sailed out in a perfect arc and wrapped itself around the advancing dragon's gun arm. It pulled the trigger, sending a flaming arc through the material and into the tunnel wall. Scott scuttled out from cover like an angry scorpion and pierced the dragon's abdomen with the knife, cutting edge up; then he gutted the stunned lizard with one swift stroke. Doc broke off a long icicle and charged like a jouster. He ran the ice javelin into the dragon's throat. It died without a hiss.

"Good work, my boy."

Scott was too busy to acknowledge praise. As the dragon hit the deck he pounced on it, pulled the laser gun's connecting cable over the snakelike neck, and, using the dragon's body as a shield, fired into the remaining squad.

Windy was no longer pinned down. He shot into the exposed ranks with devastating effect. A moment later commandos ran through the smoke on both sides of the truck and caught the remaining dragons in a deadly crossfire. In a moment it was all over.

Scott sheathed his knife as he backed away from the blood and guts pouring out of the eviscerated dragon's abdomen. Doc placed a hand on his shoulder as they surveyed the damage. Windy danced around like an egotistic prizefighter touting his victory. The Rangers ran coughing out of the smoke that was filling the tunnel. Flames licked out of the open access panels as fires fanned by the air current raged out of control within the crawl space.

Sam appeared with Helen in tow. "Well, you certainly gave us the advantage we needed."

"I was coming to warn you that the jig was up when that truck started chasing after me. Then I was afraid I was bringing you trouble instead of getting you out of it."

Sam gave her a resounding smack on the lips. "Well, you sure showed your spunk. You're the greatest."

Helen returned his kiss. "You always say that when I save your life."

As they stumbled away from the broiling fumes, Doc said wryly, "Excuse me for intruding upon your mutual admiration, but have you noticed the time transport structure?"

Scott glanced toward the center of the stronghold. The focusing nodes coruscated with the brilliance preceding a transfer. A clap of thunder echoed off the ice walls. The TTS went dark.

Something had been either sent or received. What, and when, only time would tell.

CHAPTER 25

The *Ark* popped back into real time over an Earth that was green and verdant.

Ned whistled at the downscreen. "Will you look at that?"

Rusty was too busy working the controls to admire the scenery. He glanced only briefly at the luxuriant forests seen through wisps of stratocumulus. He grunted and continued to run checks on the temporal formulations.

Britt concentrated on piloting the craft. Almost single-handedly she brought down the *Ark* in a slow, controlled descent without inducing a horizontal spatial vector. By modulating the thrusters she maintained an even keel with the utmost precision. "Dragon station below."

"I hope your timing is good," said Ned.

Rusty leaned back as the computer program ran its course. "The *Ark* is our timekeeper. The purpose of the formula is to get us off the eternal treadmill the dragons are on. If you look at time as a conveyor belt, and the various dragon installations as packages on that belt, locked in position, then you can understand the difficulties of what we're trying to do. Let's say the packages are exactly ten feet apart. If we know how much thrust is required to jump from one package to another, we can do it repeatedly and without error. But suppose we jump from package A when it's passing point twenty-seven; we don't want to reach package B at point thirty-seven, but at the point when it was first put on the belt."

"And that's what your formulation calculates?"

"Ostensibly. In actuality, I didn't have enough points of reference to make a sound statistical analysis in order to define the constant with perfect accuracy. But the temporal data gathered from this transfer will help refine the computation."

"In other words, we're temporarily unsure of our whereupon."

Rusty smiled. "I guess you could say we know our whence, but not our whenabouts." He placed his hands behind his head. Long red curls framed his face like a disarrayed Raggedy Ann doll.

"Until I factor in our temporal drift, if I hit the reversing switch we'll go back to a point as far downstream from when we started as we have flowed in this time zone."

Ned nodded, but he wore a puzzled frown. "I think I getcha. But we can't play temporal yo-yo till the capacitors recharge. How long's that gonna take?"

"The drain on the circuits is the product of the length of time traversed, the mass being transferred, and the amount of matter displaced at timefall. Recharging capacity is a straight-line function of available power, minus continued usage. If we wanted to flit a few years we could do it as soon as the focusing nodes cool. To get back to when we started, twelve hours."

"Coming into range," Britt called out.

Rusty leaned forward to study the downscreen. He set the optics to full magnification. Directly beneath the *Ark* stood the dragons' most future construct: a small time transport facility surrounded by a few scattered, prefabricated buildings. There were no outlying defense fortifications, no pillboxes, no visible armed guard, not even a reactor plant. The quarters most likely housed technicians sent ahead to erect the housing for the TTS. This station could not yet transmit; it could only receive.

"Well, we could have gotten here sooner, but it looks like we're in time." Rusty grinned like a Cheshire cat.

"Why not go back a few weeks and pick 'em off as they come out of the past?" Ned wanted to know.

"Well, by that time we could have this place knocked out."

"What do you mean by 'that time'? I thought you said there was no such thing as that time, only this time?"

"You know what I mean."

"Hell, I don't even know what *I* mean." Ned scratched his head. "You keep confusing me with all this time talk. I just figured if we went back a bit we could blow up the joint when the first dragon stuck its neck through. You know, nip it in the bud."

"Then this place wouldn't be here, now."

"That's right." Ned squinted hard. "Wait a minute, if this place is here now, it means we didn't go back and blow it up earlier."

"According to one theory."

"But suppose I convince you to do it? What then?"

"As much as I debated the point with Doc, I'm not really sure. It's one thing to argue theory, it's quite another to test it out. And when you come right down to it, mathematics is a trick: a human convenience developed by human mentality in order to create analogies for a mind that can't imagine the resultant concept. Analytical studies may have no validity in a purely objective universe—assuming there is such a thing. Of course, I'd never admit that to Doc."

Ned shook his head. "It's too much for my poor noggin. If I see it, I'll believe it. You gotta show me."

The proximity alarm went off.

"What the—" Rusty sat bolt upright. He stared at the screens with stunned intensity.

The *Ark* dropped rapidly under Britt's control. "Missile launched."

"Impossible!" In the middle of the downscreen Rusty saw the foundations of the new time transport structure; a few low sheds stood nearby. There were no external silos, and under the flame of the rocket fast approaching he saw no opening to indicate an underground launch pad.

"If you see it, you better believe it," Ned yelled. "It doesn't take math to prove what's in front of your eyes."

"I'm taking over!"

Britt relinquished control to the more experienced pilot. "It is yours."

The *Ark*'s altitude was so low that contact with the missile was only moments away. He applied lateral thrust, but knew in his heart that he could not maneuver the *Ark* out of the missile's flight path.

"It's gonna be a close one," muttered Ned.

The bridge toner alerted the gunners of impending disaster. Barrels swiveled on their mounts.

"Where did it—" Rusty tapped for full power. Only radical action was going to save the *Ark* on such short notice. "Hang on to your seats."

He switched off the gyroscope, then withdrew all power from the lifting cones on one side of the vessel and transferred it to the cones on the other side. This pitched the *Ark* into a nearly vertical glide, like a child's top on end, and nearly capsized her. Only deft manipulations kept the saucer from tipping end over end. With the upper thrusters blasting away, the *Ark* dived at a speed she had never before attained.

The missile's course veered, but not nearly swift enough to compensate for the plummeting flyer. The two machines missed each other by a hairbreadth. The missile arced out of sight on a new trajectory. It crashed in the forest with a dull thud but no explosion.

Rusty fought to get the *Ark* back under control before she crashed into the ground at more than full speed. He reversed the lifting cone power controls, switched the gyroscope into horizontal-seeking mode, waited breathlessly while she leveled out, then applied full power to all cones. Some of her momentum was transferred into lateral motion. The saucer scorched the treetops as she descended into the upper canopy.

Full thrust finally stopped her downward motion and very slowly began to lift her out of the leaves and branches. The fragile vegetation did no damage to the *Ark*'s undercarriage. Rusty began to breathe again. He looked for the first clearing big enough to accommodate the saucer's width. He made a successful if somewhat shaky landing.

Long afterward, he sat shaking his head in disbelief. "I still don't believe it."

CHAPTER 26

"Time marches on."

"A very profound statement, Henry." Sam led his troops across the bridge at a fast walk. Despite the exigency of the situation, they were still recuperating from the exertion of their two-mile jog out of the tunnel and the fight at the end of it. It did not pay to go into battle completely exhausted. "But which way is it marching?"

"As far as we are concerned, downstream, into the unknown and the unknowable."

"I'm not so sure about that anymore, Doc." Despite the pain in his leg, Scott kept up the pace. The battery pack and laser gun instilled him with confidence and a feeling of power. "I have my doubts about what was, what is, and what will be. All points in time are interrelated, like some cosmic cryptogram. We just don't know how to read the code."

"Life may be a simple cipher in both meanings of the word."

Windy drawled, "I wisht I knew what you fellas were talkin' 'bout."

"So do I," said Scott.

Helen pointed to a glade on the right side of the road. "We're holed up in there. The forest is honeycombed with animal trails. Watch out for the critters that make them: two-legged dinosaurs like giant turkeys. They run like the devil, but if you get them cornered they'll peck you to pieces." She pointed to her bare thigh; the bronzed flesh was pockmarked. "Fortunately, they don't have teeth."

Scott would have walked into the fence had not Helen stopped the procession. The strands were made of clear plastic and stretched from tree to tree to a height of ten feet. Helen took them through a gate that had been made by burning the drawn plastic off tree-mounted pegs. When everyone was inside, she lashed the strands together with sections of vine.

The sun was not yet visible because of the depth of the stronghold inside the glacier, but the sky was brightening. The tall grass in the glade wavered as scuttling creatures dashed away from the approaching warriors. Helen took them to a nook created by dense, overhanging branches. Waiting for them, with weapons drawn, were half a dozen women who were guarding supplies.

"So where's the fighting?" Sam wanted to know.

"There hasn't been any—except for the trouble you stirred up. Out here it's been quiet as a spring morn, with nothing moving but these damnable insects the dragons must have brought up from the past."

"Hell, I thought we were getting in a major confrontation."

Helen shook her head. "No, that truck must have been a border patrol vehicle. When I saw them coming down the road I ran across the bridge and hid on the parapet. They didn't know I was there. It wasn't until I saw you in the nightlights, and they started to cross the bridge, that I went to warn you."

"Well, the alarm's given now." Sam looked back at the smoke curling up from the tunnel entrance. "I asked the Nomads not to give us away, and I went ahead and did it myself. Now we're in for it."

"Our hand is certainly tipped," Doc admitted with a wry grin. "What began as a siege has just been promoted to full-scale invasion. I suggest that while we are experiencing a temporary lull in the fighting, we push our advantage toward the inner stronghold."

"Let's do it. Helen, get your gals together and follow us with all the supplies. We don't know what we'll run into. Windy, send your fastest troops ahead with the message that we're attacking in force. Work out flanking maneuvers with Broderick. And if you can catch up with Bold One tell him to—uh—hell, the jig is up. Just tell him to use his head."

Windy threw off a salute and dropped back to his platoon.

The Femme Fatales within hearing range did not need to have Sam's orders repeated by Helen. Helen said, "What about the cannon?"

Scott thought about the weeks of hard work dragging the heavy-duty laser cannon through the Pleistocene forests and swamps, across the continental ice fields, through the long glacial tunnel, until it had to be lowered by ropes down the cliff face, loaded on a raft, and paddled across the near-freezing waters of the lake. An incredible amount of energy had gone into getting it this far.

"It may be the only thing that'll knock out those armored trucks."

Sam rubbed his hands over his black beard. "You're right, Scott. Hell, we brought it this far, we're not gonna leave it now. Windy," he called out. "Detail a couple of men to cut a path for the cannon. Helen, can your gals manage to keep hauling it?"

"You try and stop them and you'll have a mutiny on your hands."

Sam gave her a quick kiss. "That's the spirit." He raised his voice authoritatively. "Okay, let's move out."

Two women slipped into the traces of the travois with the laser cannon and its battery packs. Others picked up packs of food, fuel, tools and utensils, and miscellaneous supplies. The Rangers struck out through the forest, beating a path through the brush and chasing out the dinosaurian vermin that flocked in hiding.

After thirty minutes the troops made a strip stop. Scott shed his long-sleeved tunic and cut the leggings off his trousers. Tropical conditions seemed unnatural during an ice age and in the middle of a glacier. If the dragons could not land in a time that suited their needs, they converted the environment to suit them.

Death Wind appeared among them as silently as a wraith. "Got message. We still undercover."

Sam stuck out his hand and grappled arms in traditional Nomad style. "Good to see you, Death Wind. Are all your people okay?"

The single, slight tilt of his head was an affirmative nod.

"What about enemy movement?"

"Trucks in road, but dragons stay out of woods."

Sam scowled. "We could snipe them to pieces if they'd fight on our grounds. Okay, what's the layout? How close to stronghold central can we get in the trees?"

"Some pens big dinosaurs, we avoid. Other pens little. Soon we come to end. Buildings. Roads. Much traffic now."

"You know we blew our cover?"

Death Wind nodded. "Dragons not know we are in pens. We wait for orders. Once we leave forest, all is open. No cover."

"Good work, Death Wind. Well, Henry, what's your advice? In twenty-five words or less."

Doc pursed his lips and tugged on his beard. "Quite a task, considering my penchant for verbosity." He paused to collect his thoughts. "Since we have control of this quadrant only, and since the roads between quadrants are now being patrolled, chances are that we cannot successfully execute our original diversionary tactic. Therefore, instead of feinting from opposite sides, I suggest that we make a direct frontal approach with everything we have."

"Take the ball and run right up the middle, huhn? It smacks of the kind of audacity I'd expect from you. But the troops'll be exposed to danger the whole way. And if the dragons've got those shielded vehicles to hide behind, we'll be at a disadvantage. You saw our laser beams bounce off the armor belt."

"If you want a guaranteed victory, I cannot offer it. The only guarantee in war is that of an honorable death."

Sam sighed. "I don't like to hear that, but ignoring the truth won't make it go away. Okay, let's get on with it. I want everyone massed at the innermost fence, the Rangers at one end, the Fusiliers at the other. The rest of us'll spread out in a line between."

It took an hour to get into position, by which time the dragon border patrol was in full force. Surprisingly, the actual count of enemy soldiers was not what was expected.

"You know, it makes sense in a crazy kind of way," Scott crouched by the trunk of a magnolia tree and peered through the brush at a patrol truck passing slowly along the inner circle route. His hands sweated in anticipation of the upcoming battle. "This place isn't built like a fort or garrisoned like we'd expect. The dragons couldn't have known in advance that it would have to be defended—not even by wild animals. I don't think we're going to find much resistance."

"I do not want to appear overconfident, but I quite agree with you." Doc knelt with his bad leg stretched out; he balanced himself with his cane. "The stronghold appears to be impregnable because of the sheer ice walls. Once it was cut off from the other time zones there was no way to bring in reinforcements. These armored trucks are more likely proof against escaped dinosaurs—such as those triceratops."

"Theories later. For now I'm gonna expect the worse." Sam blew a signal on his whistle. "All right, let's go get 'em. First thing we do is take out that truck."

The fence was cut in a dozen places. As the nearly invisible strands fell away the commandos slipped through and created a battlefront. Two women dragged the laser cannon out of cover and parked it at the edge of the road. The truck slowed; it was in range of the cannon, but the cannon was not in range of back-carried guns of the soldiers on the truck.

One well-placed shot blew away the grill, and destroyed the motor and the first two axles. A loud hurrah went up from the commando ranks. Sam blew the signal to charge. The entire company flowed out of the trees and onto the road, completely uncontested. They screamed like a tribe of attacking Indians in a Western movie.

Scott felt the thrill of excitement race through his body. His plastic stump whacked against the pavement, but he ignored the pain. The exhilaration of the charge obliterated all other feelings. This was man primeval: a raw, uncomplicated bundle of nerves, acting instinctively and without forethought; the deeply embedded trait that carried men into battle without fear of death; the unreasoning part of the brain left over from earlier evolutionary beginnings.

The time transport structure stood nearly a mile away, tall and coruscating. Between that and the edge of the forest and dinosaur pens lay low buildings, courtyards, alleys and pathways, and a series of thoroughfares radiating outward from the TTS like the strands of a spiderweb. The commandos raced toward the center of the stronghold screaming war cries.

Scott was unable to hop about the plastic barricades like the others, so he stayed on the main road, leading the way for the gun carriers. An armored truck coming straight toward him slowly extended its flaps and deployed marching dragons.

"Come on, let's blast them!" Scott shouted to the cannoneers.

It took but a moment for the women to pivot the travois in a semicircle in order to train the laser nozzle at the truck. The first shot blew off one of the flaps and bowled it over the soldiers hiding behind it. Scott whooped as he ran along the roadside bulkhead toward the regrouping dragons. He heard the cannon charger whining, felt a blast of heat, saw the other flap destroyed and another squad of dragons knocked onto their tails.

"Way to go!"

The truck's cargo bay disgorged another squad of soldiers. This was no nighttime patrol, but a fully loaded troop carrier. Laser beams licked the orangetop at Scott's foot; he ducked into an archway that led into a courtyard filled with lawn furniture and fleeing slaves. Hand-to-hand combat between Fusiliers and the house's inhabitants was raging unchecked.

Scott dashed up the interior ramp to the top of the roadside bulkhead. From this vantage point he fired down into the slow-moving soldiers. A flight of arrows descended into the melee as a squad of Nomads attacked from the other side of the road. The dragons were cut to pieces in the crossfire. Another blast from the cannon lifted the front of the truck straight into the air; for a moment it hung there like a rearing stallion, the wheels of all ten axles spinning madly. Then it fell forward with a crash and lay still in a cloud of smoke.

Using the bulkhead as a highway Scott raced alongside the road, vaulting the archways as he passed from courtyard to courtyard. The weight of the battery pack was offset by the flow of adrenaline. Soon he was far ahead of the rest of the troops, deep in enemy-held territory.

Another armored truck turned the corner of an intersection and bore down upon him. The laser cannon was hundreds of yards away, on the other side of the flaming debris of the demolished truck. Scott hunkered down and waited for the troop carrier to pass. He sniped at a reptilian head that stuck out above the folded flaps; the lightning bolt arced through the open mouth and out the back of the scaled head.

Scott was chased off the bulkhead by three retaliatory laser beams. He plastered himself to the parapet until the dragons adjusted their sights and fired their needle beams right through the plastic bulkhead. On hands and knees he scrambled out of the line of fire. He had never felt more alive than after that moment of escape.

The truck halted to take on the single attacker. Scott popped his head over the bulkhead, fired, ducked, and crawled away before the return shots riddled the bulkhead and left it looking like a colander. Try as he might, he could not make a hit once the dragons were aware of his presence; they stayed behind their armor and fired through tiny slits as they adjusted their aim by looking through small transparent ports. As long as the dragons stayed inside, they were impregnable to assault by small-arms fire.

The Nomads beat this technical standoff with primitive weapons that could do one thing that Scott's laser gun could not do: go around corners. They lobbed their arrows high in the air and let them curve into the open cab. Two dragons were transfixed with the deadly plastic tips. A second flight did as much damage. Under the protection of a third volley Death Wind sprang across the open space between the opposite bulkhead and the truck, and flattened himself behind the rear armor beneath the gun ports.

As soon as another flight of arrows thwacked into the cab, he grabbed hold of the top rim, pulled himself up, and stabbed his spear into the nearest head. Then he fell back down and got low. After another volley pinned the dragons in their truck, he repeated the maneuver with the same effect. One dragon stuck his laser nozzle over the top and fired straight down at the Nomad. The blast dug up orangetop, but Death Wind managed to sidestep the actual beam.

Scott stood up in full view on top of the bulkhead, stretched his arm out straight, and fired an energy beam right through the dragon's snakelike neck. It hissed painfully as it fell back atop one of its comrades. Scott gave Death Wind a thumbs-up. The Nomad returned the sign.

The truck retreated. The Nomad squad launched another volley of arrows into the troop carrier. Death Wind repeated his tactic. Scott sniped whenever he saw scales. Then Death Wind climbed onto the armor flap, straddled it with his legs, and picked off the stunned dragons with eager dispatch. Finally, he dropped inside the cab, slipped up behind the driver, and jabbed him through the back with his spear.

Scott rolled off the bulkhead, hung by his hands, and plopped down to the road surface. He climbed up the side of the truck. "Nice going, Death Wind." In a flash he was inside, putting a stranglehold on the driver. "Give me a hand."

Together they dragged the heavy lizard out of the seat. They left it in the cargo compartment with the rest of the bodies.

Scott shrugged out of his battery pack and took over the controls. "Okay, let's turn this baby around and head for the command center. Then we'll give them some of their own medicine."

By now the shouts and shots of combat filled the air on all sides. The commandos were largely avoiding the streets where armored vehicles could hold them at bay. Instead, they dashed through the living quarters raising mayhem, and headed straight for the main objective: ignoring the pawns and going for the king.

While Scott turned and backed up the truck, the Nomad squad boarded, found the hydraulic mechanism that opened the rear armored flaps, and, after removing their precious arrows from the bodies, chucked out the dead and dying dragon soldiers.

"Wait for me," shouted a familiar voice.

Scott slammed the control rod into the neutral position and let the vehicle coast to a stop. "Hop aboard, Doc. This is the express bus to the time transfer station." Scott brought the multiaxled vehicle into a sharp turn by reversing the independent wheels on the left side as the right side wheels were still turning forward. "Just like you said, Doc: right up the middle. Dragon central here we come."

The truck lurched forward. Since the armored control cabin was designed for long-necked dragons, Scott had to stand in order to see out the pilot port. It felt good having a machine under his control again.

"I must say, my boy, you have not lost any of your driving skills."

"Hey, I've been tooling these things around for sixty million years. Not to shower praise, but if you've driven one dragon vehicle, you can drive them all. They're consistent that way."

"Typical dragon uniformity. It is that predictable psychology that has allowed us to follow their temporal wanderings with such comparative ease."

"Yes, well, let's not start getting overconfident. We've done that too many times in the past—and in the future."

"I quite agree, my boy. I quite agree."

The truck hummed along the street unopposed. The sights and sounds of fighting were far behind. Death Wind stood on a platform with his head over the top of the cab; his long black hair whipped about in the breeze. The other Nomads kept a constant vigil on all sides.

"Doc, this is too easy. I'm getting scared."

"I understand your feelings. I am experiencing some trepidation myself. However, I can find no logical reason not to continue our course of action. Unless they have a cannon of their own, this vehicle is unstoppable."

Death Wind shouted, "There!"

Scott slowed down as the truck approached an intersection. Steam escaping from vents at the base of the roadside bulkhead formed heat waves in the air. Slaves and technicians milling in the alleyway appeared to dance sinuously through the inversion layer. Death Wind and the other Nomads ducked quickly, and stayed low inside the cargo compartment, so as not to give away the presence of an invasionary force.

"Look at that!" Scott shouted with glee. "They don't even know the stronghold's under attack."

"Let us not assume that those in command are as ignorant. They did not send troops in armored vehicles as an ordinary course of events."

The TTS towered before them like a pulsating blue monolith.

Because of focusing node leakage it did not pay to recharge the capacitor banks unless a transfer was intended.

"Looks like they're getting ready to do something." Scott squinted through the Plexiglas port. "Reinforcements, maybe."

Now that the day was begun, the streets were crowded with dragons lumbering to their work stations. Scott slowed and weaved through the unsuspecting dragons.

"Hey, aren't they walking a little faster than normal?"

"Listen to toner," said Death Wind. "It give warning."

"Where's it coming—" Then he saw one. Mounted on posts at each intersection were tonal repeaters, like loudspeakers that played only dragon message music.

Doc pursed his lips. "Another case of the unexpected. They are already mobilizing their defenses."

The crowds grew thicker. The dragons paid no mind to the troop carrier, apparently unaware that a captured vehicle was invading their inner sanctum. Scott slowed down even more. He did not want to give away their strategy.

"Notice that building on the left," Doc said softly. "The massive array of external piping is characteristic of a chemical factory. And it seems to me that the TTS is taller and slimmer than the others we have encountered: cylindrical as opposed to dome-like."

"Terrific, Doc, but let's forget about scientific observations and concentrate on our primary goal. Unless we knock out that missile site we can't call Rusty for backup."

"Uh, quite right, my boy. I suppose that once we are reunited with the *Ark* we will have unlimited time for future studies."

"So let's avoid trouble and look around for a launching pad or an underground silo."

"It would not detract from our objective to first disable the time transporter. At this point that is a more tangible quantity, the results of which are every bit as important."

"Well, at least it would prevent the dragons from launching an attack through time." Scott made quick decision. "Okay, let's go for it."

He accelerated through throngs of dragons that were now showing signs of anxiety: the sluggish pace had picked up, and beady eyes twitched nervously. Toned commands directed workers to emergency stations and tasks that were unclearly defined, as if no battle plan existed for defense of the stronghold.

"This time I think we caught them completely by surprise,"

said Scott, grinning uncontrollably; his cheeks were about to burst from the strain. "Dragons have been taking up too much of our time, but I think after today their dominion will be timeless."

"I pray that your prophecy is not deterred by that line of defense consolidating up ahead."

Several dragons wearing brightly colored capes directed a loose band of soldiers into ranks. Laser guns were drawn and aimed.

"Keep your heads down back there," Scott called out. "When Scott's afoot, dragons are in trouble."

The armored truck broke free from the crowd. The roadside bulkhead gave way to open orangetop that surrounded generating equipment, machinery, storage sheds, and mechanical spaces. Scott kept a steady hand on the control rod as the truck ran the gauntlet of bewildered soldiers. The first laser beam struck harmlessly against the side armor. Another blasted the front grill. The reinforced energy-absorbing plastic shields protected the truck and its occupants from small-arms fire.

"Unless they've got bigger guns than that, we're crashing this party like there's no tomorrow."

"I wish you could phrase that somewhat differently," chafed Doc. "That has such an aura of finality about it."

"There!" shouted Death Wind, pointing to the right.

A single-passenger vehicle operated by a caped administrator shot out of a motor pool. The dragon's mouth was open in a hiss that was lost in the cacophony of squealing wheels, zapping laser beams, and exploding lightning bolts.

Scott turned in its direction. "Stand by to ram."

The huge truck rolled over the hood of the roofless car, crushing the engine compartment and bringing the smaller vehicle to a grinding halt. The dragon driver was hurled through the windshield and under the truck's last two axle trains; the reptilian head was squashed like soft dough. The truck trundled on unabated.

None of the Nomads could return a shot, even with the power weapons taken from the vanquished dragon soldiers. To stick a head above the upper shield was to have it baked in the heat of deadly crisscrossing laser beams.

"Hang on, people," Scott sang out excitedly. He was so happy to be in the thick of things with Doc and Death Wind that nothing was going to slow him down. "It's going to get rough."

Doc wedged himself into a corner and held tight on to a support bar. "You mean rougher."

Dragon soldiers faded back from the path of the rampaging

troop carrier. Scott swerved from side to side, running over taloned toes or knocking lizards head over heels. One woman in the cargo compartment lost her grip and bounced off the walls like a billiard ball until another Nomad caught her. Lightning bolts bounced off armor as if they were no more powerful than flashlight beams.

"Way to go, Scott."

Scott did a double take. He stared at Death Wind for so long that the Nomad had to grab the control rod and straighten out the truck. Scott's jaw dropped; he had never heard Death Wind exhibit such emotion. He was speechless.

There were no more soldiers in front of them. Parting shots sizzled through the air, but were easily absorbed by the rear shield. The path to the TTS was clear. The truck sped across the lowered drawbridge. Mist rising off the cold water condensed in the hot air and clung like a shroud; the swirling white cloak had prevented distant observation of the TTS layout.

"What the—" A thick plastic slab rose to a height of twenty feet around the base of the elongated time transport structure. A garage door being swung shut was attended by a host of technicians, effectively sealing off the transfer area. The focusing nodes were wound to full excitement; blue static discharges crackled off the tips as if the entire structure were drooling electricity. Scott found his voice. "Whatever they're sending or receiving must be important."

Doc peered through a forward observation port. "The slab must be five feet thick. And why would they need a revetment—"

"This is no time to ask questions," Scott shouted. "Hang on, I'm going to ram the command center. Whatever that shipment is will be their last."

He hunkered down and braced his real foot against the forward bulkhead. He held on to the throttle with one hand and with the other prepared to meet the shock of collision. Doc put his back to the wall and closed his eyes. Death Wind wrapped his steely fingers around a support bar. He let out a savage scream that was the Nomad war cry. The other Nomads, hanging on to rods in the cargo compartment, whooped in chorus.

"Ready or not, here we come."

The time transport control equipment was housed in an adjoining building with a clear Plexiglas front. Two caped dragons and a pawful of technicians idled around consoles and computer monitors. Those not facing the glass turned around and hissed at the oncoming truck. They had time to do nothing more.

The armored grill crashed through the wall of glass with an awful, gut-rending jar. Shards of glass and plastic exploded inward from the force of the collision. The momentum of mass and speed carried the truck right over the nearest computer consoles and their reptilian programmers, and into the farthest, wall-mounted modules.

Scott was slammed against the forward bulkhead hard enough to knock the wind out of him and wrench a shoulder. He saw stars for a moment. When he opened his eyes he saw Death Wind crumpled in front of him; the Nomad shook his head and spit out a clot of blood. Then he looked up at Scott and gave him the thumbs-up.

Scott smiled. He heard a groan in the corner. Doc waved his hands in front of his face to clear the air. Dust and smoke filled the cabin. "Doc, are you okay?" Scott pulled him out of his fetal position and dragged him into the open air of the cargo compartment.

The doctor coughed once or twice as he groped for balance. "I am fine, but I fear that we may have damaged the transporter equipment."

"Damaged it!" Scott screamed. "Doc, we demolished it."

Nomads rose from the dust like a flock of phoenixes. None was hurt.

Doc brushed himself off. "We may have jammed the controls, but it does not look as if we have affected the present transfer."

Bits of glass and chunks of framing tinkled down from the ruined building. Scott peered through the smoke and still-falling debris at the coruscating focusing nodes that were still spitting arcs. "Well, we can fix that." He dragged a laser gun out of the wreckage, slung it over one shoulder, and clambered up the sidewall of the truck.

No living dragons were left in the command center. The crew of technicians that had been shuffling out of the revetment approached warily until they saw Scott emerge from the cargo compartment. Then they hissed, turned tail, and waddled off like mute ducks.

"Come on!" Scott called to his companions. He dropped into the remains of the control room, amid a dozen small fires caused by electrical shorts. Pipes, wires, plastic parts, and electronic components lay in a heap, their original forms unrecognizable. He waded through the smoldering debris to the central console. Flames licked up through the main control panel.

Scott stabbed the crystal eject button and pulled his hand back before his finger got burned. Nothing happened. Either the power was off or the mechanism was jammed. The console was quickly being consumed by fire. Scott pulled out his knife and jabbed the point into the bubbled facing. The hardened material did not yield easily. He pried off chunks of plastic until he exposed the locking gate, then forced the loading cam off its rails. He burnt the hair off his knuckles, but a moment later he held the diamond cube in his hand; the crystal surface was blackened with soot.

"For posterity," Scott said proudly, ignoring the pain of singed flesh.

The Nomads helped Doc down from the truck's high sidewalls. With pinched eyes the doctor gazed at the crystal surface blackened with soot. "Is it damaged?"

Scott humphed. "No way. It'd take more than low heat and a layer of graphite to rearrange the molecular lattice or prevent data entry and access." He stuck the data crystal into a pocket and resheathed his knife. "Let's go."

Scott, with singleness of purpose, did not wait for compliance, but kicked open the door with his artificial leg and stepped out into the sunlight. The air was hot, still, and humid. He strode straight for the massive door of the TTS revetment. It was not locked, but a powerful spring kept it closed. Without electricity to the hydraulic system he could not open it alone.

"Give me a hand."

It took all of them yanking on the full-length handle to swing it back enough to slip aside. They were in a huge room dimly lit by ceiling globes twenty feet overhead.

"The power's still on. Must have an underplastic feed."

"There should be a locking mechanism—"

"Forget it, Doc. Let it close." Scott wasted no time on trivialities, but strode across the cluttered room to the opposite door. Even inside the thick plastic walls he could hear the whining of the chargers; the focusing nodes were wound up to nearly full excitement. The closure on the inner door was the same. "Hey, I need a hand with this one, too."

Doc ambled along behind, poking and prodding the strange devices, crates of equipment and supplies, and partially assembled machinery. "This must be a storage facility for—"

"I said, forget it." Scott and the Nomads struggled with the other door. "We haven't got much time."

"This is curious." Doc stopped by a wheeled cradle covered with a synthetic tarp. He pulled off the covering to reveal a clear cylinder the size of a fifty-five-gallon drum. He stood like a stop-action character about to be animated.

With the Nomads pulling on the handle, the mammoth door opened enough for Scott and Death Wind to get their hands around the fat lip. They opened the door a body width. Heterodyning focusing nodes screamed; blue sparks showered off the inward pointing tips. Death Wind braced his shoulder against the door while Scott squeezed through. "Doc, are you coming?"

Doc was motionless. He stared at Scott with a quixotic expression on his face and a faraway look in his eyes. "I believe we are on the threshold of a great discovery."

"You got that right. Okay, you people stay here and hold the door." Scott stepped into the time transfer chamber. Death Wind was right behind him.

A hundred feet away stood a shimmering purple curtain that rose skyward like a round-topped granary. Surrounding it was the structure on which were mounted the focusing nodes, crackling in the charged atmosphere. The air smelled of ozone.

Scott studied a nearby instrument panel. The gauges indicated that the capacitors were fully charged: the transfer could take place anytime. He felt the vibration of machinery through his foot and artificial leg: the transmission lines, the charging apparatus, the transformers, all were buried beneath the plastic decking.

"Either it's jammed, or it's set on automatic sequencing." Scott pulled the laser gun out of its holster and fanned it across the board of meters. Perhaps if he destroyed the instrumentation—

"Come quick!"

Scott jolted at Death Wind's faraway shout. The Nomad was no longer standing next to him, but poised at the edge of the purple curtain. He waved for Scott to join him. Even as he watched, Death Wind stepped through the opaque barrier and disappeared.

"Death Wind!" Scott hobbled awkwardly because of his fake leg and the heavy battery pack slung over one shoulder by a single strap. He stopped at the edge of eternity. The static charge made his hair stand on end. He could hardly breathe. Looking up, he saw the yellow crescent of sunlight that circled the open top of the time transport structure. He felt like a microbe at the bottom of a ballpoint pen, between the cartridge and the holder.

The Nomad popped back into reality, grabbed Scott by the shoulder, and yanked him into the dead zone. The noise, the light, the odor, everything was gone: except the vibration. In the middle of the cone, where he expected to see a stack of supplies or a contingent of escaping dragons, was an empty floor that slowly slid apart like the iris diaphragm of a camera.

"What the—"

A bitterly cold mist rose out of the opening. When the floor stopped dilating it left a circular pit of unplumbed depths. Despite his goose bumps, Scott stepped close to the edge and looked down. Thick, crystalline flakes surged upward past a pointed cone. A sudden explosion was followed by a blast of heat and a blue ring of fire that vaporized the artificial snow. Then the cone ascended, imperceptibly at first, but with slowly increasing speed.

"Get out! Get out!" Scott screamed. His voice was swallowed up by the tenuous atmosphere. "Hurry!"

Death Wind needed no urging. He plopped through the curtain into the world of real time.

Scott saw the cone rise up out of the floor, heard the roar of rockets, then passed out of the semireality of impending time travel.

Death Wind shouted as he ran. "Close door!"

Scott was hampered by the off-centered weight of the battery pack. He struggled with the strap as he hobbled across the deck. He did not manage to dislodge it until he reached the door that the Nomads held open for him. He dropped the laser gun and skidded through the opening just as a tongue of flame erupted through the purple curtain and engulfed the staging area. His back was singed.

Then the door was slammed shut, and the missile rose unseen on a pillar of energy into the nebulous reaches of time.

CHAPTER 27

Rusty shoved Britt's hand aside and answered the bridge toner himself. To Ned's all-clear signal, he responded, "Sit rep."

Ned's toned situation report was concise. "Victory. Come get us."

Rusty placed his fingertips on the keys again, to ask for clarification, but realized that Ned did not want to get involved in long-range tone talk when he could report verbally in a few minutes. Ned did not understand the anxiety level of those who had remained behind in the *Ark*. He toned simply, "Acknowledged."

Britt powered up the reactor pile. "If anyone was hurt, he would say so."

"Yes, I guess you're right." Still, Rusty did not like negative communication. It often left too much to interpretation. He folded his long body into the pilot's seat and ran his fingers over the controls. "Give the all-aboard."

Britt used the intercom toner to pass the message. One by one the various stations responded. The techs in training fidgeted in their seats as they looked to Rusty for guidance. He nodded silently and prepared the ship for takeoff.

The *Ark* lifted as smoothly on her power-beam pylons as if she were being hoisted by a hydraulic ram. At first the downscreen view was blurred: intense heat produced by the lifting cones reflected off the ground, each beam intermingling with those around it. As the ship rose above the reach of her own fire, the blackened, burned-out landing zone stood out amid the lush green foliage of the surrounding forest.

Rusty leveled off the *Ark* at five hundred feet, applied forward momentum, and sat back to watch the scenery as the flyer cruised over a landscape that was pristine in the abundance of life. Herds of cattle and horses grazed on lush plains, seemingly oblivious to the saucer passing overhead. Tall oaks and taller redwoods cloaked a menagerie of wildlife. The treetops were alive with the song and the color of nesting birds. A fantastic array of ground dwellers moved like a carpet across the brush-covered topsoil. Flowering plants grew in great profusion. The land was alive.

The only scars were those left by the *Ark*'s brief touchdown and the recent dragon incursion. Left to its own devices, the Earth would soon obliterate all traces of both.

"Britt, tell the gunners to be on the alert. And watch the scanners and radarscope."

Britt nodded perfunctorily.

The *Ark* thrummed along with effortless ease. Rusty kept a sharp eye on the viewscreens. The sky was clear and blue, the outside temperature comfortable. If there was anything hostile down there, it was well hidden.

The toner sang. Ned reported that he could hear the *Ark* approaching. A few minutes later he toned that he had made visual contact. "LZ cleared."

Rusty slowed the *Ark* to a crawl, and gradually dropped elevation until she slipped over the upper canopy with just enough height to avoid singeing the leaves. As the machine coasted over the dragon advance base he saw Ned's assault troops indicating a landing zone. The *Ark* hovered directly over the clearing. The remains of two prefabricated sheds hugged the perimeter, and dragon bodies lay scattered about from the recent fight. The solid plastic pad that was the foundation for the time transport structure, whose construction had not yet begun, was a place that Rusty wanted to avoid. He did not want the flyer parked in a spot where an object transferred through time might suddenly materialize. The effect on the *Ark* would be as disastrous as the backlash to the sending unit: mathematics proved conclusively that two material objects could not occupy the same space at the same time. Displacing air at one atmospheric pressure required enormous power; in addition, the energy of arrival was dissipated by an expanding shock wave equivalent to an aerial detonation.

Ned toned landing instructions as the *Ark* settled in place. The troops backed away from the tongues of purple flame. Rusty tapped vernier buttons in reverse, gradually diminishing the power to the lifting cones. The *Ark* landed as softly as she had taken off.

"Okay, shut her down," Rusty left the purely mechanical procedures to his crew. "Come on, Britt, let's go check it out."

Outside, Rusty and Britt dashed across the still-smoking grass. Rusty should have been ecstatic over their easy triumph; instead, he was troubled by the very fact Ned found so exciting.

"Your timing was pretty good. The dragons can't have been

here more than a few days—a week at most. There was only one leader, two techs, half a dozen soldiers, and a bunch of goons. We made mincemeat out of 'em—it was nothing more than a mopping-up operation."

Rusty surveyed the crude advance base. "Where's the missile silo?"

"Ain't none. What you see is what you got." Ned stuck his hand behind his head and scratched his scalp. "Sure is a puzzler where that thing came from, 'less they had it sitting there on the TTS pad. Believe me, we checked everywhere. There's nothing within a mile of this place that didn't either grow or was born here. I wouldn't have given the all-clear otherwise."

Rusty strode toward the circular pad. "It looks blackened, and ripply. But why would they have a missile sitting in the middle of their transfer platform?"

"Beats me. But you notice they didn't have any buildings close by, either. They're all way over on the other side of the clearing."

Rusty stopped at the edge of the pad. "Is it solid?"

"Appears that way. Following orders, I didn't let anyone walk on it in case they got caught in a transfer."

Rusty nodded silently, observing.

"We found powdered mix in the storage shed. They got bags of it, and an epoxy additive, too. That's how they poured their plastic. And—"

"All right, let's get away from here in case they make another transfer. Even a small mass sent into a nonevacuated medium will cause quite a concussion."

"Could be another reason why the sheds are on the other—"

"Ned, let's saddle up and get out of here, now. I want to make a slow circuit to look for remote installations. Did you find any electronic equipment or receiver apparatus?"

"Yes, but we destroyed most of it already. Saved some for you to look at, 'cause it didn't look familiar to me. Figured you'd want to check it out yourself. All battery operated. And they got wires running off into the woods—booby traps, most likely, or alarms. We can—"

"No, we'll do that later. Right now I want your troops out of here. Until we know for sure where that missile came from, we have no way of knowing whether or not they've established an auxiliary station that can launch a missile from a remote site."

"Hey, I never thought of that. Maybe we should—"

"We're leaving now, Ned. Britt, let's get started."

Rusty left Ned to gather his troops while he and Britt double-timed to the bridge. In short order the *Ark* was airborne. This time he took her straight up to an altitude of five hundred feet. The lateral thrusters were silent. The *Ark* idled in place as Rusty and a host of lookouts scanned the horizon for signs of the enemy.

"We're so close that unless a missile is fired right under us—"

A titanic explosion erupted on the TTS pad. The flyer rocked violently and was lifted bodily on a column of expanding air. Rusty was pressed down in his seat by the sudden upward acceleration, then thrown to the floor by the *Ark*'s wild gyrations.

On the downscreen monitor he saw a bright ball of blue flame spreading outward and upward. In the middle was a dark, cone-shaped object. His shock was so great that several seconds passed before he realized that he was looking at the business end of an approaching missile. The slender projectile rose slowly at first, struggling to break the bonds of gravity. As it gained momentum it accelerated along a nearly vertical axis toward the hovering *Ark*.

"It's impossible!" Rusty leaped back to his console. His fingers hesitated over the control board. There was no way the lateral thrusters could move the massive bulk of the *Ark* out of the way in time to avoid the deadly missile. Even if the warhead malfunctioned as the last one had, a direct hit would prove fatal: the *Ark* would crash before Rusty could regain control.

Although the equation was simple, his brain burned in turmoil at the decision he had to make: if the *Ark* could not move in space, then she had to move in time. And Rusty had time for only one quick action.

He slammed his fist down on the reversing switch.

CHAPTER 28

When the flames hit the laser gun's battery pack, incineration was immediate. The capacitor exploded against the bulkhead, shattering plastic, cracking the hinge, and partially dislocating the door. Flames licked into the storage room for only a moment. Then there was a tremendous whap as the focusing nodes discharged against their target.

All was silent.

The silence went on and on.

After what seemed like an eternity Scott drew in a deep breath of air. It tasted hot and pungent. He had skidded into a stack of pallets; enough empty, lightweight packing cases had fallen on his head to bury him. He struggled out from under the pile of debris. He did not hurt, and did not appear to be injured.

"Hey, is anyone alive?"

Doc lay on the floor with a tarp covering his body like a shroud. When he sat up he looked like a third-rate movie ghost wearing a sheet. He pulled the tarp off his face. "We appear to have survived another bout against the nominally unexpected."

Nomads lay scattered on the floor like discarded dolls. One by one they picked themselves up. Death Wind felt for bumps on his head. "Okay."

Scott dug dust out of his eyes. "Doc, we've solved the missile crisis. All this time, the launching pad was *under* the transporter. No wonder we couldn't find it."

"I suspected as much, although I did not grasp the full significance of its placement until now."

"Huhn?" On hands and knees Scott shuffled through the loose crates to Doc's side. "You mean you *knew*? Is that why you wanted to shut down the transporter first?"

Doc stroked his beard. "Let us say that the existence of an underground complex was indicated by the lack of visible evidence to the contrary. Mine was not an eminently inspired idea, merely one of deductive reasoning. Nor should the concept of a subterranean launch site be difficult to grasp for one of your experience."

Scott grimaced. "I guess I've spent so much time putting myself into dragon shoes, and thinking in terms of alien psychology, that I just never thought we'd both go about something the same way. They're always so *different*."

"It was you who said that all electrons flow alike no matter who drew the wire through which they move."

Scott held up his hands in defense. "But that's not the same. An electron is a product of nature, and thereby inviolable. Technology is a method of form that's developed according to the ideology of the originator."

"According to universal principles."

"Well, yes, but—"

A hand clamped down on Scott's shoulder. "Fight when right. Admit wrong." Death Wind winked at him.

Scott sighed deeply. "Okay. I'm wrong. But I still don't understand why they— Hey, wait a minute." He leaped to his feet and rushed to the jammed inner bulkhead door. He peered through a stress crack into the time transport structure. The focusing nodes were dark and quiet; the shimmering purple curtain was gone. Bright sunlight streaming down the inside of the tower illuminated the floor; the iris diaphragm was still open. "We've knocked out the recharging circuit, but the missile— Where did it go? *When* did it go?"

"That is an answer which at the moment eludes me, at least in relation to this particular missile fired at this particular time." Doc rapped his knuckles on the plastic cylinder next to him. "But this explains why the missile that hit the *Ark* did not explode. It was not armed with a warhead—was not, in fact, designed as a weapon of offense. Together with this rather elongated time transport structure, the dragon missiles acted as the delivery system for the mass euthanasia devices."

Death Wind gently, almost reverently laid his hand on the clear, glassy surface. "Death bomb."

"Yes. And that means that the Pleistocene stronghold must have been the first future base constructed in the dragon life extension program."

Scott passed the squad of Nomads who were listening attentively. "You mean, the dragons came here—er, now—in the beginning of their temporal campaign rather than later? But why?"

"It all fits neatly into place. Our own time—the Holocene—lay at the limit of dragon time travel due to the inherent engineering design of their transport equipment. When they constructed this stonghold it was not only with the intention of leapfrogging into a further future time, but for the purpose of carrying out the practical aspects of their nefarious plan of conquest. Do you remember the distillation plant we passed on the way in?"

Scott had to think a moment before he vaguely remembered Doc mentioning it. "Sure."

"The dragons undoubtedly figured that the genocide chemical was too dangerous to produce in quantity in their own time zone—an accident could conceivably bring about the Great Dying they were endeavoring to circumvent. How convenient to manufacture the deadly product now, when a handling mishap would not affect their home world.

"However, there was still the matter of releasing the chemical into the atmosphere above the various continents a million years hence. They did not have sufficiently advanced technology to construct a flying time machine such as the *Ark*, so they did the next best thing—they devised a stationary time portal through which they could launch missiles carrying the bombs to their future destinations."

Scott's jaw dropped to his chest. "Why, that's—that's ingenious."

"Do not communicate your exuberance to Sam. He does not share our appreciation for the dragon's brilliance of concept."

"But, what about the missile that hit the *Ark*? And those others?"

Doc shrugged. "Dummy missiles without payload, modified for defense after we destroyed their home world. Dragons do not use explosives, thus they had none on hand with which to arm their warheads. I believe it was Rusty who said that a missile does not need to destroy a craft, it merely has to damage it severely enough so it can no longer fly. As you recollect, we did nearly crash."

"So you're saying these missiles weren't designed to shoot down aircraft, they were leftovers put to another use?"

"Exactly. Once they executed their devastating pogrom against life in our time zone, and planted their seeding farms to cultivate the kind of livestock and vegetation they wanted for the future, it was easier to drop later death bombs—on continents where they had not yet spread their influence—from flyers on exploratory missions. The extra missiles in the stronghold were probably being held in reserve for emergency use. You know the dragon's penchant for triple redundancy."

Scott nodded slowly, lost in thought. Then he remembered his sister. "And the crypts? Are those slaves and dragons in waiting?"

Doc nodded slowly. "Biding their time, so to speak. Remaining in stasis, in youth and good health, until the time is right—or will be right—to repopulate the future world."

"But, why wait? Why not send them right away? I mean, couldn't they colonize one time zone at the same time they were destroying another? After all, they didn't know they weren't going to succeed—"

Scott was cut off by a tremendous explosion that knocked him to the deck. An instant later a secondary shock wave more powerful than the first rocked the very foundations of the time transport structure. Compressed air forced itself into the sealed room through cracks and pinholes in the inner bulkhead; his eardrums felt as if ice picks had been driven through the membranes.

Sealed containers shattered from the concussion. The tinkling of plastic shards was mixed with the crash of collapsing shelves and cabinets. The roar and reverberation was attended by needle-like blasts of air that, restricted by the venturi effect, darted into the room like solid projectiles. The chamber filled with thick, choking dust.

Scott got his knees under his belly, but could not lift his head off the floor. He huddled on the deck with his hands clamped over his ears, gritting his teeth in pain. When he finally opened his eyes he saw nothing but dirt and debris. Strong hands yanked him up by the shoulders. "I'm—okay. Check—Doc."

Death Wind went to the doctor and pulled him out from under a blanket of clear plastic shards. "Okay?"

Doc's eyes were glazed, and his head moved jerkily as if the joints were locked together. He was speechless.

Scott climbed to his feet still holding his ears. "That ringing—" Then he stopped and stared at the pulverized remains of the death bomb. Fear gripped him like a boa constrictor. "Doc!" He could not stop himself from backing away from the rising fumes—as if he could outdistance the deadly vapor, or by sheer willpower force the genie back into its bottle. He stopped breathing.

Choking and gasping, Doc waved his hands in front of his face. "Only dust—my boy. It was emp—" He was taken over by a fit of coughing. The airborne grit threatened to smother him.

Scott staggered against the inner bulkhead; his knees shook.

uncontrollably. When he twisted around to support himself on the door handle, he saw through the dislodged hinge pin that the time transport structure had collapsed. The staging area was a giant junk heap of splintered plastic sheets, tangled electrical cables, and smashed focusing nodes. "What the—"

Across the dust-filled room the Nomad squad shoved open the outer bulkhead door. The twang in Scott's ears grew louder and deeper, like the thrumming of a dragon flyer. Death Wind picked up Doc by the waist and carried him outside like a sack of potatoes.

Scott stumbled toward the rectangle of light. Outside, he eagerly sucked in great lungfuls of air. In his peripheral vision he glimpsed a shaft of purple radiance where the yellow globe of the sun should have been. "It's the *Ark*! Where the hell did she come from?"

"Or when," muttered Doc.

There was no mistaking the flyer for any other: the surrounding pincushion of focusing nodes were distinctive.

Scott grimaced. "This is a strange time for her to appear."

The lifting cones glowed weakly, and flashed on and off intermittently. The modified flyer dropped in stages: quickly when the purple beams died out, slowly when they flickered on. The short power surges were all that was preventing her from plummeting straight down on top of the wreckage of the time transport structure.

"She's in trouble!"

The gyroscope appeared to be out of order, causing the *Ark* to wobble like a child's top running down. With a pronounced but fluctuating list the saucer edged away, hopscotching across the stronghold on short bursts of energy. She dropped dangerously close to the roof of the nuclear reactor containment building and barely scraped over the multistory administrative headquarters on the other side. Her lifting beams melted whatever they touched.

Scott grabbed Doc's free arm. "Come on. Let's go."

Death Wind, supporting the doctor's other arm, nodded wordlessly.

They and the Nomads staggered across the orangetop in the direction of the *Ark*. Dead and dying dragons lay everywhere; most were bleeding from the eyes, ears, and nose. The terrible concussion caused by the *Ark* entering the space-time continuum in the presence of a dense atmosphere was fatal to those close to the point of rupture, and who were not protected by an airtight barrier.

Everywhere the destructive force of the temporal incursion was evident. Large buildings were disjointed as if they had been picked up and dropped; small sheds and storage facilities lay flattened; exposed machinery was torn from its mounts; external piping systems had burst apart. As much of the stronghold as the eye could see suffered massive devastation.

The *Ark* disappeared from view, behind a group of distant barns.

"She's coming down too fast." Scott cringed as he listened for the sounds of a crash. "If she hits too hard—"

Since the only enemy soldiers in sight lay still in death or writhing in pain, the Nomads relaxed their bows. They ran ahead as Scott and Death Wind kept pace with Doc. The drawbridge had been knocked down into the moat, submerged except for the broad balustrade that doubled as a piping raceway. The squad crossed atop the shattered plastic rail.

"I thank you for the relief, lads, but I believe I am now able to travel unassisted." Doc tapped the plastic road surface with the cane that he had brought through so many travails. "Almost unassisted."

Scott wiped sweat off his brow now that his hands were free. "Is it me, or is it getting hotter around here?"

Death Wind nodded grimly. "Hot."

Doc observed, "The steam is thicker close to the reactor building, perhaps because that is where the heat is generated."

"No, it's—" Scott glanced around at buildings farther away. "It's not just that. There's more steam everywhere. Visibility's down to barely five hundred feet. It wasn't that bad a few minutes ago."

Vapor rising from buried vents condensed into pockets of white fog amid an overall thickening mist. The stronghold's normally clinging, humid atmosphere now took on the viscous appearance of a swampy miasma. The hiss of escaping steam became ever more apparent.

Scott had to yell in order to make himself heard. "Let's make a detour to the reactor building and check out the control room. This may be important."

The three of them veered toward the tall structure. The roof was a puddle that drooled off the edges like a cartoon caricature. The plastic melted by the heat from the *Ark*'s lifting cones was slowly solidifying into bulbous masses; the walls sagged, then refroze in a permanent outward bulge. They entered the building through an opening whose door had been blown inward off its hinges.

"It appears that damage from the pressure wave was severe," said Doc, barely audible against the screaming clamor.

"I'll say it was. And dissolving the overhead power lines didn't help any, either. This place is a shambles." Superheated steam filled the corridors and seared Scott's lungs. "Forget it. We can't get in there."

Doc faltered in the ovenlike heat. "I cannot—"

"We leave." Death Wind turned Doc around and shoved him toward the doorway.

"Wait a minute," Scott shouted. He was practically blinded by the searing heat in his eyes. He blinked away the tears, but still could not see through the veil of steam. He felt his way along the corridor. "There may be a—"

Alone, he worked his way deeper into the reactor building. He heard Death Wind's muted shout, then the roar of venting gases drowned out all other sounds. He hunched low and maintained contact against the wall with one arm. If he ever became lost in the maze of hallways he would never find his way out.

He reached an intersection, followed the corner around, and stumbled on. He tried to remember the layout of the many reactor buildings he had penetrated in the Cretaceous, when he was sabotaging fission piles. Dragons were amazingly consistent in manner and method, taking uniformity of construction to the nth degree. He soon found what he was looking for.

The main control room would be close to the reactor core so that duty personnel could be close to manual overrides. Remote auxiliary testing stations were located strategically in order to allow backup crews to monitor such functions as radiation levels, power fluctuations, and coolant activity. These were not regulatory stations, but observation posts.

Dead dragon technicians lay sprawled on the floor or hunched over their consoles. This part of the containment structure was not kept airtight: there was no need to keep negative pressure anywhere except where radiation leaks could occur. The dragons had all died from concussion.

Scott cupped his hands over his eyes in the steam-filled room. The main computer was down, and all the screens blank; high temperature had fried the solid-state circuitry, and moisture had destroyed the keypads and electronic sensors. He pressed his face close to pressure gauges, thermocouple readouts, and glass-encapsulated dials, studying the mechanical pointers of each. The data he garnered was enough to corroborate what he feared.

He worked his way back to the door, ducked through the steam into the corridor, and slammed into a resilient, moving object that knocked him hard against the frame. A mouthful of teeth glared down from a height of eight feet; sharpened talons gripped his shirt front. Scott gasped as the dragon pulled him up against its scaly chest.

Its breath was hot and fetid. The lower jaw unhinged with snakelike breadth, and the slender tongue darted vibrantly with carnivorous intent. The beady eyes were twin incarnations of hellfire. The neck arched in the shape of a horseshoe as the ugly head reared, then plunged for the kill.

Without thinking, Scott whipped out Death Wind's knife and stabbed upward into the descending throat. The razor-sharp blade slipped through the soft underflesh and into the mouth; only the hilt prevented the tip from reaching the brain. If the caped dragon hissed, it was lost in the cacophony of shrieking steam. The head withdrew into the swirling mist as suddenly as it had appeared, leaving Scott staring at his upraised arm and the bloody knife as if it had all been a fantasy.

Scott kept the knife held out in front of him as he made his way blindly along the corridor wall. His throat burned as if he were swallowing fire. His eyes teared unmercifully. He got down on hands and knees to escape the thickest of the rising steam. At the first intersection he turned and kept sidling along the plastic bulkhead.

The wall bent back at a ninety-degree turn. Panic-stricken, Scott could not remember passing another intersection. He must have made a wrong turn—

A familiar face took form in front of him. "I worry."

Scott closed his eyes in relief when he realized that he was actually outside the building in the midst of escaping steam. "You were going in after me, weren't you?"

Death Wind did not answer, but pulled Scott away from the doorway. He led him across the orangetop to a thick plastic barricade. The air was still hot, but not steaming.

"Is the nuclear pile in danger of exploding?" Doc asked calmly.

Scott took several deep breaths before replying. "No way.

Dragon reactors have too many built-in safeguards." He placed his hands on his hips, bent at the waist, and continued sucking in air. "But the radiation counters are all off scale. If you think this is hot, an hour from now we'll be glowing in the dark. At this point a meltdown is inevitable."

CHAPTER 29

"Are you sure she's in here?"

"I watched her come down. She hit pretty hard, but I didn't see no explosion."

Scott stared at the triple-canopy jungle on the other side of the severed fence. "Where's everyone else?"

"Bold One and Slender Petal, along with the rest of the Nomads, went in to scout a route. Sam an' Helen're hanging back fer Broderick an' his platoon—they got pinned down by a armored division an' lost a few troops." Windy pointed his laser gun at the trees. "Got some pretty mean critters in there, too. Big things like tanks with clubbed tails. I went in as fer as the pond. That's where I saw them giant turtles—the size o' ships they were, with heads like dormers an' oars fer feet."

"I have no doubt we can avoid water creatures, as well as slow-moving herbivores nonaggressive by nature. Did you see any triceratops? They are a bit territorial."

"Nary a one. But that don't mean they ain't in there."

Doc bunched his lips. "Dragons mix their livestock less often than you mix metaphors. With a modicum of caution and a show of aggression I think we can avoid direct confrontation."

Death Wind held up his bow. "Quiet weapons no good. Scare with noise."

"Yes, a near miss with a laser gun can no doubt frighten an entire herd. Well, we cannot do any good out here. Are your men—"

"Whoa, Doc. Here they come now." Scott thrust his finger at a group of people emerging ghostlike through the wreaths of steam. He waved his hands over his head. "Sam! Over here."

The Gentleman General approached looking more grim than usual. "I'm sure glad to see you fellows. I thought we'd never find you in this mist. What the hell is going on? First the *Ark*, then all this steam."

"Doc thinks the *Ark* made a temporal breakthrough, but why

here and now we don't know. The steam's being generated by a runaway reactor."

"Oh, great. That's all we need. Half the Fusiliers are still fumbling around in the fog. And we picked up a bunch of mutes from Charon." Sam jerked a thumb in the direction of the reactor. "Can you shut it down?"

"No more than I can turn off the sun. The radioactive core is melting right through the foundations of the containment building. The steam will stop, though, as soon as the pressure reaches the breaking point. It'll blow sky high." Scott saw the horror on Sam's face. "Not a nuclear explosion. That can't happen. But the steam vessels will burst. The heat's already expanded the turbine casing enough to lock it up, so there's no more electricity being generated."

Sam mulled the information for several seconds. "How long have we got?"

Scott shrugged. "We're out of range as far as shrapnel goes. It's the radiation that'll get us." He shrugged again. "Minutes. Hours. If we get a large enough dose we might live for now and die in a few weeks, or months."

Sam made an instantaneous decision. "Okay, I want everybody out of here. If the *Ark* is in there somewhere"—he jerked a thumb at the jungle—"find it. I'll stay behind."

"I'm not leaving you," Helen said calmly.

"Helen, we don't have time to argue—"

"Then, don't. Daddy, tell him how stubborn I can be."

Doc nodded grimly. "Sam, you—"

The general growled. "Never mind. I know what she's like once she makes up her mind. All right, get going. We've lost a lot of Fusiliers already. I can't abandon the rest. Just mark a good trail."

"A wise move, and a logical one." Doc started off through the parted fence. "Well, the decision is made. Let us act on it."

Windy yelled in his craggy voice, "Okay, troops, saddle up."

Scott said, "As soon as the steam plant blows things'll start clearing up. If the *Ark* can still fly we'll come looking for you."

As he ducked into the dense brush he heard Sam call after him, "Only if it's safe. Otherwise, save yourselves."

Scott did not answer. The question paramount in his mind was: what if the *Ark* can't fly?

Death Wind took the lead, effortlessly following the path of his tribe members. The dense brush close to the fence was more of a sight barrier and soon yielded to more open areas that were easy to travel. The soil underfoot, all of which must have been transported through time from the Cretaceous, was soft and loamy: a startling re-creation of the dragons' home world.

Turkey-sized dinosaurs scuttled everywhere, and smaller cousins clung to the bark of magnolias, dogwoods, palms, and willows. Huge insects flitted about the laurel. In a clearing they spooked an ankylosaur, a squat quadruped armed with twin rows of spikes and a clubbed tail, but it scampered off at the first sign of human intrusion. Scott wondered how long it took a forest to reach its present dimensions. Dinosaurs matured quickly, but some of the trees were over a hundred feet tall.

"Ain't gonna find no tyrannosaurs, are we?" Windy asked softly.

"Dragons did not bring predators into the Holocene, so I doubt that they had a need for them now. Just keep making noise. I am sure that most of the inhabitants will run at our approach."

"Didja hafta say 'most'?"

Doc swiped his cane through the dangling vines as if it were a machete. "It pays to be on the alert."

The steam vents were cleverly covered with thick screens that could bear the weight of the multiton denizens, and were placed near trees where they were less likely to be trod upon. Besides supplying heat, the rising mists conferred an eerie, preternatural dawn-world appearance to the jungle landscape.

"Have you noticed that there are no rotting logs or dead brush?" Doc tapped the green grass with his cane. "No decomposing vegetation as you would expect to see in a truly ancient jungle."

"I wasn't really paying attention." Scott concentrated on watching for boisterous dinosaurs and swatting gargantuan insects. He turned around to make sure the Rangers were behind him. He could see two or three, depending on the amount of the steam. "Windy, what made you break off the attack?"

"Din't break it off. We're still attacking. Sam figgered as long as the *Ark*'s here an' below missile interception height, we'd regroup an' use her cannons to fight it out. An' with all this steam we can't see nuthin' without radar nohow."

"A logical course of action," Doc said.

"Nuthin' gets by Sam. He's purty smart even if he don't like generalin'. If this war ever ends we're gonna 'lect him president."

"I am sure he will be overjoyed at the prospect," Doc said sarcastically. "Perhaps you can persuade him to—"

"Hey! What's that?" Scott held up his hand for silence. The platoon stopped in its tracks. Off in the distance Scott heard a strident tune that was not the chirp and buzz of birds and bugs. "It's a toner."

"Yeah, but it's behind us," said Windy.

A Ranger pushed through the file of motionless commandos, jabbing a thumb over his shoulder. "It's my radio. I'm getting a call from the *Ark*." He presented his back to his platoon leader.

Windy pulled the transmitter off the radioman's backpack and keyed a reply.

Scott listened intently. His pinched eyebrows gradually relaxed, then a grin broke out on his face, and finally he whooped and whirled like a dervish. "Did you hear that, Doc! The *Ark* is okay, and the Nomads have found her in a clearing due east."

Death Wind looked up at the clinging mist; the sun was completely blotted out. "Follow." He struck out in a new direction.

Doc shrugged his shoulders at Scott. "Always trust a Nomad in matters of woodcraft." He loped along after the young savage.

Bushwhacking through dense shrubbery required strength, stamina, and an inborn sense of direction. Death Wind not only broke trail, but skirted around trees and impenetrable stands of brush in such a circuitous course that to Scott he seemed to be going in circles. Like Doc, though, he had full confidence in the Nomad's orientation skills.

The next time Scott heard a toner it was in front of him. He stopped beating the bush long enough to decipher the message. The *Ark*'s external loudtoner was repeating an automatic directional call. A few minutes later he found himself standing on a burned-out sward. When he looked up he saw through the mist the business end of a lifting cone.

"Hey! Rusty! We're home."

A familiar red head jumped out of the white fog; wiry arms grappled Scott like a long-lost cousin. "I never thought I'd be so happy to see your ugly puss."

Grinning broadly, Scott hugged his companion every bit as hard. "Well, if it isn't Father Time himself. You know you scared the hell out of us when you popped into space-time like that. When were you coming from?"

"I'll tell you later. Right now we've got to go get Sam and company. His frequency's been keeping up a constant chatter ever since I toned him."

"You know your appearing act knocked out the reactor?"

Rusty nodded. "That's why we've got to hurry. The radiation counter is clicking like an epileptic clam. If we don't get out of here soon we'll all be French fried. Doc, Death Wind, I didn't mean to ignore you, it's just—"

"Tut, tut, my boy. We all have our priorities. Right now I agree with yours in abandoning this dragon abode. Windy and the Rangers should be—"

He was cut short by a muffled explosion. The ground rumbled, knocking his cane out from under him. He fell against Death Wind.

"That was the steam vessel," Scott said. "Things are going to get real hot real fast."

Windy appeared out of the fog, his eyes bulging. The Texas Rangers crowded in behind him.

"All aboard," Rusty called out. "We've got one more stop to make before, as Sandra would put it, we blow this berg."

The terminal moraine towered over the lush landscape: a sheer, white cliff face that stretched for miles across the savanna. The continental glacier was still in a stage of advance, as were all the glaciers in the early Pleistocene. But soon it would recede, leaving in its wake huge piles of boulders, carved valleys, long lines of debris, and gouges in the rock. Then, nature would do its best to cover up the scars.

Grass would sprout in windblown soil, flowers would open their blossoms to suck in the energy of the sun, brush and shrubbery would thrust their roots into the earth, oaks and redwoods would launch themselves into the sky, and animals in great numbers would reclaim the land.

That was the way of the world, that was the way of life. Nothing could stand in the way of birth.

"Relax, Sandra. Take it easy."

Sandra gritted her teeth. "That's easy for you to say."

Jane wiped sweat off Sandra's brow. "No, it is not easy. I say it because I must."

Sandra managed a smile. "Okay, I'll do the same for you when it's your turn."

Other women clustered in the warm, sunlit clearing tended their chores: stirring the cooking pot, stitching clothes, making booties and blankets. Beyond the perimeter of the campsite one woman gathered wood for the fire, while another hunted rabbits and squirrels with a bow and arrow. On a high bluff within shouting

distance, another woman stood guard; she leaned against the shaft
of her spear while, eyes cupped for shade, she scanned the horizon
for wild carnivores and returning warriors. The only animals in
sight were the two pet wolf pups gamboling about the clearing.

The pains were coming quicker now, with clocklike regularity.
Sandra grimaced as each pang gripped her groin with growing
intensity. "You know, I thought I'd be scared, especially without
my mother here. But I'm not. I'm not scared at all. It all seems
so—so natural. I'm actually looking forward to it."

"That is the way it should be." Jane patted Sandra's forehead
with a hot towel. "That is the way it must be."

Sandra felt a stab of pain worse than any of the others. She
squeezed her eyes shut and drew her knees to her breasts. When
the wave of pain subsided, she pulled the smock up to her waist.
"I think this is it," she said when she could breathe again.

Jane nodded quietly. She pulled a pot of hot water off the fire,
redipped the towel, wrung it out over the ground, and crouched at
Sandra's feet. "Whenever you are ready."

"Are you sure you know what you're doing?"

"I have helped many times. It was the way we did it—in the
barn."

Two other women sat by Sandra's side. They laid their hands
gently on Sandra's arms, to comfort her by their touch, to help her
through her trial, to share her experience.

The next spasm was stronger. Sandra gripped the two women
next to her; she clenched her teeth so she would not cry out. The
pain was sharp and severe, but somehow exquisite.

"Okay, this is it."

Jane nodded silently. She soaked a blanket in the hot water,
twisted it, and stretched it out on the ground between Sandra's
outspread legs.

Sandra tuned out the sounds of the forest; no longer did she hear
the birds singing in the branches, the insects droning through
the glade, the wind rustling through the needles and leaves. She
existed solely within herself. She had only one function at the
moment, and that would take her whole attention. She relied on
her companions to help and protect her.

She screamed, then choked it off.

"It is okay," Jane said soothingly. "Cry if it helps."

Sandra's world was one of mixed feelings: she hurt so much,
but felt so good. "Ooooh."

"You must push. Push hard."

Sandra pushed. The pain was more agonizing than she could have imagined possible. She did her best to ignore it. She pushed harder. The pain came in waves, washing over her body like flames on flesh, or like sandpaper on raw skin. How long the pain went on she could not tell; she lost all track of time. Time, in fact, had no meaning to her: whether this was the Pleistocene or the Cretaceous was immaterial. What was important was that she was here, now, experiencing the renascence of life in a brand-new world.

As suddenly as it came, the pain was gone. A luxurious sensation of peace and serenity flushed through Sandra's body: a feeling of rapture she never knew existed, nor could possibly explain. Tears of happiness welled in her eyes and slowly dripped down her cheeks. Then she heard a wail that was unlike any she had ever heard before. She blinked away the tears, cleared her vision, and looked down at her feet.

Jane cleaned the infant with a warm towel. "A boy."

Sandra swallowed hard, but the lump in her throat would not go away. She reached out for the child. "Let me hold him."

The baby continued to cry. His tiny, doll-like hands were drawn into fists, his face was flaccid and wrinkled and scrunched up into a gnomic caricature. He was the most beautiful thing she had ever seen.

When Sandra took him from Jane he was still attached to her by the umbilical cord. She cradled him proudly in her arms.

The Nomad on the hill raced down with her spear upthrust. She stopped reverently outside the circle of midwives. "Flyer come."

Sandra smiled in a way only a mother can. She thought of Death Wind, her husband, returning from war. "Boy, will *he* be surprised."

CHAPTER 30

The sun shone down on the lush, primal forest with a brilliance and a warmth that filled the land with yearning. Each green leaf sparkled with the varnished coating of spring, each flower glistened with early-morning dew. The air captured a vitality that was beyond the bounds of reason, and a crispness just enough to taste.

"Scott, I can save them. You know I can."

"I know you think you can. And I know that what you propose scares the hell out of me."

Rusty bent his lanky frame. "But they're *alive*."

"Everyone's alive—somewhere, sometime. But that doesn't mean they can be resurrected—or should be."

"I don't believe you," Rusty practically screamed. "I can't believe what I'm hearing. You think because you've given them up in your heart they no longer have a right to live. That's *insane*. That's so—*selfish*."

"No, it's not. It's a recognition of reality. I love them as much as you do, but to rip through time on some impossible scheme—"

"It's *not* impossible. Not anymore. Not after the refinements I've made after the last jump."

Scott could not look his friend in the eye. "Then it's risky. The timing is too tight. If we make even the tiniest mistake we could do irreparable damage to the fabric of space-time. We could wipe ourselves out of existence. We don't know all the ramifications—"

"That's straight-line dragon thinking, Scott. We're not reptiles, we're mammals: with the mental capacity of a brain that's more highly organized, with the ability to imagine concepts that—"

"That's right. *Imagine* concepts. Just because we can conceive something doesn't make it true."

"But we've got a time machine. We can go whenever we want—to any point in time, with absolute precision."

"That doesn't mean we can change history. The book has already been written."

227

"I'm not talking about rewriting the whole book—I just want t edit one chapter."

"Rusty, let it go," Scott pleaded, with arms outstretched. "Th past is over. What's done is done. You have no divine right t transform the world to suit your image of how it should be."

Rusty's voice was equally as loud. "This isn't a persona vendetta I'm fighting. There are human lives at stake—and no just strangers: your family as well as mine, and everyone we grev up with. For most of our lives they were our whole world. Hov can you let them die without lifting a finger to save them, whe you know that you have it in your power to do so?"

"Because I don't *know* that we have that power. I know onl that that's what you believe."

Rusty shook his head vehemently. "It's what I can prov mathematically. Figures don't lie."

"But they can mislead. They can give you answers that don't fi reality. Mathematicians proved that bumblebees can't fly becaus their wingspan couldn't support their body weight; but that didn knock the bees out of the air."

Rusty chafed. "That's a problem posed by inaccurate data an unwarranted assumptions. With a properly derived constant—"

"Oh, and we're not making any unwarranted assumption here," Scott said sarcastically. "I suppose if I told you it took hundred hours for one man to dig a hole, you'd tell me a hundre men could dig it in an hour—or a thousand men could dig it in si minutes—or ten thousand in thirty-six seconds. It just isn practical—"

"All right, I get the point. But I've been through the figure over and over. I've run computer simulations. I've checked th answer forward and backward, upstream and downstream, pas and future—"

"Are you sure you didn't start out with the result you wanted and work your way back to the question?"

Rusty ran his hands through long, curly hair. "You know m better than that. I'm telling you I can save them."

"But—they—are—dead," Scott enunciated slowly. "I sav them. And even if they weren't then, they are now. You can' bring the dead back to life except in fairy tales. Th radioactivity—"

"You think they're dead because you saw them in this tim stream. But I didn't. To my consciousness they aren't here now

What you tell me is hearsay; or, at best, circumstantial evidence. It's not proof in the overall picture of space-time."

"Rusty, we're not arguing in a court of law. This isn't a question of perceptions, it's a matter of cold fact."

"Your facts, not mine. I have no direct knowledge of their death, therefore I'm not bound by your preconceived notions of their mortality."

Scott shivered; the cold chill that coursed along his spine was not brought on by a drop in temperature. The implications of Rusty's proposal were too profound for him to visualize. "But you and I are in the same time stream. What's true for me is true for you."

"Is it?"

That short sentence carried enormous portent. Scott's mind swung like a pendulum, caught between what he believed and what he wanted to believe. His heart fluttered. "I sure wish I had your confidence."

Rusty shrugged and offered a half smirk. "I wish I had as much confidence as you think I have."

Scott shook his head. "Don't say that. I'm scared enough already." He could not keep from smiling. He brushed his shaggy blond hair out of his face. "Well, let's go talk it over with the gang."

The campsite filled a clearing that was bounded by brush and tall oak trees. Rock pits surrounded cooking fires that raged with the abundance of wood. Thin streamers of smoke rose into the air and quickly dissipated in the upper winds. People talked and lounged in attitudes of relaxation; this was the first real rest they had had in weeks.

A powwow was in progress around the central fire. Doc, Jane, Britt, Sam and Helen, Bold One and Slender Petal, Windy, Broderick, and Death Wind, Sandra, and child, all sat discussing the issue of the day.

"—rather live with mountain gorillas than with mounted guerrillas." Sandra unabashedly suckled the baby on her exposed breast. "I'm tired of war."

"We are all tired of war, my dear. War is not that which one seeks, but that which is thrust upon those who refuse to bend to the will of others."

"And I'm tired of being a general," said Sam. "This is great growing country, even with all the ice. And that, we know, won't be here forever."

Helen intertwined her arm with her husband's. "We're thinking of starting another family."

Sam winked. "Maybe this time we can have one who's not so quarrelsome."

"Daddy!" Sandra screamed so loud that she frightened the baby. He let the nipple slip from his mouth, and wailed. Sandra let her blouse drop over her breast, hugged him close, and rocked him in her arms. To her father, she said, "You'll pay for that."

"I'm sure I will."

Scott joined the repartee by first kissing his wife. He pointed his chin at the infant. "Have you decided on a name yet?"

Sandra cuddled the infant; gradually, he calmed down to a bare whimper. "He's so sweet I wanted to call him Sugar, but DW doesn't think that's manly enough. We haven't been able to agree on anything yet. Would you like to hold him?" She shoved the unnamed baby into Scott's arms.

"Well, uh—" He held out the baby as if he were a sack of wet cloth. "Sure." After a moment the crying grew louder. Scott stood uncomfortably, looking to his wife for advice.

Jane smiled at him. Her belly was just beginning to show. "Get used to it."

Sandra took back the tiny bundle. "You'll make a great father, Scott. You really will. At least you weren't afraid to hold him."

An awkward silence ensued. People stared at the ground, fiddled with their clothing, played with sticks, stirred the fire: anything to avoid eye contact. Finally, Doc said, "I suppose the time for decisions has come."

Rusty said, "We all know when I stand."

"I say it is about time we started living life instead of fighting it." Broderick doodled in the sand. "And many of the Fusiliers feel the same way. We are fairly well paired off."

Bold One was terse. "No more roam. Good land. Many herds. Hunt."

"We are healthy. We have medicine," Slender Petal said. "We will live long and well."

Death Wind folded his muscular arms across his chest. "We stay."

"And I go with my husband." Sandra put the baby back onto her breast. "Always."

"But don't you understand that it's not over?" Rusty raised his voice but restrained from making accusatory inflection. "You can't cop out as soon as you get what you want. We're all in this together."

"Rusty, not everyone at Charon, or the Outpost, joined this crusade, but we didn't hold it against them," Helen said.

Doc added, "We must each make a decision based on individual needs; short-term personal ambitions are as important as long-term group goals."

"Besides, for what you want to do you don't need an army—just a small reserve corps." Sam stirred the fire with a blackened stick. "And I don't think anyone intends to block you. We all know what's at stake. Challenging the forces of nature with the fate of the world in the balance is a responsibility we've already accepted. Otherwise we wouldn't be here, now. If you feel honor bound to fight one last battle, I trust your judgment."

"Thanks, Sam, for your vote of confidence. I appreciate your position as much as you appreciate mine. This is just something I have to do, or I could never live with myself."

Sandra said, "Rusty, I think you'll agree that I can understand the turmoil of your emotions. I've been where you are now. I know how it feels. No matter how it turns out, it's important for your own well-being that you do what you think is right. You have to find your destiny. At the same time, we have to find ours."

"Well spoken, my dear. You make me proud to have you for a granddaughter." Doc sat with his good leg bent and his bad leg stretched out. His cane was stuck under his arm so he could lean back against it. "Against such clarity of thought I have nothing further to add."

"Thank *you*, Pop, for helping me to become the person I am today. I don't think I've ever told you this before, but you've had a great influence on me. I love you."

"I love you, too, Sandra—both the girl you were, and the woman you have become. I just wish—I wish—" Doc cleared his throat. When he continued, his voice trembled ever so slightly. "I wish you all the happiness this new, dragon-free world has to offer."

Sandra swallowed hard. "Pop, it was you who said that wherever you are is home. Well, we're here, and this is where I've given birth to my son, so I'm for calling it home."

Doc nodded slowly. "And I am sure that you can help mold this world into what it needs to become."

After a long silence, Helen said, "Daddy."

"Yes, my dear."

"Does that mean that you are—going?"

Doc pursed his lips before answering. "I must. There is still work to be done."

"Isn't that what you said twenty years ago, when your wanderlust took you away from Sam and me?"

"I suppose it is. It has always seemed in my short life that there is so much to do, and so little time in which to do it. Access to a time machine has aggravated that condition; contradictorily, it does not give one more time, but more opportunities in which to spend one's time. Remember though, Helen, as I go charging off into the realm of alternate space-time, that I am removing from your life only my physical presence. The moments of happiness we have shared will be with us always."

Rusty choked. "Doc, you make it all seem so permanent. When you have a time machine, everything in the universe is temporary."

"And who are we to say what the future may bring? Or the past, for that matter."

"I don' know what'll it bring," drawled Windy. "But I know them two boys have it in 'em to change the world. Hell, I'd follow 'em to the end o' time just to see what they're gonna do with it."

Scott put his arm around Jane's slender shoulders. "Honey, we've got to do what we can. They're our people."

"It is what I expect of you. We must try."

Scott kissed her on the cheek. "Besides, we can come back anytime we want." He glanced at his lifelong companion. "So, partner, when do we leave?"

Pulling Britt close, Rusty said, "No time like the present."

"I do have a request before we go, if we can spare the time." When he had their attention, Doc said, "I would like to bequeath to my great-grandson a name from my own past."

Sandra studied her grandfather's face. After a moment of silence she approached him with arms outthrust. The babe in his swaddling clothes had sucked his fill and fallen asleep. "What's your name, Grandfather?"

"Well, in the many guises of my life I have answered to quite a few appellations, according to the custom of the day and the people with whom I lived. But the name I was born with I have not used since I was a lad. My parents called me George, after my father, who was named after his father and his father's father. I did not have a son to carry on the tradition, and do not—as yet"—he glanced at Sam and Helen—"have a grandson. Therefore, it would give me great honor if your son, my only male descendant at this time, would bear this name." He placed his lips on the infant's forehead.

Twin tears rolled slowly down Sandra's cheeks. Her chest heaved with emotion. "Then his name is George, after the greatest dragon slayer of all time. That's how we'll remember you."

Doc nodded gratefully.

Scott stood up straight and tall, crossed the circle to where Death Wind sat cross-legged, and removed his belt and knife. "This belongs in your family. I guess I'd better return it, and thank you for its loan."

Death Wind climbed to his full height. His dark eyes were deep pools of mystery. "We are same family."

"Yes, and always will be." He handed the heirloom to Death Wind. A knife would be much more useful in this world than the one to which Scott was going. "I want you to retain this knife in remembrance of our brotherhood. Use it well."

Death Wind took it solemnly. "I will miss you."

Arm held out in Nomad fashion, Scott said, "I'll miss you, too. But no matter where or when we are, we'll always be together."

Death Wind grasped Scott's forearm, released it, and rested his hands firmly on Scott's shoulders in the Nomad family greeting. Death Wind's face was expressionless, but his voice was an open book. "It is code."

CHAPTER 31

The desert air was hot, the sand hotter. Heat waves shimmered like dancing ghosts. Six pairs of moccasins crunched through the granules in the shadow of an overhanging ledge.

"It must be in here," said Rusty, looking up from the sketch.

When Scott shone his pack-powered light into the cave a metallic glint reflected the beam. He stepped into the dark interior. "Looks like a stainless steel door behind that pile of debris." He clambered over loose rocks until he reached the shiny surface. "Yes, this is it." He rapped gently. "Anyone home?"

"Scott!" Jane pulled him away from the portal.

Scott spread his arms. "Only teasing."

"Y'all give us away if ya set off the alarms," said Windy.

"No, there are no exterior proximity devices or contact switches. Every rockfall would set them off."

Rusty handed his map to Britt, turned her around, and took a magnetic interruptor out of her knapsack. "Thanks."

"Besides," said Doc, leaning against his cane. "It is always polite to knock."

Rusty ran the homemade electronic box around the exposed portion of the door frame. "The frequency is matched and nullified. Okay, Windy. Burn it."

The door had no outer knob, just a raised rectangle opposite the interior handle. "Watch yer eyes." Windy fired his laser gun at the protrusion. The narrow beam drilled a hole through the steel, then exploded as the concentration of energy spread out from the molecular impact. "Again?"

Scott leaned his shoulder against the heated metal. The door budged ever so slightly. "No, I think I can get it open." He shoved hard several times before the heavy-duty lock yielded to the force. Rusted hinges squeaked. The door moved inward about a foot before it jammed. Continued beating forced it only another six inches. "I guess that'll do."

He had to take off his battery pack before squeezing into the dank, musty chamber. Windy handed the backpack to Scott, then removed his own and passed it in. One by one the others entered the dark, steel-walled antechamber. Each carried a pocket light.

"Judging from the amount of dust and the lack of footprints, this place does not appear to have been in recent use." Doc's narrow beam showed nothing but emptiness. "As we expected."

Rusty approached the inner door, an airtight hatch built like the door to a vault but without a handle of any kind. "We'll have to burn out the locking mechanism before we can pull back the bolts." He ran his magnetic interruptor around the frame. "It's clear." He stepped back and let Windy do his job.

After half a dozen blasts the massive lock was a molten blob of steel. "That bugger's built ta last."

Scott took a hammer and crowbar out of Jane's knapsack and went to work on the exposed drive pins. When they were smashed out of the retaining grips he used the crowbar to pry the rim off the seal. Scott applied all his strength; well-tuned muscles and two feet of iron leverage gradually pushed open the door. Tortured hinges creaked and groaned. "Okay, folks, watch your step."

Scott slipped into a pitch-black space that was not a room, but the top landing of a stairwell. His powerful pack light illuminated a deep shaft and a circular staircase. He waited until everyone was inside before taking the lead. Hand-held lights bobbed down the metal steps. Rusty clung to the top rail, breathing hard—not because of the stirred-up dust, but because of what he expected to find at the base of the stairs.

"Another door," Scott called out.

Rusty inhaled sharply and slowly made his way down the steps. He did the honors with the magnetic interruptor, neutralizing the alarm systems. Then Windy and Scott did their jobs. The vaultlike door was more massive than the previous one and took twice as much effort to breach with the laser gun.

Scott stepped back after an attempt at prying. "It's no use. Internal positive pressure is keeping it closed. Windy, you're going to have to drill a hole all the way through."

It took ten blasts on the same spot before the laser beam penetrated the thick casting. A rush of air flowed through the hole like a stream of water gushing out of a fire hose nozzle. Scott worked the crowbar into the crevice formed by the hatch on the rim, pushed with all his might, and broke the seal. He fell in with the door when the suction let go.

From the base of the stairwell Rusty heard the gentle whirring of motors and the hum of transformers. As the others filed into the mechanical room he hung back, afraid of what he might see inside. The air rushing past him was stale and carried with it the animal odors of perspiration. He choked, not only from the stench, but from the memories it evoked.

"Come on, Rusty," his companion called.

Rusty forced himself to enter the room. Pumps and compressors made soughing sounds like the wind through trees. A single, dim emergency light sent out an eerie yellow glow that was overshadowed by the electric torches carried by the six-person team. Britt held Rusty's hand and led him along the narrow aisles, past a familiar-looking computer console, through an open doorway, and down a long corridor to another door. This one had no lock.

Scott turned the knob and walked into an elevator lobby. "Windy, you'd better stay here with Jane and Britt." He punched a few buttons, one of which turned on a bank of fluorescent lights, while another set in motion an electric motor. He shrugged off the battery pack and dropped it at the head of another stairwell. "We don't want to look like an invasionary force."

Doc consulted a timepiece he wore around his neck. "We had better hurry. We do not have much time."

The elevator doors opened. Scott kissed Jane before entering the cage. "Hold the fort, honey."

Doc tapped his cane on the still-bobbing floor. "It has been quite a while since I last rode in one of these."

Scott held his prosthesis in the air. "It beats footing it on the stairs. Rusty, come on."

The redhead was frozen in his tracks. He stared at the elevator car as if it were a slab in a morgue. His mouth worked, but no words came out. Britt took matters in hand and shoved him aboard. "You must do this yourself."

Scott stabbed a button and the doors slid shut. He flashed a quick wave at Jane. "Be right back."

The lump in Rusty's throat threatened to strangle him. As the elevator dropped into the depths he felt like an escaped convict forced back into solitary confinement after a short reprieve.

Scott pounded him on the back. "It's okay, Rusty. It's okay."

It was all his idea, but now that he was here he was afraid to carry out the mission he had planned so carefully. Some of the butterflies in his stomach were the result of the high-speed plummet into the bowels of the earth; most were from a bad case of nerves. He swallowed hard. Before he could protest, the doors slid open. He saw a long, well-lighted corridor whose walls were

lined from floor to ceiling with trays of plants. Trailing branches
and clusters of leaves billowed out to form a narrow, junglelike
passage. Thirty feet away a young girl tested the pH of the
hydroponic fluid. She looked up, startled.

Scott strode boldly out of the corridor. "Hi. You don't remember me, but—"

The girl dropped the siphon; the hardened plastic apparatus
clattered on the floor but did not break. Her jaw fell to a chest that
had not yet begun to sprout the buds of puberty.

"I doubt very much that she can." Doc stopped behind Scott.
There was not enough room for him to pass. "Good morning, my
dear. I am sure this intrusion is rather unexpected—"

The girl found her voice and an emergency alarm at the same
time. She pounded a fist on a mushroom wall button, but the siren
was not nearly as loud or as startling as her scream. She ducked
into a nearby cubicle and slammed the door behind her.

"That should announce us." Doc grabbed Rusty by the tunic
and pulled him out of the elevator car. "Let us head for the
meeting hall before it gets too crowded. Scott, you know the
way."

Since they were in a service corridor they encountered very
little traffic. The few heads that popped out of work cubicles
stayed out of the way; fear-struck faces watched the gruff-looking
trio in strange garb march confidently along the hallway as if they
knew what they were about.

Rusty's mind raced. The familiar surroundings were a blur, a
strange phantasmagoria reminiscent of a time and place that no
longer existed. He was hardly aware of the flashing red lights or
the wailing sirens or the awestruck people pouring into the
corridor and staring at him with a mixture of fear and astonishment. Mingled with the smell of processed air and human flesh he
thought he detected an odor he had forgotten existed—that of an
apple pie baking in a convection oven. Memories flooded his
brain, blotting out all vision of the present. He turned blindly left
and right, pulled along by Doc's warm hand as if he were the
caboose of a train. Then he was in the meeting hall: little more
than an enlarged cubicle that, as a child, he had thought was a
huge playroom with boundaries so vast that it tired him to run all
the way around it.

"Who—who are you?"

The sirens stopped; the lights ceased flashing. The sudden
silence and the staring faces were intimidating. The room was

packed with people, and the corridor outside as well. Elected leaders squirmed through the throng of humanity.

"We're—we're—" Scott's voice faltered as erstwhile friends and family crowded around him.

Rusty reacted nervously to the sheer pressure of people. He found it hard to believe that he had once lived in such cramped quarters.

"We are an advance scouting team that has come here to liberate the citizens of Maccam City," Doc said calmly. "The main expeditionary force is waiting outside. We have an aircraft standing by to transport you to safety."

Tingles ran up Rusty's spine as he recognized one man in particular, and the little girl he held in his arms. He could hardly believe what he was seeing—never before did he have to look *down* at his father. His sister Faron scrunched her eyes at Rusty as if he were a giant ogre.

The man who looked up at him made no notice of Rusty, but faced Doc openmouthed. "You're—an outsider."

"I am."

He glanced at Scott, then at Rusty. Stunned eyes took in their bronzed, sun-baked features, muscular bodies, and long hair. "Where—where did you come from?"

"I am an emissary from Washington."

"You mean—headquarters still exists?"

"It did when I left it." Doc glanced at his timepiece. "We have much to discuss, but now is not the time to do it. We must get you out of here immediately."

Caught up in his own emotion, Rusty suddenly realized how enormous a shock this must be for his fellow citizens. They had been buried underground for a hundred years without contact with the outside world—with no knowledge that people other than they still survived. Then a group of oddly dressed warriors descended unannounced into their secret sanctuary and politely invited them to evacuate at once, with no questions asked, and to forsake the only kind of life they had ever known.

Furthermore, he never anticipated that he would go unrecognized. While only hours had passed for the people of Maccam City since they last saw Scott and Rusty, years had passed for the two wandering sons. They had traveled enormous distances in space and time, and had returned to their point of origin both older and wiser. Maturity had changed them in many ways.

"How did you get in here? The doors are sealed, and the intrusion alarm—"

"We demagnified the tocsin code. But that is unimportant. You must vacate these premises at once."

Faron tugged at the thin material of her father's tunic and stared at Rusty with a jaundiced eye. "Daddy, who is that man?"

"Strangers, darling." He looked at Rusty, then at Scott. "Strangers from outside."

Rusty saw Scott's folks surging forward, with their daughter between them. He and Scott stared at each other. Scott's eyes glistened like wet opals. Rusty tried valiantly to hold back his own tears. He came here as a leader, as a savior, as an intrepid conqueror: it would not look good for him to break down and cry. Then he saw his mother . . .

"We have no time to waste. It is imperative that we get back to our aircraft and depart this time zone."

Rusty's father looked at Doc quizzically. "They still use time zones?"

"Uh, yes, but in a different context." Doc referred to his timepiece again. "We have sufficient capacity for all your people in our aircraft, but I am afraid that we do not have time for you to gather your personal belongings."

"This is all so sudden—"

Doc remained the eloquent orator. "I understand your trepidation, but we really must be going. I can explain the urgency of the situation at a later date. Now, if you can start the procession moving we will lead you out of here and into a world of sunshine and fresh air."

Scott's father shouted in glee and slapped Rusty's father on the back. "I told you it was okay to go outside. This is the moment we've been waiting for. Mister, I'm behind you and your buddies all the way. All I've got to do is get my son in the pump room and I'm packed."

Doc glanced at Scott. "Yes, well, we have already accounted for those who were working on upper-level maintenance details. Scott and Rusty, I believe they are, and a motor mechanic named Roger."

"I *knew* it was all right to go outside. I told you so." He let out a cheer that was shared by at least half the crowd. "This is what we've been waiting for all these years."

Those Maccam City dwellers who shared his partisanship needed no further urging. They in turn shouted down the protests of the bewildered opposition. It was perhaps the shortest revolution in human history. With uncommon brevity citizens cooped up far too long yielded to the victorious faction. The authoritative voice of one of their own turned a shallow tide.

With great fanfare and hubbub they filed out of the meeting room. Those still in shock, or uncertain of the turn of events, were swept along with the overpowering multitude.

"But, what about—" Rusty's father lingered indecisively. "What are we getting into?"

With a faraway look in his eyes, Doc soliloquized. "That is something that no one can predict—perhaps something we are better off not knowing. The future is ours for the making; we must make of it what we can. And this time we can do it on our own terms. The war is over. Let us hope that mankind has the wisdom to keep it from returning."

CHAPTER 32

Doc, Scott, and Rusty sat down wearily in the *Ark*'s bridge. It had been a long day: morning in the Pleistocene, afternoon in the Holocene, evening in a portion of the Holocene a few years later, in time for their own departure from then into the Pleistocene—plus a few minutes as a safety margin so they did not bump into themselves leaving for the final assault in the Ice Age. When time is your handmaiden, the only passage that counts is subjective.

"I can't believe we pulled it off," Scott said. "The window was so short. Getting there after we—that is, our previous selves—left for maintenance duty, but before the dragons arrived to pump the city full of corrosive gas. I had the jitters the whole time."

"Which self's time?" Doc asked. "Your present self, or your past?"

"Hell, I don't know anymore. Both, I guess. And every one in between. We've come a long way since this whole thing started. Every moment has been either exciting or terrifying."

"How would you classify today's activities?"

"Transmogrifying."

Doc snickered as he leaned back in his seat. "Rusty, my boy, I noticed you had your doubts for a while. When did you lose your confidence in the success of this mission?"

"About a million years from now. When I popped into the future tense to destroy the dragon advance base, what I saw then made me wonder how this venture would ultimately turn out. I admitted the possibility that somewhen we might have interrupted the continuity of the universe and wiped ourselves out for all time. I still wonder what that future may bring."

"Why? Because you saw an endless pristine forest with no signs of civilization or human habitation?"

Rusty grimaced. "Doesn't that seem strange to you?"

"Not at all. A great deal can happen in a million years. Besides, how far afield did you look?"

"I practically closed my eyes. I was afraid of learning too much."

243

"What? This from the lad who says that prior knowledge has no effect on future events. You should at least be consistent within your own prognoses."

Rusty shrugged. "Call it the Pandora syndrome. I was afraid that if I made too many direct observations of future reality I wouldn't have the courage or the resolve to make interdimensional alterations."

"Too much knowledge can be a curse," Doc agreed.

"If I weren't so scared, and if I really knew all the secrets of the universe, I'd have tried to figure a way to save Roger's life instead of letting him get beamed down by a dragon laser gun. But since I saw it happen in my own time stream, I thought it might do irreparable damage to the overall flow of events."

"But what about me?" Scott fairly shouted. "And Doc? We saw the Maccam City residents frozen in ice. Isn't it the same situation?"

"Who knows. Maybe you and I are in different continua, and what you saw or experienced has no effect on what *I* saw and experienced. Or maybe you and everyone else—every*thing* else— are only manifestations in this universe: a support system for my own personal continuum. I don't know. I'm confused."

Doc said, "Think how complex today's events would have been should the people rescued from the stronghold have been some of *your* people, instead of former prisoners from Charon."

Scott shuddered. "What does Mr. Math have to say about it?"

"It depends on how you plug in the variables."

Doc said, "Perhaps we could pick up Roger *after* you saw him. He might only be injured."

Rusty held out his hands. "Doc, as much as I'd like to believe you, and try to save him, I don't want to take a chance on running into myself out there in the desert. I don't know what effect it might have—and I don't want to know. Not until I work over the formulas a few hundred more times."

"We've got a long way to go in understanding the operation of the universe," Scott said. "The book of time is written in an incredibly obscure language we may never be able to read. It makes me wonder if we didn't make a mistake we'll pay for somewhen down the line. I mean, if we're not here in a million years, what happened to us?"

Doc nodded thoughtfully. "When you think how far man evolved in the past million years, when he had wild animals and the Ice Age to contend with, imagine how far and how fast he.

might progress without predation, and with perfect control over his environment. Perhaps a million years hence he has turned this part of the continent into a vast park, as a monument to dragon folly. Or perhaps he has left Earth for the stars. Or discovered a place in time that is incomprehensible to us. The possibilities are endless. We can, if we choose, return to that future time and seek out an explanation."

"No!" shouted Rusty.

"Perhaps we should consider living in two time frames simultaneously. Some of us could stay here to hunt the dragons' dinosaurs to extinction and seed the planet with Pleistocene wildlife, while the rest of us carry out a parallel life in that future kilomillennium."

"No!"

"Tut, tut, now, Rusty. Let us not retreat to straight-line dragon thinking. Was it not you who said that we are mammals, with highly organized brains that can conceptualize quanta that reptilian brains cannot?"

"Maybe I am. And maybe the dragons weren't so far from the truth after all. I don't know. There's a lot I don't know anymore."

"Ah, the wisdom of maturity is fast taking hold of your impetuous nature. Is it not strange that one can be born all-knowing, yet the older one gets the more ignorant one becomes?"

Rusty scowled.

"Welcome to the establishment, my man."

Scott winced. "You know, Doc, now that you bring it up, there are a few things *I* don't know anymore." He dug the computer crystal out of his pocket and flipped it in the air like a coin. "We know the dragons didn't establish base camps in other time zones, so we're not likely to find them hiding behind some future temporal curtain. But what about the Pleistocene stronghold? Why wasn't there any evidence of that in man's past?"

"Oh, but there is."

"Huhn?"

"Not physical evidence, perhaps, because the glacier has wiped it out. Once the heat was turned off, and the glacier continued its flow through the stronghold, every shred of dragon fabrication was ground to bits, separated molecule from molecule, as the many layers of ice moved downstream at unequal speeds. In a few thousand years all signs of their occupation were spread out over half a continent as tiny, indecipherable fragments of a long-forgotten puzzle; radiation as well.

"But the dragons themselves were most certainly kept alive in man's history. They have come down to us in many forms: the cockatrice, the basilisk, the snake in the Garden of Eden, the fire-breathing dragon of yore. They are the stuff of legend. The dragons in man's mind will never die; they will live on as the incarnation of all that is evil."

Scott thought for a moment. "But will they live on in the minds of the Cro-Magnons?"

"Since we are descended from the Cro-Magnons, logic dictates that they must."

"But we never saw any Cro-Magnons, or even signs that they existed in the Pleistocene. If they didn't encounter the dragons—" Scott rubbed his chin, scratching his fingers on the blond stubble. "The Neanderthals didn't intermarry with . . ."

Doc slowly shook his head. "No, the Neanderthals died out of their own accord because they were unable to adapt to the harsh conditions of the Ice Age. They were on the road to extinction long before our arrival. The presence of our people will have no effect on the Neanderthals' demise: they will neither interbreed with the Neanderthals nor hunt them down and kill them. They are two separate simian branches on the evolutionary tree."

"Then—what's the answer?"

Doc smiled demurely. "Simply that the archaeological record shows only that Cro-Magnon man *lived* during the Pleistocene Epoch, not how he got then and there, or when and where he came from. If he did not exist in the Pleistocene before our arrival then, I daresay he lives then now."

Rusty fidgeted in his seat. "What you're implying is a paradox."

"The sudden emergence of Cro-Magnon man under those circumstances is a *real* contradiction," Scott emphasized. "Not just apparent."

"Yes, he is a parent, in a course of events I prefer to call 'prevolution.' I am sure that somewhere—or somewhen—in the mathematical concept of the universe there exists an equation that correlates the continuity of space and time in such a way as to account for all observable phenomena."

Rusty squeezed one eye shut. "Do you mean that no matter how convoluted the structure of space-time seems to us, there's a viewpoint that sees it in a straight line?"

"Perhaps. Or perhaps we each create a line that in the end merges with all others."

"I still don't follow you," Scott said, bunching his lips. "You're saying that what I see and do may affect me now without affecting you, but that later it will affect us all. But if we all exist together, and we all belong to the same space, the same time, and the same universe, how can reality be anything but purely objective?"

"I cannot say. That is the beauty of subjectivity. It allows for a way out of every situation without delineating the route. There can be a here as well as a there, why not a then as well as a now? Specifically, time can be broken down into a then, a now, and a later—or past, present, and future: yesterday, today, and tomorrow. When space and time are merged into unity this implies that there is a here-then, a here-now, and a here-later, as well as a there-then, a there-now, and a there-later. There may even be a here-there, and a now-then. I do not know. I doubt that we will ever know. But one eventuality we can count on is that we are here, now—and what follows, will follow. Nothing can change that."

Silence pervaded the bridge as if it were the back side of the Moon. After a seemingly interminable time, Scott cocked an eyebrow. "Are you sure?"

Doc nodded in an exaggerated fashion. "Absolutely." He glanced from one to the other to make sure both Scott and Rusty were looking at him. Then he winked.

STEVEN BRUST

___JHEREG___ 0-441-38554-0/$3.95

There are many ways for a young man with quick wits and a quick
sword to advance in the world. Vlad Taltos chose the route of the
assassin and the constant companionship of a young jhereg.

___YENDI___   0-441-94460-4/$3.50

Vlad Taltos and his jhereg companion learn how the love of a good
woman can turn a cold-blooded killer into a _real_ mean S.O.B...

___TECKLA___ 0-441-79977-9/$3.50

The Teckla were revolting. Vlad Taltos always knew they were lazy,
stupid, cowardly peasants...revolting. But now they were revolting
against the empire. No joke.

___TALTOS___ 0-441-18200/$3.50

Journey to the land of the dead. All expenses paid! Not Vlad Taltos'
idea of an ideal vacation, but this was work. After all, even an
assassin has to earn a living.

___COWBOY FENG'S SPACE BAR AND GRILLE___
  0-441-11816-X/$3.95

Cowboy Feng's is a great place to visit, but it tends to move around
a bit—from Earth to the Moon to Mars to another solar system—
and always just one step ahead of whatever mysterious conspiracy is
reducing whole worlds to radioactive ash.

CLASSIC SCIENCE FICTION
AND FANTASY

279